NIGHT-GAUNTS

and Other Tales of Suspense

Also by Joyce Carol Oates

NIGHT-GAUNTS

and Other Tales of Suspense

JOYCE CAROL OATES

The Mysterious Press
New York

The poem "Night-Gaunts" by H.P. Lovecraft was originally
published in the December 1939 issue of *Weird Tales*.
Reprinted with the permission of Arkham House.

FIRST EDITION

Published simultaneously in Canada
Printed in the United States of America

ISBN 978-0-8021-2810-2
eISBN 978-0-8021-4628-1

First Grove Atlantic hardcover edition: June 2018

This book was set in 12 pt. Adobe Garamond Pro by
Alpha Design & Composition of Pittsfield, NH

Library of Congress Cataloging-in-Publication data is available for this title.

The Mysterious Press
an imprint of Grove Atlantic
154 West 14th Street
New York, NY 10011

Distributed by Publishers Group West

groveatlantic.com

18 19 20 21   10 9 8 7 6 5 4 3 2 1

NIGHT-GAUNTS

Out of what crypt they crawl, I cannot tell,
But every night I see the rubbery things,
Black, horned, and slender, with membranous wings,
They come in legions on the north wind's swell
With obscene clutch that titillates and stings,
Snatching me off on monstrous voyagings
To grey worlds hidden deep in nightmare's well.

Over the jagged peaks of Thok they sweep,
Heedless of all the cries I try to make,
And down the nether pits to that foul lake
Where the puffed shoggoths splash in doubtful sleep
But ho! If only they would make some sound,
Or wear a face where faces should be found!

—H.P. Lovecraft

for Janet Hutchings

Contents

The Woman in the Window

Beneath the cushion of the plush blue chair she has hidden it.

Almost shyly her fingers grope for it, then recoil as if it were burning-hot.

No! None of this will happen, don't be ridiculous.

It is eleven A.M. He has promised to meet her in this room in which it is always eleven A.M.

She's doing what she does best: waiting.

In fact, she is waiting for him in the way that he prefers: naked. Yet wearing shoes.

Nude he calls it. Not *naked.*

(*Naked* is a coarse word! He's a gentleman and he feels revulsion for vulgarity. Any sort of crude word, mannerism—in a woman.)

She understands. She herself disapproves of women uttering profanities.

Only when she's alone would she utter even a mild profanity—*Damn! God damn. Oh hell . . .*

Only if she were very upset. Only if her heart were broken.

1

He can say anything he likes. It's a masculine prerogative to say the coarsest cruelest words uttered with a laugh—as a man will do.

Though he might also murmur—*Jesus!*

Not profanity but an expression of awe. Sometimes.

Jesus! You are beautiful.

Is she beautiful? She smiles to think so.

She is *the woman in the window.* In the wan light of an autumn morning in New York City.

In the plush blue chair waiting. Eleven A.M.

Sleepless through much of the night and in the early morning soaking in her bath preparing herself for *him.*

Rubbing lotion onto her body: breasts, belly, hips, buttocks. *Such soft skin. Amazing . . .* His voice catches in his throat.

At first, he scarcely dares touch her. But only at first.

It is a solemn ritual, creamy-white lotion smelling of faint gardenias rubbed into her skin.

In a trance like a woman in a dream rubbing lotion into her skin for she is terrified of her skin drying out in the radiator-heat, arid airlessness of The Maguire (as it is called)—the brownstone apartment building at Tenth Avenue and Twenty-third where she lives.

From the street The Maguire is a dignified-looking older building but inside it is really just *old.*

Like the wallpaper in this room, and the dull-green carpet, and the plush blue chair—*old.*

Dry heat! Sometimes she wakes in the night scarcely able to breathe and her throat dry as ashes.

She has seen the dried-out skin of older women. Some of them not so very old, in their sixties, even younger. Papery-thin skin, desiccated as a snake's husk of a skin, a maze of fine white wrinkles, terrible to behold.

Her own mother. Her grandmother.

Telling herself don't be silly, it will never happen to *her*.

She wonders how old his wife is. He is a gentleman, he will not speak of his wife. She dares not ask. She dares not even hint. His face flushes with indignation, his wide dark nostrils like holes in his face pinch as if he has smelled a bad odor. Very quiet, very stiff he becomes, a sign of danger so she knows to retreat.

Yet thinking, gloating: *His wife is not young. She is not so beautiful as I am. When he sees her, he thinks of me.*

(But is this true? The past half-year, since the previous winter, since the long break over Christmas when they were apart (*she* was in the city; *he* was away with his family in some undisclosed place very likely Bermuda for his face and hands were tanned when he returned) she has not been so certain.)

She has never been to Bermuda, or any tropical place. If *he* does not take her, it is not likely that she will ever go.

Instead, she is trapped here in this room. Where it is always eleven A.M. Sometimes it feels to her as if she is trapped in this chair, in the window gazing out with great yearning at—what?

An apartment building like the building in which she lives. A narrow shaft of sky. Light that appears fading already at eleven A.M.

Damned tired of the plush blue chair that is beginning to fray.

Damned tired of the bed (he'd chosen) that is a double bed, with a headboard.

Her previous bed, in her previous living quarters on East Eighth Street, in a fifth-floor walk-up single room, had been a single bed of course. A girl's bed too small, too narrow, too insubstantial for *him*.

The girth, the weight of *him*—he is two hundred pounds at least.

All muscle—he likes to say. (Joking.) And she murmurs in response *Yes*.

If she rolls her eyes, he does not see.

She has come to hate her entrapment here. Where it is always eleven A.M. and she is always waiting for *him*.

The more she thinks about it the more her hatred roils like smoldering heat about to burst into flame.

She hates him. For trapping her here.

For treating her like dirt.

Worse than dirt, something stuck on the sole of his shoe he tries to scrape off with that priggish look in his face that makes her want to murder him.

Next time you touch me! You will regret it.

* * *

Except: at work, at the office—she's envied.

The other secretaries know she lives in The Maguire for she'd brought one of them to see it, once.

Such a pleasure it was, to see the look in Molly's eyes!

And it is true—this is a very nice place really. Far nicer than anything she could afford on her secretary's salary.

Except she has no kitchen, only just a hot plate in a corner alcove and so it is difficult for her to prepare food for herself. Dependent on eating at the automat on Twenty-first and Sixth or else (but this is never more than once a week, at the most) when *he* takes her out to dinner.

(Even then, she has to take care. Nothing so disgusting as seeing a female *who eats like a horse,* he has said.)

She does have a tiny bathroom. The first private bathroom she'd ever had in her life.

He pays most of the rent. She has not asked him, he volunteers to give her cash unbidden as if each time he has just thought of it.

My beautiful girl! Please don't say a word, you will break the spell and ruin everything.

What's the time? Eleven A.M.

He will be late coming to her. Always he is late coming to her.

At the corner of Lexington and Thirty-seventh. Headed south.

The one with the dark fedora, camel's-hair coat. Whistling thinly through his teeth. Not a tall man though he gives that impression. Not a large man but he won't give way if there's another pedestrian in his path.

5

Excuse me, mister! Look where the hell you're going.

Doesn't break his stride. Only partially conscious of his surroundings.

Face shut up tight. Jaws clenched.

Murder rushing to happen.

The woman in the window, he likes to imagine her.

He has stood on the sidewalk three floors below. He has counted the windows of the brownstone. Knows which one is *hers*.

After dark, the lighted interior reflected against the blind makes of the blind a translucent skin.

When he leaves her. Or, before he comes to her.

It is less frequent that he comes to her by day. His days are taken up with work, family. His days are what is *known*.

Nighttime there is another self. Unpeeling his tight clothes: coat, trousers, white cotton dress shirt, belt, necktie, socks and shoes.

But now the woman has Thursdays off, late mornings at The Maguire are convenient.

Late mornings shifting into afternoon. Late afternoon, and early evening.

He calls home, leaves a message with the maid—*Unavoidable delay at office. Don't wait dinner.*

In fact it is the contemplation of the woman in the window he likes best for in his imagination this girl never utters a vulgar remark or makes a vulgar mannerism. Never says a banal or stupid or predictable thing. His sensitive nerves are offended by (for instance) a female shrugging her shoulders, as a man might do; or trying to make a joke, or a sarcastic remark. He hates a female *grinning*.

Worst of all, crossing her (bare) legs so that the thighs thicken, bulge. Hard-muscled legs with soft downy hairs, repulsive to behold.

The shades must be drawn. Tight.

Shadows, not sunlight. Why darkness is best.

Lie still. Don't move. Don't speak. Just—don't.

It's a long way from when she'd moved to the city from Hackensack needing to breathe.

She'd never looked back. Sure they called her selfish, cruel. What the hell, the use they'd have made of her, she'd be sucked dry by now like bone marrow.

Saying it was sin. Her Polish grandmother angrily rattling her rosary, praying aloud.

Who the hell cares! Leave me alone.

First job was file clerk at Trinity Trust down on Wall Street. Wasted three years of her young life waiting for her boss Mr. Broderick to leave his (invalid) wife and (emotionally unstable) adolescent daughter and wouldn't you think a smart girl like her would know better?

Second job also file clerk but then she'd been promoted to Mr. Castle's secretarial staff at Lyman Typewriters on West Fourteenth. The least the old buzzard could do for her and she'd have done a lot better except for fat-face Stella Czechi intruding where she wasn't wanted.

One day she'd come close to pushing Stella Czechi into the elevator shaft when the elevator was broken. The doors clanked opened onto a terrifying drafty cavern where dusty-oily cords hung twisted like ugly thick black snakes. Stella gave a little scream and stepped back, and she'd actually grabbed Stella's hand, the two of them so frightened—*Oh my God there's no elevator! We almost got killed.*

Later she would wish she'd pushed Stella. Guessing Stella was wishing she'd pushed *her.*

Third job, Tvek Realtors & Insurance in the Flatiron Building and she's Mr. Tvek's private secretary—*What would I do without you my dear one?*

As long as Tvek pays her decent. And *he* doesn't let her down like last Christmas, she'd wanted to die.

It is eleven A.M. Will this be the morning? She is trembling with excitement, dread.

Wanting badly to hurt him. Punish!

That morning after her bath she'd watched with fascination as her fingers lifted the sewing shears out of the bureau drawer. Watched her fingers test the sharpness of the points: very sharp, icepick-sharp.

Watched her hand pushing the shears beneath the cushion of the plush blue chair by the window.

It is not the first time she has hidden the sewing shears beneath the cushion. It is not the first time she has wished him *dead.*

Once, she hid the shears beneath her pillow on the bed.

Another time, in the drawer of the bedside table.

How she has hated him, and yet—she has not (yet) summoned the courage, or the desperation, to kill him.

(For is not *kill* a terrifying word? If you *kill*, you become a *killer*.)

(Better to think of punishment, exacting justice. When there is no other recourse but the sewing shears.)

She has never hurt anyone in her life!—even as a child she didn't hit or wrestle with other children, or at least not often. Or at least that she remembers.

He is the oppressor. *He* has murdered her dreams.

He must be punished before he leaves her.

Each time she has hidden the shears she has come a little closer (she thinks) to the time when she will use them. Just *stab, stab, stab* in the way he pounds himself into her, her body, using her body, his face contorted and ugly, terrible to behold.

The act that is unthinkable as it is irrevocable.

The shears are much stronger than an ordinary pair of scissors, as they are slightly larger.

The shears once belonged to her mother who'd been a quite skilled seamstress. In the Polish community in Hackensack, her mother was most admired.

She tries to sew too. Though she is less skilled than her mother.

Needing to mend her clothes—hems of dresses, underwear, even stockings. And it is calming to the nerves like knitting, crocheting, even typing when there is no time-pressure.

Except—*You did a dandy job with these letters, my dear! But I'm afraid not "perfect." You will have to do them over.*

9

Sometimes she hates Mr. Tvek as much as she hates *him.*

Under duress she can grip the shears firmly, she is sure. She has been a typist since the age of fifteen and she believes that it is because of this skill that her fingers have grown not only strong but unerring.

Of course, she understands: a man could slap the shears out of her hand in a single gesture. If he sees what she is doing, before the icepick-sharp points stabs into his flesh.

She must strike him swiftly and she must strike him in the throat.

The "carotid artery"—she knows what this is.

Not the heart, she doesn't know where the heart might be, exactly. Protected by ribs. The torso is large, bulky—too much fat. She could not hope to pierce the heart with the shears in a single swift blow.

Even the back, where the flesh is less thick, would be intimidating to her. She has a nightmare vision of the points of the shears stuck in the man's back, not deep enough to kill him, only just wound him, blood streaming everywhere as he flails his arms and bellows in rage and pain . . .

Therefore, the neck. The throat.

In the throat, the male is as vulnerable as the female.

Once the sharp points of the shears pierce his skin, puncture the artery, there will be no turning back for either of them.

Eleven A.M.

Light rap of his knuckles on the door. *Hel-lo.*

Turning of the key. And then—

Shutting the door behind him. Approaching her.

Staring at her with eyes like ants running over her (nude) body.

It is a scene in a movie: that look of desire in a man's face. A kind of hunger, greed.

(Should she speak to him? Often at such times he seems scarcely to hear her words, so engrossed in what he sees.)

(Maybe better to say nothing. So he can't wince at her nasal New Jersey accent, tell her *Shhh!*)

Last winter after that bad quarrel she'd tried to bar him from the apartment. Tried to barricade the door by dragging a chair in front of it but (of course) he pushed his way in by brute strength.

It is childish, futile to try to bar the man. He has his own key of course.

Following which she was punished. Severely.

Thrown onto the bed and her face pressed into a pillow, scarcely could she breathe, her cries muffled, begging for him not to kill her as her back, hips, buttocks were soundly beaten with his fists.

And then, her legs roughly parted.

Just a taste of what I will do to you if you—ever—try—this—again. Dirty polack.

Of course, they'd made up.

Each time, they'd made up.

He had punished her by not-calling, staying away. But eventually he'd returned as she'd known he would.

Bringing her a dozen red roses. A bottle of his favorite Scotch whiskey.

She'd taken him back, it might be said.

She'd had no choice. It might be said.

No! None of this will happen, don't be ridiculous.

She is frightened but she is thrilled.

She is thrilled but she is frightened.

At eleven A.M. she will see him at the door to the bedroom, as he pockets his key. Staring at her so intently she feels the power of being, if only for these fleeting moments, female.

That look of desire in the man's face. The clutch of the mouth like a pike's mouth.

The look of possession as he thinks—*Mine.*

By this time she will have changed her shoes. Of course.

As in a movie scene it is imperative that the woman be wearing not the plain black flat-heeled shoes she wears for comfort when she is alone but a pair of glamorous sexy high-heeled shoes which the man has purchased for her.

(Though it is risky to appear together in public in such a way the man quite enjoys taking the girl to several Fifth Avenue stores for the purchase of shoes. In her closet are at least a dozen pairs of expensive shoes he has bought for her, high-heeled, painful to wear but undeniably glamorous. Gorgeous crocodile-skin shoes he'd bought her for her last birthday, last month. He insists she wear high-heeled shoes even if it's just when they're alone together in her apartment.)

(Especially high heels when she's *nude*.)

Seeing that look in the man's eyes thinking—*Of course he loves me. That is the face of love.*

Waiting for him to arrive. And what time is it?—eleven A.M.

If he truly loves her he will bring flowers.

To make it up to you, honey. For last night.

He has said to her that of all the females he has known she is the only one who seems to be happy in her body.

Happy in her body. This is good to hear!

He means, she guesses, adult females. Little girls are quite happy in their bodies when they are little/young enough.

So unhappy. Or—happy . . .

I mean, I am happy.

In my body I am happy.

I am happy when I am with you.

And so when he steps into the room she will smile happily at him. She will lift her arms to him as if she does not hate him and wish him dead.

She will feel the weight of her breasts, as she raises her arms. She will see his eyes fasten greedily on her breasts.

She will not scream at him *Why the hell didn't you come last night like you promised? God damn bastard you can't treat me like shit on your shoe!*

Will not scream at him *D'you think I will just take it—this shit of yours? D'you think I am like your damn wife, just lay there and take it, d'you think a woman has no way of hitting back?—no way of revenge?*

A weapon of revenge. Not a male weapon but a female weapon: sewing shears.

It is appropriate that the sewing shears had once belonged to her mother. Though her mother never used the shears as she might have wished.

If she can grasp the shears firmly in her hand, her strong right hand, if she can direct the blow, if she can strike without flinching.

If she is that kind of woman.

Except: she isn't that kind of woman. She is a *romantic-minded girl* to whom a man might bring a dozen red roses, a box of expensive chocolates, articles of (silky, intimate) clothing. Expensive high-heeled shoes.

A woman who sings and hums *tea for two, and two for tea, you for me and me for you, alone . . .*

Eleven A.M. He will be late!

God damn he hates this. *He is always late.*

At the corner of Lexington and Thirty-first turning west on Thirty-first and so to Fifth Avenue. And then south.

Headed south into a less dazzling Manhattan.

He lives at Seventy-second and Madison: upper east side.

She lives in a pretty good neighborhood (he thinks)—for her.

Pretty damn good for a little polack secretary from Hackensack, N.J.

Tempted to stop for a drink. That bar on Eighth Avenue.

Except it's not yet eleven A.M. Too early to drink!

Noon is the earliest. You have to have preserve standards.

Noon could mean lunch. Customary to have drinks at a business lunch. A cocktail to start. A cocktail to continue. A cocktail to conclude. But he draws the line at drinking during the midday when he will take a cab to his office, far downtown on Chambers Street.

His excuse is a dental appointment in midtown. Unavoidable!

Of course five P.M. is a respectful hour for a drink. Almost, a drink at five P.M. might be considered the "first drink of the day" since it has been a long time since lunch.

Five P.M. drinks are "drinks before dinner." Dinner at 8 P.M. if not later.

Wondering if he should make a little detour before going to her place. Liquor store, bottle of Scotch whiskey. The bottle he'd brought to her place last week is probably almost empty.

(Sure, the woman drinks in secret. Sitting in the window, drink in hand. Doesn't want him to know. How in hell could he not know? Deceitful little bitch.)

There's a place on Ninth. Shamrock Inn. He can stop there.

Looks forward to drinking with her. One thing you can say about the little polack she's a good drinking companion and drinking deflects most needs to talk.

Unless she drinks too much. Last thing he wants to hear from her is complaints, accusations.

Last thing he wants to see is her face pouty and sulky and not so good-looking. Sharp creases in her forehead like a forecast of how she'll look in another ten years, or less.

It isn't fair! You don't call when you promise! You don't show up when you promise! Tell me you love me but—

Many times he has heard these words that are beginning to bore him.

Many times he has appeared to be listening but is scarcely aware which of them is berating him: the girl in the window, or the wife.

To the girl in the window he has learned to say—*Sure I love you. That's enough now.*

To the wife he has learned to say—*You know I have work to do. I work damn hard. Who the hell pays for all this?*

His life is complicated. That is actually true. He is not deceiving the woman. He is not deceiving the wife.

(Well—maybe he is deceiving the wife.)

(Maybe he is deceiving the woman.)

(But women expect to be deceived, don't they? Deception is the terms of the sex-contract.)

In fact he'd told the little polack secretary (warned her) at the outset, almost two years ago now—(Jesus! that long, no wonder he's getting to feel trapped, claustrophobic)—*I love my family. My obligations to my family come first.*

(Fact is, he's getting tired of this one. Bored. She talks too much even when she isn't talking, he can hear her *thinking*. Her breasts are heavy, beginning to droop. Flaccid skin at her belly. Thinking sometimes when they're in bed together he'd like to settle his hands around her throat and just start squeezing.)

(How much of a struggle would she put up? She's not a small woman but *he's* strong.)

(The French girl he'd had a *tussle* with—that was the word he'd given the transaction—had put up quite a struggle like a fox or a mink or a weasel but that was wartime, in Paris, people were desperate then, even a girl that young and starved-looking like a rat. *Aidez-moi! Aidez-moi!* But there'd been no one.)

(Hard to take any of them seriously when they're chattering away in some damn language like a parrot or a hyena. Worse when they screamed.)

Set out late from his apartment that morning. God damn he resents his God damn wife suspicious of him for no reason.

Hadn't he stayed home the night before? Hadn't he disappointed the girl?—all because of the wife.

Stiff and cold-silent the wife. God, how she bores him!

Her suspicions bore him. Her hurt feelings bore him. Her dull repressed anger bores him. Worst of all her boredom bores him.

He has imagined his wife dead many times of course. How long have they been married, twenty years, twenty-three years, he'd believed he was lucky marrying the daughter of a well-to-do stockbroker except the stockbroker wasn't that well-to-do and within a few years he wasn't a stockbroker any longer but bankrupt. Asking to borrow money from *him*.

Also, the wife's looks are gone. Melted-look of a female of a certain age. Face sags, body sags. He has fantasized his wife dying (in an accident: not his fault) and the insurance policy paying off: forty thousand dollars free and clear. So he'd be free to marry the other one.

Except: does he want to marry *her*?

God! Feeling the need for a drink.

It is eleven A.M. God damn bastard will be late again.

After the insult and injury of the previous night!

If he is late, it will happen. She will stab, stab, stab until he has bled out. She feels a wave of relief, finally it has been decided for her.

Checks the sewing shears, hidden beneath the cushion. Something surprising, unnerving—the blades of the shears seem to be a faint, faded red. From cutting red cloth? But she doesn't remember using the shears to cut red cloth.

Must be the light from the window passing through the gauze curtains.

Something consoling in the touch of the shears.

She wouldn't want a knife from the kitchen—no. Nothing like a butcher knife. Such a weapon would be premeditated while a pair of sewing shears is something a woman might pick up by chance, frightened for her life.

He threatened me. He began to beat me. Strangle me. He'd warned me many times, in one of his moods he would murder me.

It was in defense of my life. God help me! I had no choice.

Hears herself laugh aloud. Rehearsing her lines like an actress about to step out onto the bright-lit stage.

Might've been an actress, if her damn mother hadn't sent her right to secretarial school. She's as good-looking as most of the actresses on Broadway.

He'd told her so. Brought her a dozen blood-red roses first time he came to take her out.

Except they hadn't gone out. Spent the night in her fifth-floor walk-up, East Eighth Street.

(She misses that, sometimes. Lower east side where she'd had friends and people who knew her, on the street.)

Strange to be naked, that is *nude* yet wearing shoes.

Time for her to squeeze her (bare) feet into high heels.

Like a dancer. Girlie-dancers they are called. Stag parties exclusively for men. She'd heard of girls who danced at these parties. Danced *nude*. Made more in a single night's work than she made in two weeks as a secretary.

Nude is a fancy word. Hoity-toity like an artist-word.

What she has not wanted to see: her body isn't a girl's body any longer. At a distance (maybe) on the street she can fool the casual eye but not up close.

Dreads to see in the mirror a fleshy aging body like her mother's.

And her posture in the damned chair, when she's alone— leaning forward, arms on knees, staring out the window into a narrow shaft of sunshine between buildings—makes her belly bulge, soft-belly-fat.

A shock, first time she'd noticed. Just by accident glancing in a mirror.

Not a sign of getting older. Just putting on weight.

For your birthday, sweetheart. Is it—thirty-two?

She'd blushed, yes it is thirty-two.

Not meeting his eye. Pretending she was eager to unwrap the present. (By the size of the box, weight of what's inside, she guesses it's another pair of God damn high-heeled shoes.) Heart beating rapidly in a delirium of dread.

If he knew. Thirty-nine.

That was last year. The next birthday is rushing at her.

Hates him, wishes he were dead.

Except she would never see him again. Except the wife would collect the insurance.

She does not want to kill him, however. She is not the type to hurt anyone.

In fact she wants to kill him. She has no choice, he will be leaving her soon. She will never see him again and she will have nothing.

When she is alone she understands this. Which is why she has hidden the sewing shears beneath the cushion for the final time.

She will claim that he began to abuse her, he threatened to kill her, closing his fingers around her throat so she had no choice but to grope for the shears and stab him in desperation, repeatedly, unable to breathe and unable to call for help until his heavy body slipped from her twitching and spurting blood, onto the green rectangle of light in the carpet.

His age is beyond forty-nine, she's sure.

Glanced at his ID once. Riffling through his wallet while he slept openmouthed, wetly snoring. Sound like a rhinoceros snorting. She'd been stunned to see his young photograph—taken when he'd been younger than she is right now—dark-haired, thick-dark-haired, and eyes boring into the camera, so intense. In his U.S. Army uniform, so handsome!

She'd thought—*Where is this man? I could have loved this man.*

Now when they make love she detaches herself from the situation to imagine him as he'd been, young. *Him*, she could have felt something for.

Having to pretend too much. That's tiring.

Like the pretense she is *happy in her body.*

Like the pretense she is *happy when he shows up.*

No other secretary in her office could afford an apartment in this building. True.

Damn apartment she'd thought was so special at first now she hates. *He* helps with expenses. Counting out bills like he's cautious not to be overpaying.

This should tide you over, sweetheart. Give yourself a treat.

She thanks him. She is the good girl thanking *him*.

Give yourself a *treat*! With the money he gives her, a few tens, a rare twenty! God, she hates him.

Her fingers tremble, gripping the shears. Just the feel of the shears.

Never dared tell him how she has come to hate this apartment. Meeting in the elevators old women, some of them with walkers, eyeing her. Older couples, eyeing her. Unfriendly. Suspicious. How's a secretary from New Jersey afford The Maguire?

Dimlit on the third floor like a low-level region of the soul into which light doesn't penetrate. Soft-shabby furniture and mattress already beginning to sag like those bodies in dreams we feel but don't see. But she keeps the damn bed made every day whether anyone except her sees.

He doesn't like disorder. *He'd* told her how he'd learned to make a proper bed in the U.S. Army in 1917.

The trick is, he says, you make the bed as soon as you get up.

Pull the sheets tight. Tuck in corners—tight. No wrinkles! Smooth with the edge of your hand! Again.

First lieutenant, he'd been. When discharged. Holds himself like a soldier, stiff backbone like maybe he is feeling pain—arthritis? Shrapnel?

She has wondered—*Has he killed? Shot, bayoneted? With his bare hands?*

What she can't forgive: the way he detaches himself from her as soon as it's over.

Sticky skin, hairy legs, patches of scratchy hair on his shoulders, chest, belly. She'd like him to hold her and they could drift into sleep together but rarely this happens. Hates feeling the nerves twitching in his legs. Hates sensing how he is smelling her. How he'd like to leap from her as soon as he comes, the bastard.

A man is crazy wanting to make love, then abruptly it's over—*he's* inside his head, and *she's* inside hers.

The night before waiting for him to call to explain when he didn't show up. From 8 P.M. until midnight she'd waited rationing whiskey-and-water to calm her nerves. Considering the sharp-tipped shears she might use against herself, one day.

In those hours sick with hating him and hating herself and yet—the leap of hope when the phone finally rang.

Unavoidable, crisis at home. Sorry.

Now it is eleven A.M. Waiting for him to rap on the door.

She knows he will be late. He is always late.

She is becoming very agitated. But: too early to drink.

Even to calm her nerves too early to drink.

Imagines she hears footsteps. Sound of the elevator door opening, closing. Light rap of his knuckles on the door just before he unlocks it.

Eagerly he will step inside, come to the door of the bedroom—see her in the chair awaiting him . . .

The (nude) woman in the window. Awaiting him.

That look in his face. Though she hates him she craves that look in his face.

A man's desire is sincere enough. Can't be faked. (She wants to think this.) She does not want to think that the man's desire for her might be as fraudulent as her desire for him but if this is so, why does he see her at all?

He does love her. He loves something he sees in her.

Thirty-one years old, he thinks she is. No—thirty-two.

And his wife is ten, twelve years older at least. Like Mr. Broderick's wife, this one is something of an *invalid*.

Pretty damned suspicious. Every wife you hear of is an *invalid*.

How they avoid sex, she supposes. Once they are married, once they have children that's enough. Sex is something the man has to do elsewhere.

What time is it?—eleven A.M.

He is late. Of course, he is late.

After the humiliation of last night, when she had not eaten all day anticipating a nice dinner at Delmonico's. And he never showed up, and his call was a feeble excuse.

Yet in the past he has behaved unpredictably. She'd thought that he was through with her, she'd seen disgust in his face, nothing so sincere as disgust in a man's face; and yet—he'd called her, after a week, ten days.

Or, he'd showed up at the apartment. Knocking on the door before inserting the key.

And almost, in his face a look of anger, resentment.

Couldn't keep away.

God, I'm crazy for you.

In the mirror she likes to examine herself if the light isn't too bright. Mirror to avoid is the bathroom mirror unprotected and raw-lit by daylight but the bureau mirror is softer, more forgiving. Bureau mirror is the woman she *is*.

Actually she looks (she thinks) younger than thirty-two.

Much younger than thirty-nine!

A girl's pouty face, full lips, red-lipstick lips. Sulky-brunette still damned good-looking and *he* knows it, *he* has seen men on the street and in restaurants following her with their eyes, undressing her with their eyes, this is exciting to him (she knows) though if she seems to react, if she glances around, he will become angry—at *her*.

What a man wants, she thinks, is a woman whom other men want but the woman *must not seem to seek out this attention or even be aware of it.*

She would never bleach her hair blond, she exults in her brunette beauty knowing it is more real, earthier. Nothing phony, synthetic, showy about *her*.

Next birthday, forty. Maybe she will kill herself.

Though it's eleven A.M. he has stopped for a drink at the Shamrock. Vodka on the rocks. Just one.

Excited thinking about the sulky-faced woman waiting for him: in the plush blue chair, at the window, nude except for high-heeled shoes.

Full lips, lipstick-red. Heavy-lidded eyes. A head of thick hair, just slightly coarse. And hairs elsewhere on her body, that arouse him.

Slight disgust, yet arousal.

Yet he's late, why is that? Something seems to be pulling at him, holding him back. Another vodka?

Staring at his watch thinking—*If I am not with her by eleven-fifteen it will mean it's over.*

A flood of relief, never having to see her again!

Never the risk of losing his control with her, hurting her.

Never the risk she will provoke him into a *tussle.*

She's thinking she will give the bastard ten more minutes.

If he arrives after eleven-fifteen it is over between them.

Her fingers grope for the shears beneath the cushion. There!

She has no intention of stabbing him—of course. Not here in her room, not where he'd bleed onto the plush blue chair and the green carpet and she would never be able to remove the stains even if she could argue (she could argue) that he'd tried to kill her, more than once in his strenuous lovemaking he'd closed his fingers around her throat, she'd begun to protest *Please don't, hey you are hurting me* but he'd seemed scarcely to hear, in a delirium of sexual rapacity, pounding his heavy body into her like a jackhammer.

You have no right to treat me like that. I am not a whore, I am not your pathetic wife. If you insult me I will kill you—I will kill you to save my own life.

Last spring for instance when he'd come to take her out to Delmonico's but seeing her he'd gotten excited, clumsy bastard knocking over the bedside lamp and in the dimlit room they'd made love in her bed and never got out until too late for supper and she'd over-heard him afterward on the phone *explaining*—in the bathroom stepping out of the shower she'd listened at the door fascinated, furious—the sound of a man's voice when he is *explaining to a wife* is so callow, so craven, she's sick with contempt recalling.

Yet *he* says he has left his family, he loves *her*.

Runs his hands over her body like a blind man trying to see. And the radiance in his face that's pitted and scarred, he needs her in the way a starving man needs food. *Die without you. Don't leave me.*

Well, she loves him! She guesses.

Eleven A.M. He is crossing the street at Ninth and Twenty-fourth. Gusts of wind blow grit into his eyes. The vodka is coursing along his veins.

Feels determined: if she stares at him with that reproachful pouty expression he will slap her face and if she begins to cry he will close his fingers around her throat and squeeze, squeeze.

She has not threatened to speak to his wife. As her predecessor had done, to her regret. Yet, he imagines that she is rehearsing such a confrontation.

Mrs. ___? You don't know me but I know you. I am the woman your husband loves.

He has told her it isn't what she thinks. Isn't his family that keeps him from loving her all he could love her but his life he'd never told anyone about in the war, in the infantry, in France. What crept like paralysis through him.

Things that had happened to him, and things that he'd witnessed, and (a few) things that he'd perpetrated himself with his own hands. And if they'd been drinking this look would come into his face of sorrow, horror. A sickness of regret she did not want to understand. And she'd taken his hands that had killed (she supposed) (but only in wartime) and kissed them, and brought them against her breasts that were aching like the breasts of a young mother ravenous to give suck, and sustenance.

And she said *No. That is your old life.*

I am your new life.

He has entered the foyer. At last!

It is eleven A.M.—he is not late after all. His heart is pounding in his chest.

Waves of adrenaline as he has not felt since the war.

On Ninth Avenue he purchased a bottle of whiskey, and from a street vendor he purchased a bouquet of one dozen blood-red roses.

For the woman in the window. *Kill or be killed.*

Soon as he unlocks the door, soon as he sees her, he will know what it is he will do to her.

Eleven A.M. In the plush blue chair in the window the woman is waiting nude, except for her high-heeled shoes. Another time she checks the shears hidden beneath the cushion, that feel strangely warm to her touch, even damp.

Stares out the window at a narrow patch of sky. Almost, she is at peace. She is prepared. She waits.

EDWARD HOPPER, *Eleven A.M.,* 1926

The Long-Legged Girl

On the bathroom counter she'd come to hate (it was old, beige-flesh-toned Formica, with faint cracks you could not help mistake with a shudder of repugnance for loose hairs) the wife set out the husband's prescription pills both current and years-old.

So many! The wife had foraged in the medicine cabinet and in cupboards beneath the sink. The husband's medical history in miniature: digoxin (heart), blood thinner (high blood pressure), painkiller (root canal work), Lipitor (cholesterol), barbiturates (insomnia). Plus capsules for kidney dysfunction, so old they'd begun to crack and leak their white gritty powder.

Also on a shelf beneath the sink her groping fingers found an old sticky four-ounce container of Deet.

Her plan was to grind a selection of the medications into a fine powder and this powder she would dissolve in tea. Very hot exotic tea, to disguise the taste. She'd become a connoisseur of herbal infusions and had an impressive array on a kitchen shelf: passion fruit, cinnamon apple spice, citrus zinger, pomegranate zinger, peppermint, Bengal. Even the Deet would be undetectable if she didn't include more than a drop from an eyedropper.

In this way, she would regain control of her life. Of what remained of her life.

Yes, it was deliberate: she was using the husband's medications exclusively, and none of her own.

Beautiful Wedgwood teacups she would place side by side on saucers, on a tray. One of these would contain the lethal concoction, the other just herbal tea. She had yet to work out how precisely she would do this, for she had to be very clever; she must not arouse suspicion in her visitor, for that would be catastrophic. Even if others forgave her, never would she forgive her*self.*

To the casual eye—to the visitor's eye—there would appear to be no difference between the teacups and their contents: steaming-hot pungent-smelling herbal tea. Out of Solomonic fairness the wife would so position the teacups, she would so turn the tray about, that she herself could not know which cup was which.

For this solemn transaction, as she thought it, the wife would use two of her most exquisite teacups, inherited from a long-ghosted great-grandmother: pearl-white Wedgewood with tiny pink roses. She would have to wash the cups before-hand, fastidiously—the cups had not been used in years. No one gave a damn about *teacups* any longer: in the wife's lifetime the world had coarsened to stout, sturdy-proletarian mugs for all hot drinks. Certainly the husband's thick fingers could not have handled such delicate teacups, he'd probably broken china from the Wedgwood set years ago which was why so few pieces remained. But the visitor would notice, probably: the classy visitor would exclaim *Oh! How beautiful!*

Or possibly: *Oh, Mrs. Stockman! How beautiful!*

Like the gracious hostess the wife knew herself to be, or would have been if her life had not rattled along a terribly wrong, mistaken trolley track, she would allow her visitor to choose between the cups. *She* would drink from the cup that remained.

Like Russian roulette, it was. Though radically abbreviated, and played without the opponent's knowledge. *You don't owe your adversary the first shot*—this was a principle of gun owner-ship, one of myriad fatuous catchphrases you often heard in rural New Hampshire.

What mattered was, the wife's fate would lie outside her. She would be blameless.

The music of chance. Whatever is, is.

By the time the medications are ground into fine white odor-less powder and a single droplet of Deet mixed into the powder the bright May afternoon has waned. A roller-coaster day, a rare day when the wife can *breathe*. (For the wife is asthmatic, at times. More recently, more frequently.) Now trembling with excitement, or with dread so thrilling it is indistinguishable from excitement. At the stove staring at the teakettle heating on blue flames with a vibratory hum.

She hears the doorbell. Is it five-thirty P.M.—so soon?

Hears the oldest daughter's just-slightly-mocking voice: "Hey, Mom? One of Dad's students is here."

"God damn. *No.*"

But *yes.* For everywhere in the village the wife's eyes locked onto her: the long-legged girl.

Even before the wife knew the girl's name. Even before the wife knew, could guess, could not not-know, how (intimately, outrageously) she and the long-legged girl were connected.

Along the periphery of the sprawling college campus on its several wooded hills. On leafy walkways in the village, and on pedestrian crossings on Main Street. In the college bookstore, in the frozen yogurt store, in the CVS and in Geno's Pizzeria. In the post office facing the village green, and on the graveled paths of the village green. Suddenly it began to happen that the hapless wife's eyes swerved in their sockets like magnets drawn to the irresistible figure of the long-legged girl.

An elegantly poised girl. A girl with long straight silver-blond hair that fell past her shoulders, a perfect patrician profile, gray-green eyes gliding like liquid over prim adult faces. A girl who wore black leotards, or very short black spandex shorts, or skin-tight jeans that curved down at her impossibly narrow hips to expose not only her dimple of a belly button but the soft pale down surrounding it like a halo.

A girl of (perhaps) twenty-one. A girl with a face so young, so unlined, she might've been a fetus. (The wife thought, meanly.)

Lithe, sly, graceful as a dancer even when straddling a bicycle crossing College Avenue in front of the wife's compact Nissan.

In fact, *was* the long-legged girl a dancer? One of the husband's young protégées?

Strange and unnerving, that the wife (who had a reputation for not seeming to recognize anyone in public places) should so frequently see the long-legged girl, and be stopped in her tracks by the sight of the girl.

Especially, driving had become hazardous for the wife. At such times she was particularly prone to seeing the girl and so she'd become apprehensive, distracted whenever she left the house. Lately insomniac, sleep like a tattered quilt that didn't quite cover her stubby feet, she had to make an effort to stay awake behind the wheel of her car, to brake at traffic lights and stop signs, crosswalks. Once, she'd been a quite good driver. The children would never believe it.

Mom, wake up!

But she was awake. That was the problem.

Spring was dazzling-bright and all too soon, too much after a bitter-cold New England winter of terrifying ennui. The wife was a food writer, of some small, quality renown. But food had begun to fail, as inspiration, even as she overate compulsively. (Or is all overeating *compulsive*?) Writing had become too much effort, like trying to push a coarse thread through the eye of a small needle: nerves of steel were required, and for so paltry a reward. She'd even begun to dread leaving the house where once any excuse had been enough to propel her out the door—like checking out a new organic tofu restaurant. Reckless courage had to be summoned to press the switch in the garage, to send the door upward in a roll of thunder, to climb into the car that smelled as if something small had died in it, to back out of the garage with shut eyes. An accident waiting to happen but if it was truly an accident that awaited, somewhere beyond the end of the badly cracked asphalt driveway of the Stockman residence on cryptically named Hope Street, how could the fault be *hers?*

Nothing so demoralized the wife as household errands involving groceries, dry cleaners, hardware stores. The sand fleas of quotidian life crawling up your legs, invisible and awful. And bloodsucking, in the tiniest increments.

Dreading the short drive into town. Scarcely a mile. She'd put on weight, no longer walked where once, not so very long ago, she'd not only walked but *ran*—or almost. Fast-walked, it used to be called.

So, had to drive. Had to hoist herself into the car. Damned Nissan so compact, so cheap-built, she could feel it (she'd swear) sag beneath her weight with a faint jeering protest. And as she drove toward Main Street where during the school year the procession of undergraduates never ceased, like marionettes that have broken their strings, she would begin to feel a deeper dread, as of something in the marrow of her bones begging, pleading with her—*No. Turn back. It isn't too late*—even as another time she felt the rapid-eye excitation of REM sleep, an involuntary tug of her eyeballs so that she was seeing, to her dismay, the long-legged blond girl on a sidewalk, or in the street, or on her bicycle hurtling past like the Greek goddess of the hunt Artemis . . .

Unmistakably, it was *that girl*. Though two-thirds of the undergraduates at the college seemed to be blond, and most of these were tall and long-legged, and attractive, and wore interchangeable clothes, yet the girl the wife chanced to see was invariably *that girl*.

"But I don't know who she is. I have never seen her before."

The wife spoke to herself in vexed terms, usually. Dismay with herself, mounting frustration.

At the spring dance recital at the music school? Had it been there the wife had first seen the long-legged girl who was one of Victor Stockman's senior thesis students?

With an effort the wife could remember. But perhaps she did not wish to remember.

So many dance recitals. So many senior advisees. Decades of girl-undergraduates at the liberal arts college in the Hampshire hills. And dance was a popular major of course since for virtually all majors it was a useless art, a perishable craft, an expensive vanity, a folly to be performed for visiting families, to stir pride in the foolish, and to assuage the unease over the preposterously high tuition and fees at the college.

Founded in 1879, the college could claim its history as one of the first women's colleges in the United States. On its fabled wooded hills it had been kept small and select, a handpicked fifteen hundred students, unlike the slovenly-large state university a few miles away with its democratic masses; now coed, but with far fewer young men than women and these young men, on the whole, less academically impressive than the women.

It had been purely chance. On a blindingly bright day in April not the wife but the husband was driving the Nissan. Poor Victor, like Elinor, having difficulty lately fitting himself into the car, grunting and panting behind the wheel, fat knees pressed against the underside of the wheel and belly straining against the seat belt, and he'd been fiddling with the radio dial, an NPR interview with a rival composer in residence at Yale, the wife could only just imagine what savage lunges the husband's heart was taking in his chest even as he was determined to remain stoic, unperturbed—yet suddenly he'd had to brake the car to a stop at a crosswalk near the front gate of the college, sucked in his breath and stared at a tall lithe gliding figure passing just a few feet in front of the car, in the company of two others—*the blondes*, Elinor would have called them contemptuously if she hadn't understood that to be scathing in such circumstances was to sound envious and venal instead.

She'd been blond once herself. When she'd been a single-digit age.

Now, what you'd call *dirty-blond*. Split ends, crackling-dry and casually combed. It was enough to see to the children's hair and general grooming, she hadn't time to squander on her own or on anything of hers that was merely *hers*.

Seeing the flush rising from the husband's wattled neck into his face, hearing that startled intake of breath, the wife asked coolly,

"Is that the one? The long-legged one? And is she one of a series, or is she the last of a series?" It was a wild stab, and a mistake.

For the husband did not laugh. The husband did not laugh at the wife for uttering so bizarre a remark, as ordinarily he'd have done with a dismissive wave of his hand, but instead the husband flushed more deeply and stammered: "Eli, I am sorry. Oh, God! Can you forgive me . . ."

Very still the wife sat. This was not what she'd anticipated. Caught in the God damned seat belt like an overgrown baby in a high chair. Oh, the wife could not *breathe.*

Yet she managed, in her most caustic voice, like Eve Arden of the nineteen forties: "Don't be silly, Victor. Take your foot off the brake. Look where you're going. *Drive.*"

By this time the long-legged silver-blond girl and her companions had crossed the street and were gone. Not a glance had they given to the short-of-breath middle-aged couple in the corroded Nissan whose lives were visibly unraveling like a cheap sweater given a sudden yank.

She would forgive. Of course.

She would not forgive. Not this time.

Over the course of years, now nearly seventeen at the college in the Hampshire hills, and several years preceding at the state university at Durham, there'd been a number of girl-protégées who had entered the husband's life. Not always but usually dancers. Not always but usually blond with fetus-perfect faces, unlined and unlived-in.

Most of these girls had been nameless, faceless. The wife had known, but had not-known. In his sleep beside her the husband might grind his teeth and mutter an obscure name—*Em'ly!* (Emily?) *Tiff 'ny!* (Tiffany?)—that vanished even as the wife tried to decipher it.

In fact, for all of those years the wife had been enormously busy with her own life and a good part of this life the care and nourishment of the lives of others: husband, young children. Her career as a food writer with an anthropologist's cool eye and a food lover's avidity of appetite was challenging and occasionally thrilling. *I know who I am. That will not change.* For a brief, hectic season her husband might be distracted by a girl—or two, or three—but after graduation the girls disappeared. Or so the wife believed.

Other faculty wives assured her, this was so. Usually, this was so.

Well. Possibly the husband kept in touch with some of the protégées, the most promising, the most attractive. The protégées who'd most seemed to admire him. And to need him.

Possibly the husband exchanged emails with the girls. In the city, and away overnight, he might arrange to see them. That was possible. If a girl was performing in a dance program, or in a play, naturally she would provide a comp ticket for her favorite professor Victor Stockman, and naturally, the favorite professor would accept; because she was likely to be a girl from a rich family, whose parents were underwriting her New York lifestyle, it was not unlikely that the comp ticket entailed dinners at swanky restaurants as well, following the performances. And what followed then, the wife could not know. The wife did not wish to know, enormously busy with her life in the Hampshire hills, unable to accompany the husband to New York City for such festive occasions, and uninvited. Certainly the wife had not been jealous.

Telling herself how she had her *own life*. After all.

Victor believed in monogamy, he'd often said, in jest. One wife at a time.

Truly it was a jest. Those who heard laughed, obligingly.

The Stockmans were devoted to each other, it was often said. Not by the Stockmans perhaps but by others, observing.

There was something fairy-tale about the couple. Each looked subtly deformed, yet you could not put your finger on where the deformity lurked: in the body, in the face, in the gaze, in the soul. Each was "witty"—yet clumsily shy. Each was gifted—the husband a musician-composer, very *avant-garde;* the wife a writer—a "food critic"—who published in New York City–centric publications and whose first book had had a small, cheering success, too long ago to matter. Neither had been married before this marriage that seemed to have begun in a fairy-tale childhood, as if dwarf-children had married.

That the Stockmans had children—altogether normal-seeming, normal-sized and normal-mannered children, who were mortified by their odd-looking, oddly-behaving parents—was an astonishment of which the parents could know little; though sometimes Elinor saw the wincing look in the oldest daughter's face, when slovenly Elinor appeared in public in some proximity to the slender, sardonic Isabel—*Oh Mom*! Isabel murmured with a roll of her beautiful brown eyes.

If the Stockman children knew of their mother's unhappiness, they could not have known its source. In the Stockman household, the adults never quarreled; the most antagonism their gentlemanly father revealed was a furious humming of the more bellicose composers (Beethoven, Mahler, Shostakovich) through clenched teeth while their mother, hiding away in her kitchen-space like a fat dimpled spider in its web, seethed in silence, and sampled spoonfuls and handfuls of the meals she was preparing.

Old friends of the couple knew something of the frayed nerves between them though Elinor had too much pride to complain of anything so banal as a husband romantically obsessed with blond teenagers. Indeed, Elinor made it a point to amuse house guests and visitors, complaining wittily of the New England town "perfect on the surface" as a Norman Rockwell Christmas card—"We do 'quaint' here very nicely," Elinor told them. "We have plenty of practice."

Yet, Elinor took a perverse sort of pride in living there. In having persevered, in this remote New England place to which her (then-young, ambitious) composer-husband had brought her, with a promise that it would be for only a few years—until Victor Stockman was established as a brilliant young composer, with invitations to join the music faculty at Juilliard, Curtis, Princeton.

"Well. We are 'still waiting.' We do that well, too."

Driving by the music school, a squat gothic building with leaded windows, Elinor gave the impression of being undecided about whether to drop in to say hello to Victor—"He'd love to see us of course, but probably it isn't a good idea without calling first. He's always so busy—teaching, in rehearsals, auditions . . ." Her bright voice faded, trailed away.

Teaching. Its verbal proximity to *leching*. Shame!

Sometimes, to the astonishment of a friend to whom Elinor had hinted no unhappiness or unease, scarcely even a characteristic crankiness, she began crying with no explanation. God *damn*.

Quintessential New England, Elinor told her friends. The residents did not see themselves as "quaint" but rather as "realists"— their suspicion was bred in the bone, like certain types of cancer.

"They believe in expecting the worst. That way they're rarely surprised and never disappointed."

Elinor quite enjoyed playing the cynic. It gave her a small mean pleasure to hear her friends laugh appreciatively, sometimes warily, at her witty remarks. *Oh*, they went away marveling, *Elinor Stockman is so* funny.

So brave, and so funny. But what a shame, she must have gained forty pounds in the past year alone . . . Her graying hair was coarsely and crookedly braided and her face looked as if it had been scrubbed, sallow and plain, defiant. Her favorite article of clothing was a sacklike denim jumper worn over a black sweater with a frayed neck; in cold weather she wore a red quilted down coat that resembled a small, strangely ambulatory tent, from which the children hid their eyes.

One of the visitors would recall how quickly Elinor began to pant walking uphill across the village green on a mild spring day. How oddly Elinor stared at several college girls who were talking and laughing oblivious of Elinor and her friend a few yards away.

When the friend asked Elinor if she knew the girls Elinor said irritably of course not, she'd never seen them before.

"There are hundreds of them at the college. You can't tell them apart. Spoiled little rich girls with long straight hair and perfect orthodontia."

Elinor spoke with such venom, the friend thought at first that she must be joking. But there was Elinor trembling with something like indignation, turning away from the sight of the girls.

Quickly, the friend changed the subject. Though thinking how unlikely it was that there could be hundreds of girls quite like these with their long straight corn-silk hair, so striking and so self-confident, so beautiful, even in all of New England.

It had become a not-funny joke. Where was Daddy, Daddy was *away*.

Where was Daddy, Daddy was *not having dinner with them that night*.

Unfair, Elinor thought. Why do they blame *me*.

A flame of pure senseless hatred for the children swept over her, their hurt faces, accusing eyes as they stood in the kitchen glaring at her and preparing to sneer at whatever she'd prepared for them to eat.

Then, in a contrary motion, a wave of love for them deeper and more profound than any love she could have discovered for herself came over her, leaving her faint. *They are of my body, we are bonded forever. I am responsible for their happiness, and I am failing them.*

For it was her fault, essentially. The woman's fault, failing to satisfy the man. Failing to be enough for the man. No matter that the man is not nearly enough for *her.*

In the children's eyes the mother was humbled, humiliated. In the eyes of the oldest girl Isabel, especially.

In the girl's face a look of anguish, mortification that hardened into the jeering mask—"Oh, Mom. For God's sake."

It was Elinor's very existence that exasperated the girl, and turned her heart against her mother.

Since the previous November the husband had often been *away.* What was worse, he was rarely far away—just in his damned studio at the college where he frequently worked so late (teaching, meeting with senior advisees, conducting rehearsals), it was easier (as he reasoned) to remain there all night sleeping on a couch than to "hurry home" to sleep for just a few hours.

But what about dinner. Don't you want to eat with your family. Why don't you want to eat with us? YOU ARE US.

She wanted to scream at him, when he did return home. But that would only drive him away again so she hid in the shower filling the drafty bathroom with steam, or in an attic room she'd fashioned into a study. Her first book had been titled *Comfort Food: Favorite Recipes of Childhood.* Her second book, at which she'd been working for years, would be titled *After Comfort Food*: *Recipes for Adult Survival.*

In a rash and uncharacteristically vainglorious gesture the wife had accepted an advance for this second book, that promised (her editor believed) to be a "runaway" bestseller. The advance had long been frittered away, lost.

The husband had always been Elinor's first reader. He'd been a most enthusiastic reader before Elinor had begun to publish in such places as *The New Yorker*, *Harper's* and *The New York Times Magazine;* he seemed less certain of her talent now, more critical and grudging with his praise. Not that it mattered greatly for Elinor wasn't writing much any longer, and had only a scattering of notes and outlines for the second book.

In case of death of author: DNR (do not resuscitate) manuscript.

This notice she'd tacked onto a wall beside her desk. Not sure if it was intended to be funny.

"Elinor, you have changed my life. You have made my life possible."

In an earlier phase of his life Victor Stockman had been one to make such grandiose pronouncements. Shy, yet stubborn; clearly very intelligent, yet naive and gullible; sexually inexperienced, as Elinor was also, and therefore easily led, seduced. A fattish young man with owl-eyed glasses, a weak chin and a faint stammer, in his early twenties when they'd met and Elinor had perceived in him a musical genius of an arcane type, unworldly, unexpect-edly kind (at times) and (at times) childishly short-tempered. Above all, she had perceived in Victor Stockman an *inexpert* with women, which was to her advantage as she'd been certainly *inexpert* with men.

Victor was a passionate theorist and composer of "new music"—a protégée of Milton Babbitt (the experimental composer who'd once given an interview titled "Who Cares If You Listen?") and one of a very small, elite circle of contemporary composers: electronic, minimalist, aleatory, "atmospheric." Of Victor's myriad compositions only one had been singled out for acclaim, a chamber quartet influenced by Babbitt, John Cage and Philip Glass, which, by one of those flukes that occurs occasionally in academic music, was awarded a Pulitzer Prize in 1987. (Later, Victor would learn that Milton Babbitt had been one of the jurors on the Pulitzer committee. Mortified, he had wanted to turn back the award but had been dissuaded by Elinor, among others.)

The CD of this prize-winning work would sell less than a thousand copies; Elinor's *Comfort Food* sold nearly a hundred thousand copies in hardcover and paperback. Yet, within the Stockman household, as within the college community, it was Victor Stockman who was the renowned, primary spouse, and not Elinor; Victor was the designated genius of the family while Elinor was the faculty wife-and-mother with an "interesting" career on the side.

Since the Pulitzer, now twenty years ago, Victor had completed few ambitious compositions. It had seemed easier, certainly more emotionally rewarding, to concentrate on teaching. He advised on senior honors theses. He codirected the dance program. He'd established a center for young composers and coauthored music with some of them—"Aleatory Harmonies for Farm Implements" was a notable title. His lecture course Experimental Music of the 20th Century from Stravinsky to Glass became so popular it had to be moved into an amphitheater with three hundred seats; his lectures, meticulously prepared, rapid-fire in delivery and bristling like his stiff, graying whiskers, were considered "brilliant"—"cool"—"genius." The less his admirers understood, the more evident the "genius."

Elinor did not think it much evidence of genius that Victor was reluctant to ask for a raise in his salary at the college. No one at the famously liberal college was paid what you'd call "well" but Victor was reputed to be a star, one of just a few. His salary raises were minuscule, insulting.

He exasperated the wife by declaring that he'd gladly have worked for half what they paid him, he so loved teaching and working with young people.

Working with young girls, he'd meant. Elinor knew.

"'An administrator is one who knows how to take advantage of the foolish idealism of another. An idealist is one who knows only how to be taken advantage of.'"

Asked who'd made this sardonic remark Elinor retorted, "H. L. Mencken." But of course, the remark was purely Elinor.

Yet Victor was a man of pride, including sexual pride. That was the irony. No man however middle-aged and fattish, short of breath, suffering from hypertension and erratic heartbeat, discouraged about his career as by life in general, with badly deteriorating teeth, is totally lacking in sexual pride.

The long-legged girl was not a figment of the wife's imagination but indeed a dancer, a senior advisee of Victor Stockman's. One of a lengthy series of "talented" young people with whom he'd worked—the wife told herself—not anyone *singular, special.*

Yet, the girl's work was indeed unusual. Her thesis was an adaptation of Herman Melville's dark allegory "The Paradise of Bachelors and the Tartarus of Maids" as an eerie and starkly sexual ballet set to little-known music of Bartok, which her advisor Professor Stockman had arranged. Not only did the long-legged girl dance the lead role but she'd painted the set herself in blood-red streaks. The costumes (which she'd made herself) were blood-red, in tatters. Male dancers wore black leotards. There was much rushing from one side of the stage to the other. Undeniably, the long-legged girl was outstanding in the lead as a figure trying to free herself from the clutching of others, who seek to drown her or (it wasn't always clear) mate with her. Beside Elinor, in the first row, Victor stared and stared and stroked his whiskery jaws in a way that seemed to Elinor far too intimate, verging upon the obscene.

At the curtain the girl bowed in a graceful pose of humility from the waist and her long straight silver-blond hair fell about her face shimmering like a falls. And there was Victor Stockman, summoned by the triumphantly smiling girl to stand beside her, that the amphitheater might applaud them both: student dancer, professor/advisor. The two of them—(could it be?)—grasping each other's hand.

Afterward Elinor accused the husband of holding the girl's hand in front of a gaping audience—"How could you, Victor! *I hate you.*"

"That's altogether ridiculous, Elinor! Nothing of the sort happened. Stacy and I *did* not *touch.*"

(So the girl's name was Stacy. Elinor had not been able to avoid this demeaning knowledge.)

She'd seen what she had seen. Looks of blatant adoration passing between the long-legged dancer in the tattered red leotard and the husband in an ill-fitting suit.

Or indeed, was Elinor imagining it? This past year the children had begun to speak of her in the third person as if she weren't present. *Mom is losing it. Mom is too weird. Mom is having a meltdown. Mom is pitiful. You have to feel sorry for her—poor Mom.*

Following this public humiliation, private humiliations.

Heavily the husband sighed. Dared to roll his eyes.

A new habit of Victor's, stroking his whiskery jaws. Hard little drum of a belly so low, he had to maneuver his belt beneath it. Which made walking just slightly difficult.

Swaggering confidence and yet (if you observed closely) a nervous tic in every pocket waiting to be tugged out like a magician's handkerchief. The wife tried not to notice how eagerly the husband checked his emails and text messages. Like a teenager, how he could not bear to be separated from his cell phone.

(Elinor had misplaced two cell phones out of indifference. But then she was Elinor, an old person's name.)

Weeks had passed since "The Paradise of Bachelors and the Tartarus of Maids." Weeks of subterranean resistance on the part of the husband and a stiff wounded silence on the part of the wife. As if she were to blame for his behavior.

Please look at me. Please acknowledge what you have done.

Though it wasn't clear, it had never been clear, exactly what Victor had done: if his erotic obsessions were what you'd call *consummated*, or just wishful fantasizing.

In calmer moods the wife reasoned that an actual *love affair* with one of his students was (probably) not likely for prissy fussy clumsy short-of-breath Victor Stockman with his scratchy whiskers and (occasional) flatulence; even if Victor could overcome his physical clumsiness and timidity, how likely was it that a beautiful young girl could succumb to his charms? *Why* would a beautiful young girl make herself sexually available to him?

Yet: such affairs happened. Dismayingly often, even routinely. Marriages dissolved, wives were left behind—*dumped* was the ungracious term. Elinor dreaded the possibility, could not bear to consider the probability: *dumped*.

And perhaps it was insulting to her simply as a woman, as a wife, as one who'd been impregnated by the man and bore his children, that Victor was infatuated with any girl, mooning over her like a lovestruck puppy while Elinor stood before him trying to make conversation like an adult. Trying not to notice how distracted the husband was, clearly impatient to escape the house, before even the children left for school. Always he was saying, avoiding the wife's eye: "Don't wait up for me tonight. Please."

And the husband's ridiculous *humming*. In the shower especially. Like a hive of bees gone berserk.

"There is no girl. You are confused. You're looking feverish, Eli. Maybe you should see a doctor."

This was *gaslighting*. Elinor knew. She'd plied the technique herself more than once.

Had he forgotten, Elinor had already seen a doctor? Doctors? Who'd prescribed medication to calm her nerves, stir her cognitive abilities, allow her to sleep past dawn, quell suicidal thoughts. *Make her feel good about herself again.*

She'd tried diet pills also. For years. Prescription and over-the-counter. Might've worked if she'd mainlined amphetamine directly into her carotid artery, otherwise no. The more jumpy, edgy, depressed and angry, the more the raging appetite, like a fire into which someone has tossed kerosene.

She'd considered, then decided against, using some of her own medications in preparing the lethal tea. But the long-legged girl belonged to Victor exclusively.

Pulverizing pills and capsules, and a droplet of Deet. Who would know?

None of the previous girls had called the house, so far as Elinor knew. It had been a radical, bold step, the dancer who'd choreographed "The Paradise of Bachelors and the Tartarus of Maids" under Professor Stockman's direction—the long-legged girl herself!—had dared to call and leave a message asking if she might drop by to leave Professor Stockman a token of her esteem and gratitude.

Not wanting to bring the gift to the professor's office. Not wanting to give it to him in person. Just—*Thought I'd leave it for the Professor. And you could give it to him after graduation—after I'm gone . . .*

Elinor had listened in astonishment. The nerve of this girl! A flimsy excuse for her wanting to come to Victor's house, to see where he lived; to flaunt her youth, beauty, poise in the very face of the betrayed wife . . .

It was intolerable, a devastating insult, and yet the wife called the number the girl had left, to set a date. Feeling the cunning of a hunter when through some confusion, misunderstanding or plain accident his heedless prey is approaching *him.*

And so in the kitchen of the big wood frame house on Hope Street the wife is trembling with excitement, apprehension. Staring at the old, dented teakettle on the stove beginning to whistle a plaintive upbeat tune: first the vibratory hum rising sharply, then the pent-up breath before the actual whistle penetrating Elinor's eardrums.

Doorbell. Already five-thirty P.M.? Five thirty-*five*?

She'd meant to answer the door herself but Isabel has gotten there first which is just as well (the wife thinks) for seeing the thirteen-year-old daughter, taking in the fact that Elinor appears to be a normal wife-and-mother, the long-legged girl is even less likely to be suspicious of her invitation to tea.

"Mrs. Stockman! How do you do . . ."

The query is polite, forthright. Clear-blue-eyed. Here is a very poised and self-confident young woman, and *tall*.

"How do I *do*. 'Well,' I guess. Though not exactly 'very well'— that would be excessive."

Elinor laughs, as one might laugh standing on the tilting deck of a ship in a windstorm. She sees the girl blink at her quizzically as her own children often blink at her when she says something witty with a deadpan expression.

Gaiety in the professor's wife's laughter, and something like a shark-flitting shadow beneath.

"Come this way, dear. Please . . ."

"My name is Stacy, Mrs. Stockman. You know—Stacy Donovan. We met after the dance recital . . ."

"Did we? I don't think so, dear. I'd remember, if we had."

Calling the girl *dear*. Best to deceive, disarm. And smile, smile. The witch inviting Gretel inside the gingerbread house, quick shut the door.

Good that the husband is *away*. For once the wife is damned happy that the husband will be *away* for hours.

How pleasant the professor's wife is to her long-legged silver-blond patrician visitor. Pebbles wouldn't melt in the woman's scrubbed-looking resolutely un-made-up mouth.

Probably, the wife thinks, she is no older than the girl's mother. Yet, the wife doesn't doubt that she looks much older than the girl's mother in the girl's eyes.

"In here, dear. You will stay for a few minutes, I hope . . ."

In her arms against her flat chest the girl is carrying a tinselly gift tote bag containing something fairly sizable and heavy, probably expensive. The wife recalculates—*certainly* expensive.

Possibly, the girl would like to leave the gift and escape. Possibly, she is somewhat nervous, not quite so self-confident as the wife has imagined.

". . . don't want to take up your time, Mrs. Stockman . . ."

Not at all! Not at all. The wife insists, she has been looking forward to the visit. The wife was *so impressed* with that "remarkable, original" dance thesis based on the Melville story.

(This is true. The wife was indeed impressed with the dance adaptation, and bitterly jealous of the long-legged dancer.)

Away from the front door of the house, away from the hall where there is the danger of family traffic, the wife and the long-legged girl find themselves in a little parlor where "tea things" have been laid out very prettily. Imagine a nineteenth-century daguerreotype of young ladies at tea: that would be it.

Two very dainty, antique-looking teacups on matching saucers, a plate of macaroons, red paper napkins in the shape of valentine hearts. Certainly this is an occasion: Mrs. Stockman has even groomed her (usually disheveled) hair, to a degree. She has changed from the perennial denim jumper to something resembling a dress, waistless, with billowing sleeves and a long skirt, of the kind a captive wife in a cult might wear, with a bright unwavering smile.

The perfect girl is seated on a worn velvet love seat. The imperfect wife sits facing her in a cushioned chair that seems but grudgingly to contain the wife's heft, her fleshy thighs that spill over the edge of the cushion like an excess of pudding poured into a mold.

". . . just thought I'd leave a little gift for . . . 'token of my esteem' . . ."

Glancing about like a curious little bird wanting to see and to know what is not her business. Where the great Victor Stockman lives, how he lives and with whom.

Such a messy house. Not to be believed.

It smelled like—I don't know . . . old, musty things.

And his wife! The wife is so, so—awful . . .

Having obsessively planned her stratagem for days, weeks, perhaps years the wife sees her hands moving briskly, deftly above the tea tray. If her visitor thinks it odd that the teacups appear to be half-filled with tea even as she and the wife sit down, the visitor gives no sign for she is easily distracted by the wife's chatty remarks (weather: lovely; graduation in twelve days: so exciting) and her own audacity in being in the home of the adored Professor Stockman.

Charming old teacups, pink rosebuds on white. As boring as you'd expect a great-grandmother to be but comforting.

"I hope you like herbal tea, dear? My favorite at the moment is quite exotic—Bengal. Have you ever tasted it?"

From out of a squat tortoise-colored teapot the wife pours steaming liquid into both cups. A rich, spicy singed-orange aroma wafts to their nostrils.

"'Bengal'? I—don't know. It smells delicious."

With a display of childlike eagerness the long-legged Stacy reaches for one of the steaming cups. (As the wife might have anticipated, the girl reaches for the cup on the right.) If the husband could know the wife's plan in theory he would applaud it. For the husband is one of those American minimalist composers for whom "chance"—"the aleatory"—is a crucial element in creativity.

The music of the aleatory, of chance.

Whatever *is*, is *meant to be.*

God is expressed through chance.

Was that John Cage? Henry Cowell? Milton Babbitt? Stockhausen, or—Stockman?

None of them believed in God for a moment. Yet it was common in such avant-garde circles to evoke God as a hypothetical agent, to diffuse one's responsibility for a work of alleged art.

"'Bengal'—it's meant to evoke India, tigers. It's noncaffeine but tastes as if it might have caffeine—that tartness on the tongue."

"Y-Yes. It does . . ."

The hapless girl takes a tentative swallow. The wife holds her breath as the girl coughs, just a little. But then, emboldened, wishing not to offend the wife who is staring so strangely at her, the girl takes a larger swallow, and manages not to cough.

"Please take a macaroon! I didn't make them myself."

The long-legged girl laughs startled at this remark, which the wife intends to be witty and disarming, not ironic or (self-)belittling.

Politely the long-legged girl selects a macaroon to nibble like a rabbit.

Probably, the girl is anorexic: eating a macaroon would be a reckless act for her. The wife resists asking her how much she weighs reasoning that she would not wish the girl to ask *her*.

Not wanting to think that the girl might weigh one-third of Elinor's weight. Just barely.

The wife's heart is beating rapidly. The wife's heart feels enlarged to near-bursting.

All this day she has been entranced. A very special day in the wife's life she cannot (quite) believe has actually arrived.

Breathing deeply and fully and with joy. A brazen sort of joy. In the upstairs bathroom and then in the kitchen on the first floor, the wife's special places.

The unused medications returned to their original places upstairs including the Deet to the shelf beneath the sink.

No one will know. No one will guess. How possible? Why?

With dogged inanity Elinor asks if the long-legged girl likes the Bengal tea and the girl murmurs enthusiastically—*Yes*. Elinor has grasped the remaining Wedgwood cup by its delicate handle and brings it to her lips.

This is the cup to the girl's left. Which is the cup to Elinor's right.

Still, it is pure chance. Perhaps in a sense all is chance.

Saying, as if this were a remark of some profundity, "Usually, my favorite is cinnamon apple spice. I also like peppermint."

"Yes—peppermint. I do, too."

The girl seems cheered, drinking tea. The macaroon, though stale, must not be excessively stale, for the girl is eating it as a doll might eat, if a doll could eat, daintily, with self-conscious gestures.

If the scene were a ballet, what sort of music would be played? Not Bartok—too strident. Not Stockhausen, or Stockman. Possibly, the lone pure enigmatic piano notes of Erik Satie that suggest something-to-come of a catastrophic nature.

But how numb Elinor's lips are starting to feel!

Only her imagination since she has swallowed a very small quantity of tea.

Crucial not to falter. Not after so much planning.

(The tea does not taste strange. At least, no stranger than Bengal tea usually tastes.)

(It is indeed tart, somewhat stinging. Which is why the wife has chosen it.)

Since the dance recital the wife had done some research. She'd discovered that Stacy Donovan is the daughter of rich parents. Grandparents who'd donated so much money to the college that the library was (re)named for them—*Donovan Library*.

It has been said that if the girl is asked about her last name, is she related to the Donovans who'd given money to the college, she will smile mysteriously and change the subject *as if embarrassed.*

Of course, Stacy Donovan isn't in the slightest *embarrassed*.

At the college no one can recall what the library had been called previously. So quickly memories fade.

Probably, Victor Stockman can't recall the names of some of the undergraduate girls with whom he'd been in love, so desperately in love years before. But now, the long-legged Stacy has replaced these. The wife has no doubt, the husband knows Stacy's name.

Close up, the long-legged girl is indeed perfect. The wife can't (reasonably) object to the husband's infatuation with her except (of course) the wife is not reasonable. It is *not fair* to expect the wife to be reasonable.

Patrician smile, flawless skin, clear pale-blue eyes, beautiful mouth. Dancer's slender and poised body. Even the silver-blond hair falling straight beside her face seems to be natural, judging from the girl's eyebrows and lashes.

(No flaw anywhere? Really? The wife's hungry eyes dart about the girl looking for a blemish, a pimple. A hidden tattoo peeking out of a sleeve.)

Well. Here we *do not have* the cliché of the husband's new love replicating the wife of thirty years ago. Fact is, Elinor never remotely resembled the long-legged girl at any age.

Nor would any girl who looked like this have given a second glance to Victor Stockman in his early twenties. It was Stockman the genius, the avant-garde composer, Pulitzer-Prize-winning poet whom students tried to impress, bevies of young-girl students vying with one another to win the lustful attentions of Daddy.

In her forties, or is it her fifties, the wife has gained weight about her hips, sides, breasts. Even as she has seemed to lose height. Once she'd been one of the taller girls in middle school; now she would be one of the squat dowdy girls, prematurely adult at twelve. Waist and hips have become indistinguishable, like camouflage. Breasts resemble foam rubber pillows that have begun to collapse from overuse.

Swollen ankles, legs thick as an elephant's and stippled with varicose veins. (If the beautiful visitor glances at these legs she will look quickly away, shaken.)

The wife has been asking the visitor what she will be doing "next year"—a question so frequently asked of graduating seniors you would expect the girl to gag hearing it another time. But the long-legged girl is too well-bred not to give a sincere answer involving the word *intern* to which the wife does not listen.

Difficult for the wife not to become distracted. Though telling herself it does not matter really—essentially—which of them has been drinking the lethal tea yet she is thinking *Oh God what if. It is me.*

She had not planned beyond the gesture. Had been thinking it would be over in an instant but of course, no.

Thinking how it is the husband's fault of course. Should have poisoned *him*.

The coward hadn't had the moral courage to declare—*I have something to tell you, Elinor.*

Bastard has been incapable of saying—*It's wrong to continue to deceive you when I love you.*

Moony-eyed. Dreamy-mouthed. In the bathroom in the shower humming loudly, obscenely. Oh, she can't forgive him!

Wife wants to bang on the bathroom door with both fists crying *Do you think I don't know what you are doing in there? You are disgusting—you make me sick.*

Well. She'd been pregnant after all. Several times. Which has contributed to her alarming weight gain. Her belly had never quite recovered from being so huge you'd have thought she was a kangaroo mother carrying twins in a pouch beneath a billowing smock.

Something to tell you, darling. It isn't easy. I am not proud. But I think—I think I will get over it, soon. Her.

He has not said this. Will not.

Instead, the long-legged girl is declaring in her trilling voice that Professor Stockman changed her life, totally—"He had faith in me when I did not have faith in myself . . ." Wiping at her eyes. Laughing thinly. The wife is impressed that the girl can utter such banal clichés, the auditory equivalent of detritus if not excrement, with no awareness that they have been uttered countless times before, by girls very like herself.

Out of nervousness the girl has drained her cup of Bengal tea. She has nibbled two macaroons. Is the wife imagining this?—the girl's hands are shaky.

". . . bad time last fall, tried to keep it a secret . . . Tylenol . . . Lucky that I got sick to my stomach and no one ever knew. I did not tell Professor Stockman of course. But he gave me an extension on my senior thesis, he was sympathetic and seemed to *know . . .*"

Elinor is pouring more Bengal tea into their cups. Splashing into the saucers. Her hands are shaking. Runaway heart in her chest feels swollen to the size of a basketball.

Thinking, as she'd gained weight since the last of her pregnancies she'd become more fatalistic. Or perhaps it was her fatalism that was causing her to eat and drink more. (Especially drink. Near-empty bottles in the kitchen cupboards hidden behind canned goods.) Once, she'd been deeply in love with what's-his-name, the owl-eyed young man with a clean-shaven weak chin, the musical prodigy who'd seemed to adore *her*. Or perhaps he had never been intimate with any girl before her and naturally he'd imagined it was the real thing—*love*.

Each of the pregnancies had been an accident. Aleatory.

He'd encouraged her to write about food as culture, food as pleasure, food as fetish, food as custom, ritual. Food as compensation for what is inaccessible, or has been lost.

Here is the truth: the husband had loved Elinor, once. He had been proud of her, once. As he'd been a young, ardent composer once, intent upon creating a profound and original body of work.

Folders of notes she'd assembled for her second book. Research slow as picking up grains of sand with a tweezers. Captivating, so slow. But finally she'd lost her way. Eating at the computer. Drinking. Online she'd begun to follow in secret several white supremacist websites. Deluded people, mostly male, who seemed sincerely to believe that there is something inherently valuable, God-ordained about an attribute so trivial as the hue of their skin.

Amazing to Elinor, and gave her hope in a way: she, too, could be happy about something, take pride in—something.

Hi! I am an overweight homely unhappy woman with a husband who is in love with a girl young enough to be our daughter and with children who quickly turn a corner if they see me somewhere outside the house. But I AM WHITE—so there!

In cyberspace, this (piteous) declaration was taken at face value. Several Aryan males had written to Elinor seeking to befriend her.

What is the long-legged girl going to do "next year"—attend dancing classes in Manhattan. Juilliard?

Maybe it isn't the husband's fault entirely. A paradise of bachelors, but a Tartarus of maids. Love is biology, fate. Love is just metabolism. Flesh-eating bacteria in the heart.

Must mean something that *fat* and *fatal* echo each other.

Fat the essence of *fatal*.

Fatal containing *fat*.

The wife is facing the long-legged girl, teacup in (shaky) hand. Hoping that the perfect girl does not see the wife's uneven, bitten, dirt-edged nails, or peer too deeply into the wife's mildly bloodshot eyes.

Girls at the college are so wealthy, they make a fetish of dressing shabbily. Faded T-shirts, torn jeans. There are at least a dozen rents in the long-legged girl's designer jeans. Yet there are unmistakable touches of wealth: the newest smart phones, expensive wristwatches, sports cars. Smiles flashing like scimitars, the gleam of expensive teeth.

It had become a fad that year, wearing pajamas to class beneath coats. In warm weather, going barefoot.

"Professor Stockman opened my heart . . ."

Professor Stockman opened your legs.

And what long beautiful legs, smooth as swords. Elinor feels faint imagining them wrapped about the portly, dense-fleshed Victor who frequently smelled of his underarms after he had been at the college too many hours, immersed in his work.

". . . the most wonderful, generous teacher . . ."

Most wonderful, generous lecher.

The wife has to laugh, imagining the husband's myopic expression while having sex, that prissy frown he directs at the newspaper in the morning most mornings to avoid having conversations with his family.

Oh, how could the husband *have sex*. The man is so out of condition he could not execute a single push-up on the floor.

As if the long-legged girl knows exactly what she is imagining, the wife pauses, coloring faintly. The girl seems to have been moved by her own, inane words. The wife supposes that even spoiled rich girls succumb to emotions now and then, unavoidably.

Like one wielding a paddle a little too energetically the wife takes up the conversation, causing it to veer off-course.

"You're hoping to continue as a dancer, you say? Bound for— New York City? Good that your parents can pay your way. It's a cruel world, dancing—you're already too old, I think. If you're twenty, still less twenty-one, that's *old*. You'd have to have a genuine talent to overcome your age but I have to say, I don't think that you—quite do."

Blankly the long-legged girl gapes at her. The wife smiles as you'd smile at a gaping infant in a crib who has not the slightest idea what you are saying to it, so that you can say anything.

"Of course, you have *nerve*. Audacity. Dancing the way you did—stomping around half-naked—that takes guts."

This is very pleasurable to the wife. Like playing Ping-Pong with a badly handicapped child who can barely grasp the paddle.

The Bengal tea is very tasty. But so hot, it has slightly scalded the wife's mouth. It has caused the wife to perspire inside her baggy clothes.

"When you have your first babies, Tracy," Elinor says pleasantly, "your figure will slacken, as mine did. You will become flaccid, flabby—you will gain fifty or sixty pounds. That's the point of the female body—to have babies, and to become flabby. Following which, the normal response of the male is to seek younger victims, I mean females, to impregnate. It's the way of the world without which there would be no evolution of Homo sapiens."

That is not true, precisely. The wife knows better.

"You are not the only girl, you know. You shouldn't feel guilt. (You don't feel guilt? Well, good!) Victor has been a lecher for so long, his girls have become mothers; their offspring could be his grandchildren. And we wonder—will the man have sex with his own grandchildren? The girls, at least? Will he *try*?"

What's-her-name—not Tracy but Stacy—is shocked. The perfect jaw hangs open. The long-legged girl has met her match—and more. Except that she has been trained to be polite to her elders, no-matter-how-slovenly-elders, Stacy would jump up and flee the house on quaintly named Hope Street where her idol Victor Stockman resides with his witch-wife.

"I—I think that I should leave now, Mrs. S-Stockman . . ."

"What an original idea, dear! Yes. I think you are correct."

Small comfort in being snide. Small comfort in revenge. But small comfort is all that a betrayed witch can expect.

Now on her feet the long-legged girl resembles one of those long-legged birds that seem always to be about to teeter, and fall. She is confused, embarrassed. Perhaps (Elinor thinks) Stacy has never been spoken to in quite so blunt frank unabashed a way in her privileged life. Perhaps (Elinor thinks) the lethal potion has begun to course through her delicate veins.

"Here—this—for Professor S-Stockman . . ."

In the tote bag is the gift the long-legged girl is leaving for the Professor who so changed her life. Elinor sees that it is a briefcase or attaché case of some impossibly elegant soft leather with gold trim—Gucci.

"There's a c-card inside . . ."

The girl speaks softly, apologetically. Lowering her eyes.

The wife is determined not to register all this chagrin, self-effacement. Briskly she takes the tote bag from the girl: "Thank you, dear. It will mean much to Victor, to add to his collection."

"His collection?"

"Gucci is something of a cliché, as leather-goods gifts from grateful students go. But you couldn't have known this."

"Oh, I—I'm sorry . . ."

"Why should you be sorry? You couldn't have known."

The long-legged girl laughs awkwardly. Her face is mottled with the heat of embarrassment, adolescent shame. One of the little valentine-napkins has fallen to the floor and she stoops to pick it up.

"You can leave now, dear. You have made your point."

"Oh. Did I s-say, there's a card inside . . ."

"Yes. You said. Victor will be especially intrigued to read the card."

The long-legged girl looks as if she is about to cry. She is a nice girl really. She is much too old to take dance lessons in Manhattan, it is good that someone has been frank enough to tell her. The wife feels a rush of sympathy too late, she has hardened her heart against all long-legged girls.

Ushering the dazed-looking visitor to the front door, and so out onto the front stoop. So little time has passed since her arrival!—scarcely a half hour.

An eternity. Never again repeated.

Behind the window watching the long-legged girl walk away. Not so confident as she'd appeared in previous weeks, months when the wife had sighted her everywhere in the village like an assault of delirium tremens. Does the wife imagine it or is the girl less than steady on those long perfect legs? Is the girl pausing at the end of the walkway, to lean against a post as if drained of energy? The silver-blond hair obscures the pale face, the perfect profile.

The wife had not realized, the girl had bicycled to Hope Street from the college, a distance of about a mile and a half; there is her smart Italian bicycle propped against the front gate.

With a wave of guilty excitement Elinor imagines the long-legged bicyclist on Main Street, and on College Avenue where there are trailer-trucks: the bicycle careening, falling. The front wheels turning sharply and the girl losing control, falling in front of a thunderous truck. A terrible scream, and silence. *She seemed to lose her balance. The bicycle jackknifed. I couldn't stop in time. God help me, I couldn't stop in time.*

So vivid the trucker's earnest voice, the look in the man's eyes, the look of a stricken father. He will be aghast, his life will never be the same. The wife feels sorry for this stranger, deep sympathy for him; but not for the long-legged girl who'd dared to come beneath her roof bringing her husband a token of her banal esteem, boldly entering the wife's domain with the Gucci label in hand.

Not the trucker's fault, a careless college girl has died beneath the gargantuan tires of his trailer-truck.

A bulletin would be issued by the township safety officer. *Bicyclists have been warned many times about riding on Main Street*

(Rt. 31). The speed limit is thirty miles an hour. Trucks can't possibly stop in time if bicyclists turn into their lane. This is a tragedy that might have been avoided.

"God help her. God help *us*."

The wife is no longer feeling so airy, ebullient. The basketball-heart has begun to shrink. She has become too tired to walk outside, let alone peer down Hope Street to see how far the bicyclist has gone. (Before Stacy has collapsed? But has Stacy collapsed?) Her head is riddled with light like bullet holes. Yet, she is having difficulty holding her head upright for it seems to want to sink down, downward to her feet.

Well, it's funny!

(*What is funny?*) (*Everything.*)

She will lie down for a while, she thinks. Plenty of time before she needs to start supper and anyway her family doesn't respect her.

The teapot is still hot, half-filled with pungent Bengal tea. Red paper napkins on the tray. The matching Wedgwood cups in their saucers, with cracks thin as hairs.

Difficult to climb to the highest floor of the house—what is it called? Halfway up the first flight of steps she is panting. Thighs ache, knees ache, back aches. Head.

What is the name she seeks—*attic?*

An *attic. Antiquity.*

Lowering her bulk-body onto a stained nubby sofa. Why is she so warm, sweating as if she'd been toiling in a field like a beast. The springs beneath her moan as if surrendering to love.

Yet perhaps it is a joke, one of those cruel jokes people make about fat girls.

No matter. She will wait for her deliverer, whoever he is. Whoever they.

Later, a door slams open two floors below just dimly waking her from a sleep heavy as concrete—"Mom? *Mom*?" The little darlings' voices are edged with irritation, concern. They have reason to be annoyed with their mother—of course. Who does not have reason to be annoyed with a mother?

Crouched on little skiffs the children are borne by the river current past her. Looks like the Amazon River—that swift curling mud-colored current, and beneath the surface predator-shadows (piranhas? alligators?) darting and drifting.

She is safe from them, for now. Love of them has lacerated her heart, but no more.

Sign of the Beast

1.

It was a time of sin. It was not a time of innocence.

It was a time of *physical disgust.* For I remember well.

The birthmark on my (left) cheek like a pustule was shameful to me.

It was not large, I suppose—the size of a copper penny. And it was of the hue of a penny that has become damp having been gripped in a childish hand.

The sign of the beast it was called in laughter, by one who should have known better, and who caused me much hurt and chagrin in my twelfth year.

This cruel individual was our Sunday school teacher at my parents' church. We were to call her "Mrs. S___" but I did not call this individual any name at all. I did not and do not ever utter this name. When I'd first started Sunday school our teacher had been an older white-haired woman my grandmother's age, who had known my grandmother and so was kindly disposed to me and not uneasy with me for my size, as adults sometimes were. ("And what do you think, Howie?"—very courteously white-haired Mrs. Pearson would inquire of me in our Bible story discussions; but still I was shy in answering, and mumbled my reply.)

But then, one Sunday Mrs. Pearson was not in the classroom and we were told to go away and return the next week and when we did, Mrs. S___ had taken her place. (The rumor was, our teacher had gotten very sick with something terrible like cancer. We were not supposed to know this.) Mrs. S___ was excited and nervous and friendly-seeming, with a quick sharp laugh like the sound a fox might make and damp bared gums.

"Hello, children! I'm here now."

And, when we sat silent and staring: "You could say *hello* to me, too. *Hello and welcome.*"

And so we murmured *Hello and welcome.*

"How about, *Hello and welcome Mrs. S___.*"

And so we murmured *Hello and welcome Mrs. S___.*

In her behavior Mrs. S___ was youthful and loud-talking which made us uneasy, for children are not comfortable when adults behave as if they are not adults. Often it seemed that Mrs. S___was *winking* at us as if there was some joke between her and us, unexplained.

"How-*ard*!"—so Mrs. S___ soon acquired the habit of calling upon me in class, for she could see how I slouched in my seat, staring at the floor and hoping not to be called upon.

Knowing that I was clumsy in my speech, and could be made to stutter while reciting Bible verses though I was one of the older children. And that my face flushed in a way to provoke laughter in the others.

(Why is the misery of a child so hilarious to other children? Even more unnaturally, it seemed to be hilarious to Mrs. S____.)

Though Mrs. S____ was scornful of my efforts, or amused by them, I did try to memorize Bible verses as we were instructed. But even when I knew the verses my tongue felt strange in my mouth like something dried-out like an old sponge and I could not speak clearly so that Mrs. S____ would interrupt, "How-*ard*! Is that chewing tobacco in your mouth?"—and so the others would giggle.

At other times I would sit in my desk with my head bowed and eyes lowered, and my left hand pressed against my cheek to hide the birthmark as if innocently. My silent prayer was *Jesus, do not let Mrs. S____ call on me!*—but much of the time Jesus paid no heed, or may have been in league with Mrs. S____ to make me squirm in misery.

Hunched and downcast grinding my back teeth in rage against those who laughed at me.

It was strange—though Mrs. S____ was scornful of me as one of the poorer students in the class yet she seemed well aware of my identity. Or rather, she seemed well aware of *me*. As we entered the classroom at the rear of the old red-brick church our teacher would stand at the door to greet us in her friendly-seeming manner, to most of the students calling out gaily, "Hello!"

or "Good morning!" as if she had not troubled to learn their names; but invariably she said to me, with a little wink, "Why, How-*ard*! How handsome we look this morning!"

Handsome. My face flushed with heat—such mockery was hurtful to me. For there was nothing *handsome* about my face and particularly the birthmark on my cheek that throbbed with resentment.

Once when I had to pass close to her, to take my assigned seat in the first row, Mrs. S___'s hand leapt out to stroke my cheek. "Why, How-ard! Are you *shaving*?"—(which of course I was not). Again, all of the class laughed.

(I had it in my mind that Mrs. S___ had really wanted to touch the discoloration on my cheek as if to determine if it was a birthmark or just a pimple, and this made me very angry.)

Especially it was embarrassing to me that Mrs. S pronounced my name in a singsong mocking voice—*How-ard. How-ARD Heike.* I did not understand what was so funny about my name except perhaps it was an older person's name, yet she did not call me *Howie* as Mrs. Pearson had done.

Mrs. S___ was confusing to us for resembling our mothers while behaving very differently from our mothers. She wore clothes of a kind our mothers might have worn for church or "dress-up" but her clothes were tight-fitting, showing her shapely body, especially her bosom and hips; around her waist she often wore a shiny black patent leather belt cinched tight. Her face too was shiny as if it had been polished. Her eyebrows were plucked and penciled into thin pale-brown arches and her "permed" hair was shiny-black as if dyed. Restless as glittering water in a stream her eyes moved over us and there seemed always something mirthful about us to make her smile.

"Boys and girls, always remember: Jesus loves you, when no one else does!"—this was a typical remark of Mrs. S____'s, called out to us gaily, as if it was happy news and not hurtful.

Sunday school lasted one hour, in an overheated room at the rear of the old red-brick church on Price Street, followed by church services at ten A.M. Even before Mrs. S____ made my life miserable it did not seem fair to me that I had to endure two hours of sitting very still while my parents and other adults had to endure only one hour. Already as a young child I was big for my age, and restless if I had to stay still for just a few minutes let alone an hour. Though I had been told many times that God loved me, and Jesus loved me, I did not know what that might mean. I did not doubt that there was a God in the sky above us watching us at all times but I could not imagine God (or His son Jesus) caring for me or even being aware of me any more than walking along a path you might step on scurrying ants without noticing or giving a damn if you did happen to notice.

If I did something to draw God's attention to me, that would be a mistake. There was a vague uneasiness among the Sunday school class that you could make God very angry and He could *smite* you dead as He did with Old Testament people.

In her singsong voice Mrs. S____ read verses to us from the Bible creasing her forehead if the subject was very grave like the afflictions of Job or the crucifixion of Jesus and the flames of Hell but making another sort of face if the subject was somewhat comical like Jonah in the belly of the whale, or Moses surprised by the burning bush, or Jesus driving the "moneylenders" out of the temple which Mrs. S___ demonstrated by pretending to be wielding an invisible whip and crying, "Out, devils! *Out!*" like a crazy woman on TV.

We were surprised by such vehemence in our teacher, and did not know what to think. Most of us had never seen our mothers behave in such a way.

"D'you not think that 'moneylenders' are devils? Well! You will learn."

And Mrs. S___ would wink at us, most pointedly at *me*.

(I could not understand why except maybe Mrs. S___ believed that my father owned Heike Lumber which was a family business mostly owned by an older uncle. My father did work for Heike Lumber but it was a bad joke to think that he made much money, as my father would himself have said. And so maybe Mrs. S___ thought, or was pretending to think, that my parents had more money than they did, and so it made sense for *money* to be associated with me. It was not right, I thought, to be teased and tormented for *that*.)

There were times when Mrs. S___ broke off reading a Bible verse as if she'd lost her place or hadn't been paying attention to her own words. Seeing us gazing at her blankly she would say, "What are you all gaping at? Haven't your mommas at least taught you that it's rude to *stare*?"

Something mocking in the word *mommas*. Like you might say the word *monkeys*. It was known that Mrs. S___ did not have children herself for she'd allowed us to know that on her first day teaching Sunday school.

"How-*ard!* What do you say?"

When Mrs. S___ asked Bible questions we were expected to raise our hands to answer. But then Mrs. S___ would look past the bright eager children waving their hands to single out those others, like me, hunched in our seats trying not to be noticed.

It was like being slapped. Like being *kicked*.

I would mumble a reply, stammering and feeling my face burn.

"Speak up, How-*ard*! You are one of the older students in this Sunday school class and should be a model for the others."

So mocked, I could not speak at all. My heart beat hard and furious against my ribs like a fist wanting to hurt.

Mrs. S___ was always warning us she would speak to Reverend Boxall about us. The minister of our church was a stern-faced man older than my father who looked in upon the Sunday school class from time to time, but did not stay more than a minute.

Nights before Sunday school, I could not easily sleep. Already I would begin to worry, Mrs. S___ would single me out for the laughter of the others which had grown more scornful over the months so that even the younger children who should have been afraid of me were not.

Not that I would have hurt a younger child. A smaller child. But I was big, and might (almost) hurt someone by accident, shoving or grabbing with my strong hands if one of them got in my way, or looked at me the wrong way, when no adult was around to see.

One night trying not to sleep because I was fearful of closing my eyes yet I must have fallen asleep for when a daddy longlegs walked over my face brushing against my lips causing me to wake with a start my eyes flew open and I saw that it was Mrs. S____ who'd trailed her fingertips over my face . . . *How-ard. How-ard Heike! How handsome we are.*

To my astonishment I saw Mrs. S____'s jeering face above me. For a moment I did not know where I was—in my bed at home, or in my desk at the Sunday school. I wondered at the unnaturalness of an adult woman who teased and ridiculed a child of eleven.

Horrible to me how Mrs. S____ would come to my desk and lean over me to see where my Bible was opened, as if (maybe) I was surreptitiously reading in the Old Testament and not the New (which we were supposed to be reading). In a mockery of motherly solicitude the woman would lean close so that I had no choice but to inhale her smell, a cloyingly-sweet talcum powder or perfume; daringly, Mrs. S____ would touch my shoulder, the nape of my neck, stroke my side even as she kept up a barrage of nervous chatter no one could follow. It was shocking to me that, in the classroom, where those children seated closest to me could surely see, our teacher would slip her hand into my stiff-starched shirt, to "tickle" me to attention, in a pretense of punishing me for not volunteering to speak or answer her questions.

Or maybe this had not yet happened? Yet, I understood that it would happen, soon.

And in the night, my hands would move of their own volition to touch myself in ways that were forbidden. And Mrs. S___ laughed at me and pushed at my hands when I tried to keep them away, saying *Oh How-ard aren't you a bad boy, a very bad boy, we know what a bad boy you are How-ard don't pretend.*

And next morning in our Sunday school classroom, as if it was still my dream: "How-*ard* is very quiet today! 'Still waters run deep.'"

And, "How-*ard* has his secrets, eh? For shame!"

Shaking her finger at me, laughing. As others in the class stared at me not knowing if they should laugh with her, or recoil in disgust.

I did feel shamed. Stricken with shame like a paralysis.

As if the woman could know what it was to *be me.*

Meekly I would lower my head. Eyes cast down but (in fact) fixed upon Mrs. S___'s legs which were tight-encased in nylon stockings; yet, in warm weather, seemingly *bare*—or so they appeared to me, for I could look nowhere else. And her small, fattish feet in "stylish" shoes.

If I dared to lift my eyes I would likely see tiny beads of sweat on Mrs. S___'s face. And the smile faded as in a face you have caught unprepared to be looked at.

"How-*ard?* What are you looking at so *hard?* Has your mother never told you that staring is *rude?*"

Adding, "Especially one who bears the 'sign of the beast' on his face for all to see."

But laughing then, to show that she did not really mean this, but was only teasing.

In warm weather in the airless interior of the Sunday school classroom you might see half-moons of dampness beneath Mrs. S____'s arms. And sometimes when Mrs. S____ turned her back you could see (without wishing to see) dampness in the back of her dress, and a faint crease in her buttocks where the dress was caught. (I had learned the coarse word *buttocks* and liked to say it to myself. It would be years before I would realize that men could have *buttocks* too.) Her bosom was heavy and soft-seeming like foam-rubber. Around her neck Mrs. S____ wore a gold cross on a thin gold chain that moved and shone with her breathing.

When at last the Bible lesson was over it would be nearing ten o'clock. The bells of the church would be ringing so loudly, I would want to clamp my hands over my ears. Mrs. S____ would dismiss us, that we might hurry to join our families for the service. But Mrs. S____ would sometimes keep me behind, claiming that she needed a "big, husky boy" to help her push desks back against the walls. When she smiled at me the pink wet tip of her tongue appeared between her bright-crimson lips.

I stammered that I had to leave, deeply ashamed. For in the pit of my stomach there was a sharp sensation, and in the area between my legs that stirred and was painfully tight inside my underwear. Through the remainder of the day the strong, sharp smell of Mrs. S___ would remain with me, like a thick sweet smoke that had soaked into my clothes and my hair, and the sensation between my legs was even slower to fade.

Until that night in my bed, the sensation swept back upon me, and Mrs. S___ pushed my hands where I did not want them to go, but could not prevent.

Yet: I did not tell my parents any of this—the Sunday school teacher's teasing. I did not tell my parents that Mrs. S___ treated me differently from the way she treated the others, for it seemed to me that Mrs. S___ was disgusted with me because of the birthmark on my face, that she could not help seeing, and blamed me for.

I did not actually think that *I did not deserve being teased.* When a bad thing happened to me, to hurt or injure me, or when I was sick, even if others were sick, with a stomach flu for instance, or a bad hacking cough, it would seem to me that this was a punishment (from God?) that I deserved. When I was not punished, I was waiting to be punished. For I did not feel good about myself. I could not think that Jesus had really died for *me.*

My parents did not like to be touched, I think. And so, I did not like to be touched *because it was not right to be touched.* If you deserve *to be touched*, then your parents would touch you. But if not, not.

In school, children sometimes stared at me. Even older children, who should not have been fearful of me. Yet they stood apart from me, as if wondering at the mark on my face, whether they were safe to make fun of it, or better not.

I did not ever back away from any confrontation. I was not "aggressive"—but I did not back away. I had been known to shove boys back against a wall, or a fence—if they fell, I did not take mercy on them but might stand over them hitting with my fists, kicking. Because I was likely to be "slow" in class (sometimes) did not mean that I was "slow" in other ways. A fist can move fast of its own volition, the way a dog snarls and bites, or a cat scratches, without needing to think. Soon then, by middle school the other children knew to keep their distance from me, and to respect me, for there was a look in my face they learned not to challenge.

Older girls, in the high school, did not seem to be afraid of me so much. They would sometimes smile at me, and talk with me in the 7-Eleven where we went after school, laughing when I blushed for I was shy in their presence, and did not know how to speak without stammering. It was surprising to them (they claimed) that I was only in middle school with such *little boys*.

But I could not laugh with them, I did not understand their jokes. And so they were disappointed with me, I think.

Not only other children, and strangers, but my parents too would sometimes stare at me without seeming to know who I was. Especially when I began to grow taller, at the age of twelve.

If I came into a room not watching where I was headed, and collided with a chair, for instance in the kitchen, my mother would give a little cry and flinch from me, as if she had not been prepared for such a big boy, or rather for me. *Oh—Howie! It's you . . .*

In her face an expression of relief as if she had expected someone else and not me. A nervous smile.

Beside my father who was a tall heavyset man, I did not look so unusual. But beside my mother, who was a small woman, and would one day barely come to my shoulder, I did seem unusual, out of place in the family. The kind of boy who, if a chair was going to break, would be the one to break the chair by just sitting in it.

Though my mother tried to "discipline" me. Especially when we were together at church. For that was what a good mother should try to do, she believed.

Howard, don't wriggle! You are in the presence of the Lord.

Howard, don't slouch! You are in the presence of the Lord.

Howard, you must not look around at girls! They can see you, and they can read your thoughts.

And never forget—you are in the presence of the Lord.

That last summer of Sunday school flies buzzed overhead striking themselves against the ceiling with little *pings* that captured my attention. From the church came the sound of the choir practicing a hymn—"A Mighty Fortress Is Our Lord."

"How-*ard!* Tell us the story of . . ."

A shiver would run through me, of dread and excitement. For the Bible stories which we had to memorize were familiar to me as if they had happened in my own life—Moses in the bulrushes, Moses and the burning bush, Samson in the temple, Daniel in the lions' den, Jesus as a boy, Jesus and John the Baptist, Jesus tempted by Satan, Jesus dividing the fishes and the loaves, Jesus betrayed by Judas, Jesus crucified and Jesus resurrected—yet I could not retell them easily, or could not retell them with Mrs. S___ staring at my mouth with her strange twist of a smile.

I tried to recount the story of Jesus betrayed by Judas, which was the story Mrs. S___ had requested, except that my voice was cracked and faltering, and after a while it ceased altogether, and Mrs. S___ shrugged and laughed and called upon another student to continue, as if it had meant nothing to her anyway, and that nor was she surprised at my poor performance. Leaving me sweating and shamed and grinding my back teeth.

This last time, Mrs. S___ dismissed the class early but asked me to remain behind so that I could help her return our desks to their original positions, she said. Why the desks were moved about, and moved back, scraping against the floor, was never clear to me. But I did as I was instructed for it seemed easier and when I was pushing desks, I did not have to face Mrs. S___ and might even have my back to her.

There was a *special report* between us Mrs. S___ said. I did not know what Mrs. S___ meant by a *special report* but I did not inquire.

That day, Mrs. S___ was wearing a yellow-stripe dress like a sundress with a sash that tied behind her back, like a young girl might wear. And a neckline that dipped down, farther than any neckline my mother might wear. I tried not to look at Mrs.

S___'s chest—*bosom*—but my eyes kept moving in that direction like marbles rolling along an uneven table.

Mrs. S___ saw me looking, I think. She was fanning her heated face with a Bible pamphlet. Asking me if I had a girlfriend?—and if I "knew" about girls?—and to this, I could think of no reply. Questions Mrs. S___ asked me about my family I could not answer either. If my father and mother were "happily married"—I had no idea, the very thought of considering such a thing made me feel agitated, as I would have felt if someone had asked me how much money my father made, or if my parents loved me.

And then as if by accident Mrs. S___ touched me—drew her fingers along the nape of my neck, to make me shiver; and brushed my stiff, thick hair back from my forehead, where it grew low. With a little laugh she discovered a button on my shirt that had become unbuttoned. And leaning into me, breathing onto my face, as if by chance she seemed to lean too far, and lost her balance, and lightly brushed the back of her hand against my groin where my trousers had become tight like a vise.

And when I pulled away she laughed sharply and said, "Howard. There is the 'sign of the beast' right there on your cheek. You can't hide *that*."

A deep shame passed into my soul. Like mold in a wall, that will rot and fester and never be made right unless torn open and exposed to the air.

All this while church bells were ringing in the belfry overhead. Crazy-loud ringing, like jeering laughter. With my head lowered I pushed the woman away, blind and furious. Butting against her belly, all but cracking her ribs with the force of my need to get away from her before something happened between us, this *special report* Mrs. S___ had prophesized.

The woman cried out in sudden fear—"What are you doing! No"—falling backward, clutching at a table, only just able to prevent herself from being thrown to the floor, hard. Her breath came ragged and panting and I did not glance back at her hurtling myself at the door like a wild creature that has gotten trapped in an enclosure, and will kill to get free.

It would be the last time I attended Sunday school. If my soul was damned to Hell, I did not care.

And I did not go to church services that morning, either.

Ran away, out behind the churchyard. Down a steep hill, into a ravine. Made my way wading and splashing in a shallow creek, three miles to home and when I got there sweating, disheveled and dirty, exhausted like an animal, sank into sleep in a storage shed where no one would find me until I wanted to be found.

And later when my parents did discover me, like an animal eating ravenously out of the refrigerator, they looked at me in disgust and disdain. Out of such disgust with their son, they did not even ask me what had happened or where I had been instead of meeting them for church. They did not scold or accuse but allowed me to slink off, in shame.

Maybe seeing something in my face like a fist, they knew not to provoke.

Those days of waiting for Mrs. S___ to tell on me.

To tell my parents of my behavior, or Reverend Boxall who was our minister.

My father would be obliged to punish me. *Discipline.* No matter his disgust he would call me to him, and strike my face once, twice. His hand might be open, or closed. The blow might be hard, or glancing. An opened hand, a slap, more insulting somehow than a fist, as if I did not even merit such a blow but rather a slap such as you would give to a young child, or a girl. And he would say—"The woman told us what you did to her."

But that did not happen. Though I waited for my father to call me to him, it did not happen. Mrs. S___ did not report me!

And now there came over me a sense of helplessness and rage, that the woman's power was greater over me in not speaking of what had passed between us than if she had. For now the incident, Mrs. S___ touching me as she had, and my shoving her, touching her, would remain secret between us.

When I was alone I could not keep Mrs. S___ out of my thoughts. *How-ard! Hel-lo. Are you—shaving?* The mocking sing-song voice, the touch of her fingertips like a daddy longlegs brushing against my face. It was hellish to me, to lie in my bed unable to sleep, sweating and twitching and failing to keep my rough hands from myself despite the shame of it, that I believed it to be hurtful to me. And so my eyelids drooped during the day, I was not able to focus my thoughts, or walk steadily. . .

"Howard, what is *wrong with you*."

In exasperation and wariness my mother addressed me. She had ceased calling me *Howie*—now, no one called me *Howie*. In the kitchen coming up beside me where I was staring out the window when I believed I was alone, my mother had seemed, almost, to be touching me, or about to touch me, and though she did not touch me it seemed that I felt her touch—almost . . .

Wrenching myself away from her, feeling a stab of fury, repugnance like a dog that has been surprised, baring its teeth to snarl, bite.

Staring at each other, then. The one poised to attack with his fists, the other poised to flee screaming.

Of course, that did not happen. I would not ever have raised a fist to my mother.

But shamed then, and stammering in embarrassment *Sorry sorry Ma.*

Overhearing, later—*There is something wrong with him. Howard.*

Her voice dropping, near-inaudible—*Scares me, he is so angry* . . .

Or did Ma say—*Scares me, he is so ugly.*

Vaguely it was said among the relatives that I had become *too big* for Sunday school, that was the reason that I no longer attended. Yet, my parents insisted that I continue to attend church services with them each Sunday morning out of a fear that I would go to Hell or (maybe) out of pride, that their neighbors and relatives would see that I no longer attended church, like a heathen or a pagan, and this would reflect badly upon them.

In a pew near the rear of the church we sat, with a scattering of Heike relatives and my mother's older sisters and an elderly uncle. Always I was made to sit between Ma and Pa like a small child who might have to be *disciplined* if he squirms or yawns in church or cranes his head to look around.

Of course, I would see Mrs. S___ in church for she always attended the ten o'clock service in the company of an older stout bald-headed man who (I supposed) was her husband or (maybe) her father.

I did not want to see the hateful woman and yet, I could not stop myself from searching for her, just to determine where she was, and look away from her, and not look back. Until at the end of the service when the congregation rose, and all sang hymns together, except for me, for with my cracked voice like gravel I could not sing, and did not want to sing, but this was a time when it was natural to glance around, and so I might see Mrs. S___ on the other side of the aisle, a row or two closer to the front of the church than our row, five or six seats in, holding a hymnal in her hand at which she never glanced, and singing with the others, or pretending to sing.

Holding my breath, that Mrs. S___ might glance back at me. Biting her lower lip in a smile as her eyes greedily sought me out.

How-ard has his secrets, eh? For shame.

The sign of the beast on his face for all to see.

My hatred for Mrs. S____ was such, I had never asked any questions about her, for I did not want to know anything about her, I did not want to think of her at all. Yet there was a kind of satisfaction in establishing that the woman was in church, as I was, twenty feet away.

After the hymn, there was another time for glancing about the church, a time to see who was behind you, or on the far side of your pew, and then too I could look openly at Mrs. S____, and it would not have seemed strange, and my mother would not have nudged me—*Howard! Don't stare.*

Sometimes yes, Mrs. S____ did see me. Or seemed to see me. Though so quickly I looked away, or shut my eyes, it was not possible to be certain.

The small bright eyes like a snake's eyes moving upon me, in secret. Unmistakably the woman's thoughts rushed through me like an electrical current—*I know what you do when you are alone, How-ard! What thoughts you have of me. What a bad boy, what a disgusting boy, and the sign of the beast in your face to identify you—everyone knows.*

Irritably my mother gripped my arm and gave me a nudge asking what on earth was wrong. For I'd seemed to be paralyzed, unable to move.

My knees were weak, and my back teeth were heated from grinding my jaws. Sullenly I mumbled to my mother that I was OK but that it was too hot for me in the church, I could not breathe.

Later, outside the church, I overheard my parents speaking worriedly with Reverend Boxall and a vague reply of the minister's—*A phase he is going through. Boys do. He will get over it. God sets us these tests, as parents.*

It happened that I would follow Mrs. S___ when I saw her.

By accident when I saw her. I did not *seek the woman out.*

In town, on the street. In a parking lot. In a store.

She did not see me, I think. Most of the time.

Yet: moving her hips as if she knew that someone was watching, but did not want to let on.

Happened that Mrs. S___ shopped at the drugstore, at the grocery store, at the Target store. By accident sighting her, standing at the edge of the lot behind a Dumpster. And soon then, I knew to identify her car which was a dull-silver compact Nissan.

Exciting to me, to see Mrs. S___ park her car, climb out with a flash of her legs, walk across a parking lot in her bright clothes. Her hair was shiny-black, her mouth very red. In warm weather her arms were bare to the shoulders. Like a scene in a movie it was, when you know that something is going to happen to the person in the scene but you do not know exactly what it will be, and when.

I know you are watching me, How-ard!

We know what it means—the sign of the beast.

Rode my bike to the church, Sunday morning before nine o'clock. Dragged the bike behind a storage shed in the churchyard and slid down into the ravine, to hide.

For an hour then, squatting on the creek bank and throwing stones into the shallow, slow-moving water.

In the classroom at the rear of the church, Mrs. S___ was teaching Sunday school. I had not dared to peer in a window but I knew. It was exciting to me, to think of how I could come into the classroom slamming the door open—the looks in the faces! If it was a movie, there would be a gun, and the gun would fire.

How-ard! How-ard, no!

After a while I climbed up out of the ravine, and returned to the rear of the church. By this time churchgoers were starting to arrive, parking their cars. They would enter the church, and take their places in the pews. Like ants they seemed to me, taking their place in a hive. I would not be one of them that morning.

I had not given any thought to it, that my parents would wonder where I was, and if I was hiding from them in order to stay away from church.

Crouched behind a gravestone. Watched the rear door.

Children were leaving, Sunday school was over. Through the scope of a rifle they could be viewed, and picked off one by one without any more knowledge of what was happening to them than the knowledge of a grazing deer that is shot with its head lowered to the grass.

Last of all was Mrs. S___ who was lighting a cigarette as a man might do, shaking out the match. (Smoking was not allowed on the church property! I knew this.) It was surprising to me, and exciting, that Mrs. S___ was smoking in secret, and that I had not known this before.

Very quickly the woman smoked holding the cigarette to her mouth as she inhaled, exhaled smoke in little puffs. She was wearing a bright-green dress and around her waist a black patent leather belt cinched tight. On her feet straw-colored high-heeled shoes with no backs. As she smoked the cigarette staring at the ground at her feet it did not seem to me that Mrs. S___ looked so confident as usual but rather subdued, frowning.

Then for some reason Mrs. S___ glanced over to where I was crouched behind the gravestone. Somehow it happened, she saw me, and a flash seemed to come into her eyes such as you see in an animal's eyes, reflecting headlights.

"Why, How-*ard* Heike! Is that you?"

The voice was not so mocking, but rather surprised-sounding, almost happy.

"How-*ard?* Hel-*lo.*"

Mrs. S___ was staring in my direction, where I was cringing down behind the gravestone. I could not understand how she had seen me clearly enough to identify me.

Shamed by being so recognized, I crawled on hands and knees to the edge of the graveyard. Then scrambled to my feet to run, run.

"How-*ard?* Where are you going? *I see you.*"

Laughing after me, until I could not hear her any longer.

Following this, I was determined to stop thinking of Mrs. S___. For she had seen me, and would be prepared for me now. And still she might complain to my parents or to Reverend Boxall or even to the police and I would not be able to explain myself, why I was following Mrs. S___ when it was a great relief to me that I no longer had to attend Sunday school. Just to think of that was to feel a rush of happiness.

Now, I did not attend church services either. My parents had not tried to argue with me though (I knew) they had been talking about me in their room, my father's voice raised and my mother's voice quieter, pleading.

Clamped my hands over my ears. Laughed, what the hell did I care about *them*.

Somehow it happened, I learned where Mrs. S___ lived: in a weatherworn clapboard house on Cottage Street across from a vacant lot littered with trash. Also scrub trees grew on the lot, I could easily hide behind.

The plan came to me: I would ride my bike into town, hide it behind bushes. I would see if Mrs. S___'s Nissan was parked in the driveway of the clapboard house and if it was not, I would dare to walk to the house to ring the doorbell believing that no one would be home but that I could peer into the house through the ground-floor windows and maybe, if no one was watching I could go to the rear of the house, and look in the windows there.

I would try the door to the house, at the rear. If it was not locked, I could open it . . .

A wave of dizziness came over me, at the thought of what came next.

And so at the S___ house where the Nissan was not in the driveway I did not think that anyone would be home. It was rare that my father was home in our house during the day, but rather at work at the lumberyard and this was true for my relatives' houses where all the men worked. And even on a Saturday, a man would probably not be in his house for much of the day.

It did not occur to me that Mr. S___ (if that was who the bald-headed man was) might be home and that he would not only open the door but see me through the window as I approached the front door.

So, I rang the doorbell—which was the first time in my life that I had ever rung a doorbell!—and almost at once, the door was flung open, and a bald-headed man stood in the doorway, not smiling. "Yes? What do you want?"

I was a husky boy, five foot six or seven. My hair had been shaved close to my skull for the summer. I was wearing soiled bib overalls with no shirt or T-shirt beneath. (Some days, I worked at Heike Lumber. But not every day, and not full days.) The bald-headed man who'd opened the door was only an inch or two taller than me and might have felt some worry of me, why a stranger like me was on his doorstep.

I could not think of any answer to his question. I was not a good liar. I began to stammer, and felt blood rush into my head.

Again the bald-headed man asked me what I wanted, who I was, and I managed to tell him that I was Mrs. S___'s student at Sunday school, and she had told me that she would leave a "special Bible" for me, to pick up that day.

Special Bible! Where this notion came from, I had no idea. My face was hot with blood and my eyes were moist with tears for my words were a terrible effort for me, like dragging a heavy plank with my bare fingers.

Yet, the bald-headed man had seemed to believe this. At the mention of a *special Bible* his features softened and were not so harsh and so he even smiled, or stretched his lips in a kind of smile, such as you might make at someone who was annoying to you but harmless, and perhaps pitiful, like a retarded child or a crippled person.

Telling me he hadn't heard of any *special Bible.* His wife was not home. She had not left anything and had not said anything to him about it.

OK, I told him. Already I was turning away, eager to be gone.

In the doorway the bald-headed man looked after me. I did not look back but felt his eyes on my back.

Then calling after me, "Excuse me? What's your name?"

But I was far away enough not to hear, or anyway I did not seem to hear, waving my hand without turning back to him, and walking fast away.

He will tell her. She will know who I was. Who I am.

Waited a while before doubling back, to get my bicycle in the vacant lot. By that time the sky was darkening and a wind had come up. It was late August, there had not been any rain in weeks. Crouching in the underbrush waiting to know what to do next for I was not (yet) ready to go home and the thought came to me how easy it would be to drop a match behind the S___ house. At night when she was asleep, when no one would see. Grasses were dry as straw and the leaves on all the trees were dry and brittle.

Except I did not have a match. I had come away from home with no matches. And now the wind was coming up, and the sky was massed with dark thunderclouds, it would be the end of the drought—I had waited too long, and now it was too late.

For some time then, after school began I did not see Mrs. S___. I did not linger by the drugstore, the grocery store, the Target store where I might see the woman. I did not return to Cottage Street for fear that the S___s had reported me to the police and would be waiting for me to return and would call the police again and have me arrested.

Then, after school one afternoon when the days were starting to get dark by five P.M. I was cutting through the parking lot at the 7-Eleven, and there was Mrs. S___ coming out of the store carrying plastic bags, and I stopped and stared at her with (I guess) a funny look, and Mrs. S___ laughed and said, "Hello, How-ard." There was a trace of mockery in her voice but I was bigger now, not cowering at my desk like a baby, and I felt the fear in the woman, the way she was gripping the plastic bags against her chest as if to protect herself, saying with a nervous laugh, "I hope you aren't following me, Howard. Are you following me?"—like it could be a joke too, if it was taken that way.

Shrugged my shoulders and laughed like yes, it was a joke. And Mrs. S___ said, "It's just that I seem to see you often . . ." and her voice trailed off and I said, "I c'n take those for you, ma'am," like a grown man might say though I had never done anything like this in my life and could not have imagined doing it until that moment. And so I went to where Mrs. S___ was standing very still like a rabbit will freeze when you approach it, if there is no way out for the rabbit.

From Mrs. S___'s arms I took the packages (which did not weigh much but were clumsy to carry) and walked with her to her car (knowing which car it was, the dull-silver Nissan, but pretending that Mrs. S___ had to lead me to it) and put the packages in the trunk of the car and all this while Mrs. S___ was moving kind of stiff and her face was not the mocking face of Sunday school but the face of a woman of some age younger than my mother, but not much younger, that was looking strained, tense. Still her mouth was a bright crimson and around her neck she wore a white and red polka dot scarf.

"Thank you, Howard. That's very kind of you"—her voice was not steady.

Saw her eye move to the birthmark on my cheek, that had been itching and so I'd scratched it, and probably it was reddened, or even bleeding, but if Mrs. S___ was about to make some comment on *the sign of the beast* she thought better of it, just murmured *Bye!* and got into her car and drove away.

At the rear of the house. At that time of dark when lights are not yet on. Trying the door, discovering that the door is open, and this is a sign—it is meant to be, you can enter.

And in the house, like a dream that is not clear at the edges but sharp and clear where you are looking, a room that was the kitchen, a room with a Formica-topped table looking like the very table in my mother's kitchen; and through a doorway, a shadowy space that was the living room, and a TV on a table and headlights from outside the window reflecting in the TV screen. And there is a stairway—there is a railing to be gripped.

It is an old house, needs repainting and roofing, and the stairs are creaking, needing new stairs, planks. Because I am heavy, the steps give beneath my weight, and I am afraid to breathe, the woman in the bedroom upstairs will hear me and begin to scream before even she sees me before even she sees the sign of the beast knowing it is meant for her.

2.

Final year of school for me, when I'd drop out without graduating.

In vocational arts my grades were B+. In other subjects, mostly D's.

But I did not need a high school diploma for already I was working at Heike Lumber and would soon work full-time.

In the locker room after gym class the guys were talking about a woman in our town who'd been found dead in her house, that was only a few blocks from our school. One of the guys had an older brother who was a cop so he'd heard before anybody else, before the newspaper or TV, about how a woman who lived on Cottage Street had been found dead in some kind of storage space where her body had been crammed, and the body was *badly decomposed,* and nobody had missed the woman though she hadn't been seen in weeks. And none of her relatives even had missed her. She'd had a husband but he had died and there were no children.

How her body was found, somebody had smelled it. Next-door neighbor had actually *smelled it.*

Looked pretty much like she'd been murdered . . .

The guys did not know the woman's name but at once I thought, this had to be Mrs. S___.

In recent years all I knew of Mrs. S___ was that she no longer taught Sunday school at the church. She'd had some disagreement with Reverend Boxall or with some parents of her students, my mother had said, and had been dismissed.

She'd been acting strange, people said. Saying things to children they repeated to their parents that did not sound like a Christian speaking.

Then later that day I would learn from TV news that yes it was Mrs. S___ who had been found dead. The county coroner did not yet know how she had died. Her body had appeared "battered" and "wasted"—her face had been "unrecognizable." A relative called to make the identification had fainted from shock. The coroner had not yet determined if the woman's body had been carried after death into the storage space which was crammed with junk, or if the woman had crawled there of her own volition, to die.

Woman's body. It was shocking to me, to hear Mrs. S___ spoken of in this way.

As you might speak of some object, or thing—laundry, gravel, garbage. *Woman's body.*

The wild thought came to me—*Did I do that? Did I kill her? My fists, my feet?* (For I wore heavy work boots when I worked at the lumberyard. Once the woman had fallen it would take only minutes to kick, kick, kick her until she ceased struggling.)

My mouth went dry, with thinking of this. A wave of dizziness passed over my brain.

But then, I chided myself—*No. I did not do such a thing! I did not.*

I had wanted to enter the clapboard house on Cottage Street but I had not done it. I had wanted to surprise the woman in that house, in a (shadowy) room in that house, in a way in which she could not have known who I was while at the same time guessing who I was which was a dream of mine that came to me when I was half-awake in my bed in sweaty rumpled sheets. *How-ard! Is it you?*

But it had never happened. I was sure.

In my face my mother saw something for I was standing very still staring at the TV though on the screen now was a noisy advertisement. Asked me if Mrs. S___ had ever said *strange things* when I had gone to Sunday school and I told her sharply that I did not remember.

That evening I did not have any appetite for supper. I went upstairs to my room and fell onto my bed without undressing or even removing my work boots for it was important to be vigilant, if the police came for me. What I would hear (I imagined) was a pounding at the door and my father going to open the door, then raised voices, and a sound of excitement, and footsteps on the stairs leading to my room . . .

This room in darkness, this bed with its lumpy and stained mattress was a special place for me, and for Mrs. S___ who dwelt in the shadows here, though not in the daylight—you could not have detected Mrs. S___ in the daylight. (And so my mother could have no idea. For always I removed my soiled bedclothes from my bed and stuffed them into the washing machine before my mother could change the bedclothes once a week on Monday mornings and so accustomed had Ma become to this routine, she rarely entered my room, at least so far as I knew, and our secret was unspoken between us.)

Woman's body. Woman's body. Hours passed and I did not move for I was feeling a strange dizzy sickness and then when I tried to stand, this sensation deepened, the way you sometimes feel after being in a boat, a rocking boat, in turbulent water, and when you step out of the boat and onto land you feel suddenly nauseated—seasick on the land because it is so still.

Though at the lumberyard I was one of the strongest workers a terrible weakness suffused me as I reached for a light switch, my legs gave way and I fell, hard . . . Then, my parents were in the room crying out to me frightened as I had not ever seen my father asking what was wrong, what had happened to me, and when I could sit up, and when I could speak (for my mouth was so dry, it was as if I had swallowed sand) I told them that I was the person who had killed Mrs. S___—"I was there, that was me. Hid her in the wall where nobody was supposed to find her."

This would be a part of my life like a sickness that begins with fever, chills, nausea so strong that, even when the worst of the sickness has passed, the memory of that time will always be the worst of the sickness, and not what comes after.

For days then they would question me—"interview" they called it.

At police headquarters where some of the officers knew the name "Heike" and were respectful of my father who'd brought me in and remained with me for most of the time.

Did Pa believe that I was the murderer of Mrs. S___, I did not know. Did Ma believe?—yes, I think so.

(Past 11 P.M. of the night of my confession Pa drove me to the police headquarters leaving my stunned mother at home. For things were so upset, it was believed better for him to get me out of the house as soon as possible.)

In a stammer I tried to answer questions put to me. Why had I killed the woman, how many days ago had I killed the woman, how did I know the woman, had the woman invited me into her house, what had I done with the knife? And the ransacked house—what had I stolen? It was like Sunday school, being asked questions and everyone staring at my mouth and out of my mouth came—what? Words like phlegm to be coughed up, spat out. Words that were not my choice for I could not think clearly, my head was stopped with greenish phlegm that was disgusting to me and also to the men who stared at me as they might stare at a rabid animal.

It was a bright-lit room. Fluorescent lighting that hummed and crackled. The eldest of the police officers (who had known my father since they'd been boys, and was a "detective") spoke kindly to me, patiently, but over and over the same questions were asked, that I could not answer definitely for I could not seem to calculate what answers were "right"—what answers were expected.

How many days ago had I killed Mrs. S___—I had no idea.

Why had I killed Mrs. S___—I had no idea.

(Because she was mocking to me?—because I hated her?—this was too weak an answer to seem believable to adult men, from a husky boy like me. Too shameful.)

(It had turned out that Mrs. S___ had also taught elementary school for years. But that she had taken "early retirement" just the previous year. Her husband had worked at the New York Central railroad yard but he'd retired also with a disability.)

Had I had a "relationship" with Mrs. S___?—shook my head *no.*

Had I had a "sex-relationship" with Mrs. S___?—shook my head *no!* (This was very disgusting to me and shameful, with Pa right there listening. Could not even meet Pa's eyes.)

What had I done with the knife?

I said, in the creek . . .

The words came to me. Clumsily my tongue moved. I had thrown the knife into the creek, I told them. For suddenly that was obvious.

Where in the creek? Near where?

This, I could not recall clearly. My brain hummed and crackled and I could not hear what I meant to say.

In a police car they drove me along the creek roads. Both sides of the creek. Mostly there was underbrush and no paths leading to the creek except where people lived, where it was not likely that I had gone to throw the knife into the creek. For an hour and more, we drove along the creek, crossing at the Mercyville Bridge to return, until finally it occurred to me—I must have thrown the knife into the creek from a bridge . . .

Of three or four bridges in the vicinity all were well known to me. It was believable that I would have thrown the knife into the creek from the Firth Street Bridge which was not so far from Cottage Street, and so I told the detective this, and in the police car we drove to Firth Street but when we parked and walked out onto the bridge (a plank bridge, slick with wet, and the dirt-colored water below like sludge, tree limbs and trash rushing past so it made me dizzy) I told them that I was not sure which side of the bridge it was, I could not remember. The depth of the creek was twelve, fifteen feet below the bridge. At this time of year the current was swift. A terrible roaring rose in my ears from the creek which I could glimpse through the planks. I could not hear a word put to me even by Pa who stood close beside me touching my arm as if to comfort me, or restrain me from climbing over the bridge railing though at that moment I had not made the slightest motion to do such a thing though later it would occur to me, when I was back in the interview room like a body trapped in a vise.

Was I sure there was a knife? Was I sure that it was a knife I had thrown into the water?

This was a trick question, I thought. For the men were doubtful of me.

But then, it seemed to me that the East Street Bridge was more likely for that bridge was on my way home if I had my bike, that was where I must have tossed the knife.

But when they took me to the East Street Bridge, again I was not sure. Began to stammer and they saw the confusion in my face and were not so patient with me.

Almost I could hear them—*Jesus Christ, How-ard! What the hell is wrong with you!*

From the start Pa had been telling them he did not believe that I had murdered that woman Mrs. S___. He *did not* believe it. When had it happened?—how many days ago? I had been home every night, he said. And after school, I worked at Heike Lumber.

The corpse had begun to decompose inside the wall, it was said. The coroner had not yet determined how long for the weather had been cool, it was November and rainy, and that would preserve the corpse longer than in warmer weather. . . . I did not want to think of this. My Sunday school teacher *rotting*.

Yet it was fascinating to me, that Mrs. S___ who had so teased and tormented me and dared to touch me with her fingers light and quick as a daddy longlegs was now just a *corpse*. Men would examine this *corpse* with instruments, I supposed. An autopsy would mean sawing through the chest and rib cage and that place between the legs that was rimmed with wiry hairs.

I had not ever seen that part of Mrs. S___. But I had felt it, the stiff-wiry hairs on my fingers and against my tongue.

My son would never harm another person, Pa was saying. His voice strange and hollow like the voice of one standing in a deep well.

Insisting that I had not behaved strangely or any different than usual. Not ever!

Insisting that I had never hurt anyone, that he knew about. If I had been in trouble at school it had been caused by other boys picking on me, of course I'd had to fight back.

A few times, I'd been sent home from school for fighting. But I had not been expelled as other boys had been expelled including boys who were my friends.

How many fights? What kind of fights? Had anyone been seriously injured?

No! No.

(I'd wanted to protest to the police officers that son of a bitches had thrown stones at me after school plenty of times. Actual rocks. Bricks. I'd been hit by a piece of brick on my forehead, scar in my right eyebrow never went away. But no, this had not been reported. There was no record with police or at the school. Nobody gave a damn about *me*, if I was hurt.)

The most embarrassing thing was, Ma was interviewed also. Not in my hearing, but Pa related to me what she'd said to the police. Somehow I had not thought that my parents would be questioned if I confessed, I had not thought about the consequences at all. My mother was emotional insisting that I had not murdered Mrs. S___. All she did now was cry and pray, and pray and cry. God had assured her that she would have noticed bloodstained clothes in the laundry if her son had murdered anybody. She would have noticed "strange behavior."

Ma could not ever speak of Mrs. S___ without breaking down and crying in a helpless way like a baby, and her face crumpling like a cake left out in the rain. The police officers were sorry for her at first but then embarrassed and annoyed by her for they considered her testimony "next to worthless." (As Pa told me.)

During the days of questions it was not always clear to me what was happening. It was not like TV crime programs—very different from these as there was no ending to anything, questions were repeated and nothing seemed to be concluded. Many times I explained to the police officers that I was the one, I had killed Mrs. S___ yet still they did not seem to understand.

Why did you kill the woman?—tell us.

Because I wanted to rob her house.

Rob her house. But what had I taken from her house? What was missing? Money from her purse? Pieces of jewelry wrapped in velvet cloth in a bureau drawer? The little gold cross on a chain I'd have liked to tear off the woman's neck leaving a raw red laceration in the white skin?

And why had I dragged her body into the storage space? How had I even known that the space was there?

This was a strange question to me. It was perplexing what answer they wanted. (Though later it would be divulged that the storage space was behind a cupboard door behind furniture shoved against a wall with just enough space left to open the door a few inches.)

Later it occurred to me, maybe I had not thrown the knife into the creek. So far as I knew the police might have been looking in the creek by the bridges (though no one had told me that they had) but they had not found the knife, or any knife (so far as I knew). Maybe I had tossed the knife into a ravine instead. Into a landfill—there was a landfill on Horse Farm Road where we rode our bikes. Maybe I had buried it under trash where we searched for treasure in the landfill. If I shut my eyes (so tired, my eyes would shut by themselves) I would see suddenly sharp as a picture on TV news where I had buried the knife—a clean sharp blade glittering in the dirt.

But where did you get the knife, Howard?—so they asked me.

I guess—it was there. In her kitchen.

It was there? In the woman's kitchen? How did you know it would be there?

This was a nonsensical question. I wondered if it was a trick question. For of course there would be a knife in a kitchen, there could not be a kitchen without a knife. Why were they asking me such questions.

I told them all that I knew: the knife had belonged to Mrs. S___.

And what kind of knife was it? A long knife, a shorter knife, a bread knife—?

A long knife, I said. A steak knife.

Ah, a *steak knife*. You know what a *steak knife* is?

I thought that I did, yes. Or was I thinking of a carving knife, that Pa used to carve turkeys and hams.

When I stammered answers to their questions they glanced at one another. The room was so bright with fluorescent lighting I could not decipher what messages or signals they were sending to one another.

So many times asking me did you murder the woman because you knew her or because you just wanted to rob her. But why did you choose that house to enter, of houses in the neighborhood where no one was home?

You stole from the woman's purse, you took things from her—what did you take?

I said, I took money. I took dollar bills.

Not change?

Not change. I took dollar bills.

And where did you put these dollar bills?

In my pocket. Pockets.

Which pockets?

My jacket.

Which jacket?

Corduroy . . .

How many, Howard?

How many—what?

Bills. Dollar bills.

I—don't know. I didn't count them just put them in my
pocket . . .

And what did you do with these dollar bills, Howard? Do
you still have them?

N-No . . .

Did you spend them?

Yah I guess so . . .

Where? What did you buy?

All I could think of was the 7-Eleven store where we hung
out after school. From younger kids I knew who were kind of
afraid of me, I could get money, a few dimes and quarters just
enough for a Coke. And that afternoon Mrs. S___ came out of
the store carrying the plastic bags.

Ma'am c'n I help you.

And her looking at me.

And her red mouth, opened in surprise.

In the night sometimes she'd said to me opening the door of
her car *OK, How-ard. Get in.*

Get in, we're going for a ride.

Fucking ride, How-ard. D'you know what fucking *is?*

Between my legs it was hard as a Coke bottle. Tears started
from my eyes, the sensation came so fast and could not be
stopped.

All the dollar bills are gone, Howard? Is that what you are saying?

Yah. I guess.

What did you buy, Howard? Can you itemize?

But I could not answer. To tell them a Coke, a bag of corn chips, to play *Death Raider* with some other guys was a pitiful reply.

In the lavatory emptying my guts into the toilet. Hot-scalding guts. Then washing my hands until the skin was raw. *Filthy boy we know what is in your heart.*

Picking at the ugly blemish on my cheek, trying to loosen it. For it seemed to me that *the sign of the beast* had gotten larger, like a pimple or a boil that might come to a head.

In the lavatory mirror there was a kind of film, like grime or mist. It was not possible to see my face clearly even the birthmark, that I was scratching with my nails.

Howard?—just wondering where you were, son.

Yah. I'm here. Where else'd I be?

Yet they did not arrest me. A day and a night and another day. Asked the same questions over and over to wear me down I supposed but since I had already confessed I did not understand this.

Pa was exhausted for (he said) he could not sleep at all, at night. Could not even lie in bed unless he drank one beer after another and even then, his nerves were not steadied. My mother had gone to stay with one of her sisters, she could not bear to remain in the house alone when Pa was at police headquarters. Pa had not gone to work at Heike Lumber since the night he'd driven me to the police.

On our front lawn garbage was dumped. Who did this would never be known.

By now everybody in Bordentown knew. News had been released, that the fifteen-year-old son of local parents, a ninth-grade student at the high school, had been taken into custody by Borderntown police.

Taken into custody was not the same as *arrested*.

Interview was not the same as *interrogation*.

When would I be *arrested*, I was eager to know. I hoped that it would be soon so that I did not have to return to school.

Some of the relatives were saying, Pa should hire a lawyer for me. Pa said that was easy for them to say, the sons of bitches wouldn't be the ones paying.

Pa said he could not afford a lawyer. Ma said if we hired a lawyer it would look as if my parents thought I was guilty.

Another police detective came to interview me, from the State Police in Albany. This detective's questions were like the others but there were further questions I had never heard before, and could not think how to answer.

Was I confessing to this crime, the detective asked, fixing me with cold blue eyes like I was an insect, under coercion?

Under coercion. I was not sure what this meant but supposed it meant that someone was making me do it.

No, I said. I was not.

You are not covering up for someone else, are you? Someone in your family?

N-No . . .

Did you know that your father had often been in the S___house? Did you know that your father and the woman S___ knew each other well?

Was this so? Or was the detective lying, to trap me? Staring at me like he was so much smarter than me but the son of a bitch was not.

I was very tired now. I wanted only to sleep and could have slept on the floor of the interview room that was dirty and stained with muddy footprints.

Then later, when the State Police detective asked again about *coercion*, I began crying. It was a surprise to me (as to him) but I could not stop.

Heaving sobs that made my chest ache. It was not that I believed what the State Police detective had said about my father for I did not believe him, but rather that such words might be said, and heard by others, and not ever erased from their hearing.

Not the son but the father. The real murderer!

It was allowed then, I could lay my head down on my arms in the interview room. At once there came Mrs. S___ toward me with a red moist smile. Her waist was cinched tight by the black patent leather belt. Her bosom jutted out like actual fists. The little gold cross glittered against her white skin. Her fingernails were polished to match her lips and her hands opened to me, to touch, and to tickle. But the floorboards broke beneath her feet, the rotted planks collapsed. Her red mouth opened like a wound—*Oh How-ard!*—but she did not scream loud enough to be heard by anyone else.

Fell into the collapsed plank floor and was lost to me.

A door was opened at my back. They had brought Pa with them. Loud voices woke me.

"Time for you to take your son home, Mr. Heike. You people have wasted enough of our time"—the State Police officer spoke disgustedly.

We could not believe this! I could not believe it.

"That woman wasn't killed with any knife, son. You made that bullshit all up. She was killed in a different way, that is not yet released to the public. But nobody stabbed her. There was no knife. And nobody stole anything from her. You can all go home now"—with contempt the State Police officer spoke.

These words were so shocking to me, I could scarcely get to my feet. Since being brought to the police station that night I had not eaten regular meals but things from the vending machines. Ma had not been well enough to prepare any food for me, for Pa to bring. So my legs were weak, I could not walk without swaying.

Looks of such disgust in the officers' faces, even in the face of Pa's detective friend. And pity.

Trying to explain to those faces: "It wasn't a knife. I didn't mean to say a knife. It was my fists and my feet—my boots. I beat her to death. Beat and kicked her. That was all I needed—my fists, my boots. Couldn't stop beating her until . . ."

"Get him the hell out of here. Get him *out*."

"Then I hid her in the wall—inside the wall. Where nobody was supposed to find her . . ."

Laid their hands on me and walked me out of the room half-dragging me and my father fuming and cursing in disgust of me and behind me their voices rising in incredulity and fury.

Get that crazy cocksucker out of here just get him OUT.

3.

Ma would say, He could not help himself. Something came over him, to confess to something he had not done. God will forgive him. We pray and pray to understand. But Ma did not ever want to see me again in any way in which the two of us were alone together and even then, Ma could not bring herself to look at me.

Pa would not speak of it at all. Pa was shamed and knew himself derided by his closest relatives and friends. He would not work at Heike Lumber ever again on a full-time basis. He would walk out of the yard if something pissed him. He would drink himself to death a can of Molson's at a time he'd say laughing, Fuck, he was in no hurry.

Forever it would be known in Bordentown that I had confessed to killing Mrs. S___ who'd lived on Cottage Street, a former elementary school and Sunday school teacher. A widow who'd lived alone in a house filling up with trash with no children and no relatives to look in on her, to see how she was.

As a younger woman she'd been some kind of *glamor-girl*. People spoke pityingly of her, recalling. *Putting on airs. Pathetic.*

She'd been Howard Heike's Sunday school teacher years before. Children had complained of her, she'd scared them with her stories and made fun of them though afterward claiming it was because she'd liked them so much, and wanted them to like her.

Maybe that was why Howard Heike had killed her?—people speculated.

Or, no. Howard Heike *had not killed her*. He had only confessed that he had.

Years would pass. The house on Cottage Street would be sold, and then razed. Dump trucks of debris hauled away. Howard Heike would drop out of school, leave Bordentown in disgrace and return and still how exactly Mrs. S____ had died was not known. The coroner had not established an absolute cause of death. It was possible (though not absolutely provable) that there had been *foul play*. The bruised, battered and emaciated body weighing only seventy-three pounds when discovered crammed into the storage space had been partially decomposed, the face had seemed to cave in upon itself as if beaten with something blunt and hard though not (evidently) a fist. (A brick, wrapped in a towel?) (Pounded against a wall by the woman herself, a towel over the face?) The chest and rib cage showed signs of breakage and trauma (as if kicked by a booted foot) though possibly the injuries were self-inflicted as the malnutrition would seem to have been self-inflicted and the hair on the head stiff and matted with grease, unwashed for weeks, a haven for lice.

Enlisted in the U.S. military. For I had no police record, I had not been arrested but only taken into custody and then released when my confession was rejected.

If I am not the murderer of Mrs. S____, then the murderer of Mrs. S____ was never discovered. Now that I am discharged (honorable!) from the army and returned to Bordentown I am sure that I will see him, or he will see me, in a bar, on the street, at the 7-Eleven. Laying awake nights excited to wonder what the look will be that will pass between us. Which of us will make the first move—"Hey. You. Do I know you?"

The Experimental Subject

1.

She was a solid-bodied female of perhaps twenty years of age with a plain face, an unusually low, simian brow, small squinting eyes, tentative manner like that of a creature that is being herded blindly along a chute. In a bulky nylon jacket, unzipped. Rust-color frizzed hair. Approximately five feet three, weight one hundred forty pounds. Full bosom of an older woman, thick muscled thighs and legs, thick ankles, large splayed feet and a center of gravity in the pelvic region.

Entering the lecture hall, alone. Blinking nervously as she glanced about for an empty seat. Or for someone to smile, wave at her and invite her to sit with them . . .

But no one. Not likely. And so, taking her seat in the fifth row, settling her bulky backpack at her feet.

There it is—she is. Our subject. Like an electric current these words ran through the technician's brain as (covertly) he took several quick pictures of the girl with his iPhone.

*   *   *

It was a season of protracted heat, drought. No precipitation for months and since early September a hot, arid wind like a persistent cough.

Behind the green-tinted glass columns of Rockefeller Life Sciences Hall the temperature was fixed at 66 degrees Fahrenheit. From vents in the twelve-foot walls humidified air moved like invisible caresses.

The first to sight the girl—the (potential) *experimental subject*—was the senior technician in the Professor's (restricted, government-funded) primate laboratory. Liking to think of himself as a scout—a peregrine falcon—in the service of the Professor, anticipating solutions to problems which the Professor had not (yet) considered.

For the distinguished Professor was so intensely absorbed in his work he seemed often not to know whether an experiment was nearing completion, was only midway, or had just begun, considering the most complicated experiment but a sequence of steps like bricks in a walkway to bring others to the destination at which the Professor already waited like a Buddha basking in his own enlightenment.

Of course! An experiment is not a blundering to discovery but a confirmation of what is already known.

The search for the new *experimental subject* had not officially begun. But the senior technician N____—(name unpronounceable—Chinese? Korean? Vietnamese?—too many consonants crowded into a single syllable for the non-Asian ear to grasp)—had been keeping his falcon-eyes open.

Alone of his colleagues N___ was in the habit of wandering in the lower University campus where he wasn't likely to encounter anyone he knew, or who knew him. A tall (six feet, two inches) dark-clad knife-blade of a man, lithe as a shadow flying across a walkway, exquisite in *aloneness* as a figure in an ancient Asian woodcut. Though *visible* to anyone who actually looked at him yet N___ had the advantage of *invisibility* that is the particular prerogative of his species: deceptively bland Asian face, wire-rimmed eyeglasses, short-cropped very black glossy hair, dark flannel sweatshirt or hoodie, running shoes.

His age?—could be mid-twenties. No one could have guessed late thirties.

Even in the primate laboratory N___ did not always appear *visible*. Standing only a few feet from the Professor he'd heard the Professor inquire irritably, "Where is N___ when I need him?"

At which point N___ did not smile (visibly), cleared his throat and said in his most courteous nongloating voice: "Professor, I am here."

He'd sighted her, unmistakably. He was certain.

After the lecture lingering at the front of the amphitheater. As undergraduates streamed past waiting for the low-browed girl that he might (unobtrusively) follow her.

Having grasped instinctively that the girl was of that sub-category of young female who was not likely to have friends; certainly, not male friends. *She will be grateful for attention. She will not ask why. She will not suspect a motive.*

The subject of the Professor's lecture that day had been the phenomenon called *mitosis*. Stages of cell mitosis, stages of cell cycle, *meiosis*. All of life is involved in the replication of life: that is the meaning contained in the word *life.*

No one understood the *why* of such a process. But they were beginning to understand *how.* And very exciting it was to them, the Professor's handpicked team, the process of *how* which they were learning to replicate.

At the lectures it was N___'s custom to sit at the very end of the first row of seats in the semidarkened amphitheater, that he might observe the faint glimmer of hundreds of computer screens cast upward on young, earnest faces. The Professor's carefully chosen words, uttered through a microphone, further amplified by the PowerPoint presentation (which N___ had helped prepare for the Professor) were channeled through the neurons of the young, fingers rapidly typing on laptop keyboards as in a mass hypnosis.

And then, after fifty intense minutes, the spell was broken. The lecture was ended. Lights came up in the amphitheater, the Professor exited the stage. Laptops were shut, backpacks gathered. Where there'd been respectful silence, relieved chatter began.

Biding his time until the low-browed girl passed in the aisle descending steps with an awkward sort of care and gripping her bulky backpack to her chest. Of course, oblivious of N___.

Exiting the amphitheater, following the girl outside. Like a practiced predator taking care to keep others between them and following at a distance of about thirty feet.

It was not difficult to keep the low-browed girl in sight: frizzed rust-colored hair that looked as if she'd brushed it with rough, random strokes of a brush, stolid mammalian figure, slightly rounded shoulders, a way of pushing herself forward that was both "perky" and defeated. The girl wore an unflattering University jacket of some grape-colored nylon fabric, which she kept unzipped and open, for she was overweight and inclined to be warm on even a chilly autumn morning; perhaps bizarrely, in a gesture that should have been embarrassing to her, the low-browed girl hoped to draw attention to her sizable breasts as if not grasping (of course, the ideal *experimental subject* was not intelligent enough to grasp) that she was at least thirty pounds beyond the undergraduate ideal for a twenty-year-old female, even if her earnest simian face had been attractive. On her sturdy thighs and legs were jeans that looked stiff and new, also unattractive.

How different this female specimen was from most of the undergraduate girls at the University! If they adhered to a type, regardless of race or ethnicity they were likely to be slender, with long straight silky hair, flawless skin. They were not hesitant but confident. They did not exude *aloneness* even when they were walking alone.

It was something of a mystery, N___ thought. That the girl with the low forehead, quizzical eyes and diffident manner had dared to enroll in the introductory biology course, competing with premed students, biochemistry majors, neuroscientists . . .

N___ felt a pang of pity for the *experimental subject*. But by definition, no specimen who so matched the requirements for the *experimental subject* could be anything other than pitiable.

How slowly the girl walked! No more than half N___'s normal speed. If he weren't vigilant, he'd have easily caught up with her.

Following the girl across campus and into the student union, a featureless cube offensive to an eye attuned to the elegantly minimal architecture of Life Sciences. Relieved at least that the girl hadn't returned to her residence hall where N___ couldn't have followed her. Hoping she wasn't meeting a friend for lunch which would ruin his plans.

But the *experimental subject* would not have a friend, ideally . . .

Having to wait, at a little distance, as the girl entered a women's restroom.

This, N___ resented. There came into his pristine mind an unpleasant vision of the restroom interior: crumpled paper napkins (and worse) in a trash bin, hairs in sinks, a smell of toilets and drains, the plain, pasty-faced low-browed girl peering at herself anxiously in a communal mirror, primping her hair, puckering her fleshy lips . . . Admired in the Professor's lab for his fastidious care in prepping experimental animals for the insertion of electrodes into their brains, as for making sure that his tech assistants kept the animals' cages as clean as possible, N___ felt a rush of repugnance, indignation. If there'd been the faintest glimmer of romance in the prospect of befriending/seducing the *experimental subject*, minuscule as bacteria flourishing in a petri dish, this vision would have killed it.

In the lab, among his colleagues who were both appreciative of the technician's help when they required it and resentful of his close (if scarcely verbal) relationship with the Professor, it was speculated that N___ was, whatever age he was, not so much "virginal" as "asexual." No one had ever seen N___ with a woman in what might have been romantic circumstances, nor indeed with a man.

N___ had a vague sense of this reputation. So long as the Professor held him in high regard, he did not so much mind what others said of him though it amused him to think that anyone should consider him a virgin.

"Asexual"—yes. Probably.

The cafeteria was only just beginning to fill. Casually N___ fell into line behind the low-browed girl who appeared hungry for lunch, at five minutes before noon. A good appetite! A healthy female specimen made for breeding, wide-hipped and with a (probable) high threshold for pain.

N___ was taller than the girl by a head. This was good—(was it?); authority exudes from superior height in Homo sapiens as in other mammalian species. Moving a sticky black plastic tray behind hers, seemingly by accident giving her tray a nudge.

"Hi, h'lo—thought I saw you in Intro Biology, was that you?"

Exactly what a fellow student might say in these circumstances. Composing the bland-inscrutable Asian face into a *friendly smile* and hoping the girl would not perceive immediately how forced and insincere these banal words were.

Startled, the girl looked up at N____. Stammering, blushing—
"Yah . . . yes. Intro Biology, I just came from the lecture . . ."

Surprised that N____ was speaking to her. Touchingly grateful
for the *friendly smile* from the tall neatly dressed handsome (?)
young Asian man.

". . . like, my head aches from trying to make sense of . . . what's
it . . . *miyotis* . . ."

"'Mitosis.'"

"'Mi-*to*-sis.' Yah."

Looming tall, not too close to the low-browed girl, friendly
but polite. *Gentlemanly.* Pushing his tray behind her tray as if
they were casual acquaintances and not total strangers.

It was the girl's wish to present herself to this unexpected fellow student as overwhelmed by the biology lecture. Imagining
that, to N____, seeming even less intelligent than she probably
was would appeal to him as male.

But it was a way for N____ to connect with the girl, a stratagem to deflect her suspicion. Falling in with her tone of wry
puzzlement N____ volunteered cheerfully that, of the Professor's
lecture that morning, he'd understood just a fraction himself—
"Eleven percent."

A joke: eleven percent. To glance at N____ would be to guess
that N____ was hardly of that cohort who have difficulty understanding an undergraduate science lecture; a more experienced
individual than the low-browed girl would have guessed *postdoc,
research science, Chinese?—Korean?—Vietnamese?—quirky but
brilliant.*

Unsuspecting any stratagem on N____'s part the (naive) girl imagined N____ as a kindred undergraduate though surely—for so N____ perceived the girl's brain cranking into action like a computer of another era—smarter than she was. Just possibly, potential help to her in preparing for exams. *Tutorials. Study dates.* Nodding fiercely in agreement, "Oh, gosh, I know! The same with me. He's, like, a famous professor, a scientist—they say . . . I try *so hard* to understand him but it slips through my brain, I guess. Sometimes I try so hard it *hurts*."

As if the girl meant to be funny N____ laughed. Not very convincingly but in her excitement the girl took no notice. Like an actor reading a script he has never seen before N____ said that he felt the same way—"Except it's my back molars that hurt, from grinding."

Wincingly unfunny but the girl laughed as if she'd been tickled. Her mouth was large as a pike's mouth, her hilarity breathless and overdone.

"You mean, like—at night . . . Yah, sometimes I grind my teeth too, it used to be worse when I was a little kid . . ."

Smiling at N____ coquettishly now. Oh, this was *flirting*!

N____ had not been in such intimate quarters with a female for some time. The Professor did not encourage females in his primate lab—even gifted female postdocs had been turned away, and female research scientists in Life Sciences were pursuing their own subjects. N____ had little contact with undergraduate girls enrolled in the lecture course for he was not one of the Professor's team of teaching assistants; he'd more or less forgotten the (hypothetical) sexual imperative that a male naturally seeks a female mate, to reproduce his own kind. N___ did not care much for *his own kind—his DNA.* Yet he felt the pathos of this so clearly lonely and love-starved girl who not even smiling could make pretty. He would have to harden his heart against her, not to succumb to pity.

Of all human emotions, pity is the least useful.

For the scientist whose research involves experimental animals, pity is particularly not-useful.

Asking the girl if she was having lunch with anyone and when she shook her head *no* asking if he could sit with her and she laughed in sheer confused delight (it seemed) as blood rushed alarmingly into her face. Eagerly she said, "Yah—yes."

"Well. Maybe we could sit together . . ."

"Oh—yes."

Deftly N___ guided them into a corner of the cafeteria, where no one was likely to intrude.

Rare for N___ to have lunch in so public a place. Usually he ate in the lab, take-out food in Styrofoam packages and not what might be designated as "lunch." Just ate when he was hungry, or rather became aware in the midst of work that he was hungry.

Like characters in a broadly humorous, brightly lit TV situation comedy they introduced themselves: N___ with a plausible-sounding name—"Nathaniel" for wasn't that an Anglo name, slightly formal, archaic?—and the girl with a name that suited her: "Merry Frances."

Merry—?

But no, the name must be "Mary Frances."

"That's a nice name . . .'Mary Frances.'"

"It's for my grandma. I mean, it was. I mean—my grandma is—isn't—alive . . ." Pausing, breathless. "'Nath-an-yiel'—*that's* a nice name."

N___ smiled. Tried to smile. Not recalling how Asian boys smiled at Caucasian girls.

Not that N___ had been a boy for fifteen, twenty years.

In so public a place, amid a babble of undergraduate chatter, N___ felt exposed, absurd. Here was "Nathaniel Li" in the alarming company of "Mary Frances Bowes." If anyone from Life Sciences happened to see the Professor's chief technician in the clamorous student union, sitting across a table from the smiling, stolid undergraduate girl—how astonished they would be! Unless the colleague was from the primate lab, and could guess what N___'s motive was . . .

During the course of the cafeteria meal by asking discreet questions N___ was able to determine that 1) Mary Frances had few friends at the University; 2) Mary Frances did not have a "boyfriend"; 3) Mary Frances was living some distance from her family which was a "broken-up family" and she was "not real close" with them; 4) Mary Frances was enrolled in the College of General Studies yet had signed up for Introduction to Biology with the (questionable) hope that it would aid her application to nursing school—"I always wanted to be a nurse 'cause I want to help people all I can. It's what Jesus wants us to do—I mean, Christians . . . It's real hard to get accepted in the nursing school here but my advisor said they'd be impressed if I took Intro Biology and got a good grade . . ." Her voice trailed off wistfully at *good grade.*

So that was why the girl was in the Professor's lecture course, valiantly trying to take notes amid a sea of premed students and science majors murderous-competitive as sharks. A responsible advisor would have urged her to take only courses in the College of General Studies in which, in fact, she might receive good grades.

N___ pushed himself to sound sympathetic, convincing. "Well. If you work hard . . . maybe—somebody could help you . . ." Picking with a plastic fork in the "Asian salad" swill he'd selected in the cafeteria line, lifting his eyes to meet hers, shy-Asian-boy smile: ". . . Maybe I could help you."

Have you no mercy for her? Once, you were her.

But no. No mercy. Not in Life Sciences.

Recalling the girl's eager eyes on his face when he'd told her he could help her. Feeling a shudder of guilt and self-revulsion that the *experimental subject* was so unwary, so easily led and so tractable.

But it is not in the nature of the peregrine falcon to pass up its prey.

Especially if the falcon is hunting in the service of his master who expects much of him, that is not outwardly stated.

For there was the understanding that, if the Professor's renowned primate lab violated certain legal restrictions, committed certain acts that might be ruled "scientific misconduct"—not often, but occasionally, in the service of scientific progress—it would be the chief technician N___ who took the blame, and not the Professor. In the many years of the primate lab it hadn't yet happened that any outside authority had challenged the Professor's findings, still less his methods, for the primate lab was one of the crown jewels of Life Sciences, bringing in approximately twice as much money in research grants as its nearest competitor, and so the University had no wish to look too carefully into the "ethics" of its experiments even if the University had had the means to undertake an investigation, or could have known where to begin.

In any case, N___ would be the individual held *responsible*. N___ would be the member of the team to be disciplined, even "suspended"—"terminated"—for he was not a PhD appointment to the University, but rather an employee of the Professor.

This possibility N___ understood and accepted tacitly though he and the Professor had never discussed it; just as N___ understood that, in the event of an investigation, a harsh ruling, ugly public exposure and the loss of his appointment, still N___'s coveted Green Card would not be rescinded, for the Professor would protect him from deportation to the birth-country he had not glimpsed in more than thirty years. And, in time, there would be a considerable reward for the chief technician. He was sure.

It helped that in this affluent adoptive country, under the protection of the Professor, N___ had forgotten his origins.

There'd been "war"—"civil war"—a terrible air bombardment. A sky churned into havoc, clouds bleeding guts. Not once. Not twice. Countless times.

Collapsing walls. Clots of flame. A refugee camp, with a muddy burial ground. Before that a protracted escape-by-boat, or had it been the reverse, or had there been more than one desperate escape-by-boat, and more than one squalid camp. And more than one death. More than one language and N___ had forgotten them all. His brain refused to process these lost languages so that the name on his Green Card—"N___"—had come to seem mildly preposterous to him, too many consonants packed into a single syllable, a *foreign name.*

All that was changed now. N___ could barely recall his adolescence, let alone his childhood. Let alone his young childhood. The English spoken in his adoptive country was his language now. He had no interest in any other language. He had no interest in any other country. Vaguely he was aware that he had relatives who shared a surname living in Canada, possibly in Vancouver, a cousin his own age who was a research scientist like himself. But he had no interest in any other N___ for (in fact) "N___" was (almost certainly) not his birth name but a refugee-camp name given to a mute parentless child not (evidently) terminally ill and so worth "naming."

Instructive to remember too that N___'s surname was, or rather is, the most common of surnames in his native country. One of the most common surnames in the world. Not much pride in this and indeed, N___ was not one to *take pride.*

Like removing a CD from a player, such memory. Sliding in another CD. A phase of life: slice of neural memory in the brain. In an autopsy you could slice—very thinly—such neural matter. Store it, with care, in formaldehyde. Hardly necessary to recall, let alone record. So long as he had his Green Card and the identity that went with it: "N___." So long as he had the protection of the Professor who was his sponsor/employer in this affluent adoptive country.

Sending a rare email to the Professor: *Something to report on preliminary scouting for Project Galahad.*

Next morning at the weekly lab meeting there was N___ with a proposal.

Taking the others by surprise. For that was the Professor's chief technician/right-hand-man for you—crafty and unpredictable. In the way that N___ hid his smile somehow up inside his deceivingly bland Asian face so that you felt it rather than saw it, *inscrutable.*

Informing them that he'd sighted, he'd vetted, at least to a degree, a very promising female specimen for (classified, confidential) *Project Galahad.*

The female was twenty years of age. A first-year student in the College of General Studies with a (quixotic?) hope of being accepted into the nursing school. By her own account she had virtually no friends. She and her roommate "didn't get along." Most crucially she had no boyfriend, fiancé, husband.

She did have a family, but not living close by. And no close ties.

She was tractable, credulous, eager to please. Not very bright. Not very attractive. Physical type: wide-hipped, sturdy-boned.

N___'s proposal: with the permission of the lab, he would move forward in securing the girl as the *experimental subject*.

But no: objections were immediate. For N___ had adversaries in the lab. Rivals for the Professor's esteem. Pointing out that initiating even the first stage of the experiment was in violation of University policy regarding classified research, since the primate lab did not (yet) have permission to move forward; also, the schedule for *Project Galahad* hadn't yet been established . . .

But yes of course. Permission would be granted eventually. A schedule could be drawn up within a few days—N___ could compose a draft. It was unwise not to take advantage of the female specimen he'd discovered for she appeared to be ideal, and if they lost her through an excess of caution they might not find another.

But—*no*. It was months too soon for *Project Galahad*, there wasn't yet a budget . . .

But—*yes*. The Professor's NIH (National Institutes of Health) grant could be tapped for miscellaneous expenses.

The senior members of the primate lab were meeting in the Professor's office on the eighth floor of Life Sciences. Sitting at an oak conference table heatedly discussing N___'s proposal as with a bemused expression the Professor scrolled through images of the twenty-year-old female specimen on N___'s iPhone.

As others debated the issue the Professor remained silent. Stroking the crisp white goatee that gave him at a little distance the (misleadingly) benign look of a wire-haired terrier.

At such times the Professor's brooding silence did not indicate that he was listening to his younger associates, who spoke as much to impress the Professor as to reason with one another. Yet, the contemplative way in which the Professor stroked his goatee did not indicate that he was not listening, perhaps very carefully to each word.

The father is most powerful when he does not indicate his preferences among the children. Only the most subtle hints, but these must be conflicting hints, fertile for endless speculation.

At last putting N___'s iPhone down on the table and pushing it in N___'s direction.

With a terse nod of his head, *yes.* The female specimen was ideal.

Around the table, a ripple of assent. Even those who'd most opposed N___ now agreed, it was wisest to begin at once.

"So, N___—will you be the one to prep her?"

Gravely N___ said: "Of course, Professor. I have already begun."

It is known that Homo sapiens shares 95 percent of DNA sequences, and 99 percent of coding DNA sequences, with certain ape species; and in some human beings, the simian kinship seems more evident than in others. Many times this thought has occurred to N___, seeing the *experimental subject* waving to him, blushing at the mere sight of him—"'Nath-an-yiel.' Hi!"

Meeting at the student union. In the main library. In a coffee shop on campus. In a coffee shop off-campus. Never in her residence hall since N___ did not want to be seen by girls who knew her, in her company.

The delight in the coarse-skinned face, the glisten in the small close-set eyes. The thrilled smile.

"Mary Frances. *Hi.*"

Seeing, to his embarrassment, that Mary Frances's chapped-looking lips began to turn rosy. Her rust-red frizzed hair began to be more frequently shampooed, brushed.

In her pudgy ears, pierced earrings.

The nails of her stubby fingers, filed and polished.

An attractive sweater, fitting her sizable breasts snugly. An attractive shirt. Necklace, scarf. Whiff of something cheaply sweet like lilac.

(The pretext for) their meetings was N___ kindly providing help for Mary Frances with the biology course. *Securing her trust. Making her grateful, indebted.*

For all his intelligence N___ wasn't a natural teacher. Research engaged his interest, not teaching. To teach another, you have to *care.*

Yet, in the service of *Project Galahad* and what it might mean for scientific progress as well as what it might mean for the careers of everyone in the primate lab, N___ was determined to *care.*

Over the years he'd acquired a sympathetic and instructive manner with younger students in the lab. His natural disdain for persons less intelligent than himself he'd learned to disguise. Though he was impatient with stupidity he could sympathize, to a degree, with ignorance; it was astonishing that Mary Frances knew so little about science, but he was impressed by her determination to learn, and volunteered hours of his time tutoring her in elementary principles of mitosis, meiosis, gametes, chromosomes, genetic diversity though he felt (he could not help it) a faint revulsion for the girl, both physical and intellectual . . . and also a sort of angry pity for her, that a girl who looked like Mary Frances could sincerely believe that a young man like "Nathaniel" was genuinely interested in her.

He hoped that she wasn't boasting about him, at least. Hoped she had no one to whom she might boast.

By degrees N____ began to take some (small, grudging) pleasure in teaching the girl something valuable about biology. Enough at least to prepare her for lab quizzes and exams.

Mary Frances did not seem to grasp principles or abstract theories but she had a capacity for memorization, at least for temporary memorization. N____ could coach her to repeat something enough times to get her through a limited period of time—a day, a few hours—before it began to fade.

Despite himself he began to take a sort of pride in his tutoring. And indeed it was flattering, to see that look of adoration in a (white) girl's face, which he'd rarely seen before in any face.

Running to greet him one day as he approached the coffee shop, with childish joy waving a sheet of paper—"Oh—Nath'iel! Oh gosh! Look! Look at this! Thanks only to *you*."

Startling N____ by hugging him, pushing herself breathless and heated and smelling both frantic and fragrant against him, laughing as the two came close to toppling over on the walkway.

In red ink on white paper, a beautifully rendered B–.

It was only a weekly biology lab quiz graded by a postdoc but a B was impressive, for a student of Mary Frances's capacity. N____ was himself impressed.

"It's, like, you are saving my life, Nath'iel. Oh gosh—*I love you.*"

How soon then, to initiate the *impregnation.*

By measured stages *seduction, sexual relations, impregnation.* And if *impregnation, gestation.*

Birth, and beyond birth.

Of course, much had to be spontaneous, or seeming-so. With the Professor's approval N____had drawn up a tentative schedule based upon a normal nine-month gestation, birth sometime the next summer if all went as planned.

If successful *impregnation*, an engagement ring. If necessary, plans to marry after the birth.

Promise her whatever is required. You will know her very well by then.

Soon, N____ steered the female specimen away from campus. He preferred to spend time with her less publicly, he said.

Soon, meals together in (inexpensive, ethnic) restaurants and cafes where N____ wasn't known. For certainly that was the next step, *taking out the* experimental subject *on "dates."*

(Of course, N____ kept receipts for all expenditures and was reimbursed weekly out of the Professor's "miscellaneous" fund.)

Tutoring the girl in biology was still crucial but was not the only, or even the primary subject of their conversations.

How did one *fall in love*? N____ had no more personal experience of *falling in love* than he'd had of personally experiencing impregnation, gestation, birth in laboratory animals whom he oversaw in the Professor's elaborate experiments.

Drawing a deep breath one evening as they sat at a small table in a Chinese restaurant awaiting their meal N____ took hold of Mary Frances's hand that lay, like a small animal in a pretense of sleep, on the tabletop. Steeling himself for the immediate pressure of her (hot, moist) hand, grasping his as a drowning person might grasp for life.

"Oh—Nath'iel. *Gosh*!"

A single heartbeat thudded between them. Suddenly, they were a *couple*.

Soon then, Mary Frances dared to slide her arm through his as they walked together. Leaning against N____, giddy and clumsy as in a three-legged race.

Together, crossing a street. At a pace that left the girl breathless trying to match N____'s long-legged stride.

"Oh, Nath-iel! You are so *tall*."

Such inane remarks the girl made. There was something childlike in her naivete that made N____ want to protect her.

"People are always saying, Asians are so *smart*. Not like the rest of us. And, know what?—they are right." Pausing, leaning against N____. "And handsome, too. And *sweet*."

This was bold. This was unmistakable. Yet, N____ did not wish to take advantage of the girl, just yet.

He was fearful of her emotion, that threatened to overwhelm him. Her warm, often overwarm body, leaning against his, denser than his own and (possibly) more resilient. Her eyes he saw were mud-brown, shiny with feeling.

Like a precious coin that has been covered by the thinnest soil the girl's soul was too easily exposed. Seeming to take no notice of how guarded N____ had been in speaking of himself she did not hesitate to open her heart to him, confiding her most private secrets—bullied in middle school, friendless in high school, lonely and "miserable" at the University until she'd met *him.*

Oh, there'd been some guys at the University—"frat boys, real assholes"—who'd asked her out to "disgusting 'keg parties,' they call them"—but she'd had enough sense at least not to say *yes.*

"Really bad things happen to girls at 'keg parties.' All along Posner Avenue—those damn frat houses . . ." Mary Frances shook her head wryly, with an expression both disgusted and wistful.

N____ wondered uneasily if Mary Frances was a virgin. The very term *virgin* was quaint, faintly ludicrous to the ear, like an old-fashioned clinical name for a disease.

"Guys can be mean. Nasty. Back in middle school they'd tease us—try to scare us. 'Pig-snout'—they called a friend of mine. She'd run away and cry. Just *nasty."*

Shaking her head, such disgust that N____ had to suppose it had been Mary Frances herself called such a name.

Once begun, the girl could not seem to stop. A faucet turned on, and farther on. Soon confiding in N___ all he might wish to know, and more, of her life.

Except for cousins in the navy she was the first of her family to leave her small town, and she was definitely the first to go to college; everybody in the family thought she was "snooty" for going to the state university and not to a community college. They weren't "supportive" of her at all, in wanting to become a nurse. But she planned to surprise them by becoming a nurse and not returning home but (maybe) living in the urban area near the University.

"D'you think that's a good idea?"

"A good idea—what?" N___ had been listening so intently to Mary Frances, watching the odd twitchy movements of her mouth, he'd lost the thread of what she was saying.

"Living around here. After I graduate."

"Y-Yes. It's a great idea."

"'Cause I am getting to like it here. Getting to know you . . ."

No idea how to reply. N___ murmured a vague smiling assent.

"But I have a lot of work to do, I guess . . . to get admitted to the nursing school. To pass Intro Biology . . ."

"Well. I can help you, Mary Frances. Like I have."

"Oh, gosh! Oh, I am so lucky . . ."

Deeply moved, Mary Frances grimaced, shook her head mutely, swiped at her eyes

Where had N___ seen this gesture before? Had to be one of the primate lab animals. A female chimpanzee named

Maude who'd learned to mimic human mannerisms with eerie precision—a way of courting favor with her masters, they'd thought.

In an aggressive male chimp, like the alpha male Galahad, such a gesture might be meant in mockery. If his teeth were bared, an outright gesture of defiance against his jailers.

But Mary Frances was wholly sincere. Nothing meant more to her than nursing school, she said repeatedly; it was the predominant theme of her life, her dream of *helping other people.* Though N___ had known Mary Frances only about three weeks he'd heard her speak in this way countless times, and could have finished her sentences for her.

"'Course, I might just end up married . . ."

Boldly Mary Frances spoke, casting a coy/hopeful glance at her companion who seemed at first not to know how to reply; then asked, gamely, with a weak smile, if she thought she might like to have children, and Mary Frances said, "Oh *yes.* A family. I do."

N___ heard himself ask, as if this were a perfectly normal conversation of the sort he had frequently: "How many?"

"How *many*? Children? Oh gosh, maybe three . . . Maybe four."

N___ was smiling foolishly. A dull blush had come into his face which Mary Frances saw, and misinterpreted.

"'Course, that's all in the future, Nath'iel. We're having a really nice time *now* . . ."

The rest of the evening passed in a blur. Crossing a street on the way back to campus and to her residence Mary Frances slid her arm into N___'s, and came close to leaning her head against his shoulder. A faint stir of desire in his groin, like a young snake waking.

Rehearsing what he would say to the *experimental subject*, soon. *I love you, Mary Frances . . .*

But *no.* He could not.

For one thing, how could N___ fashion his face, uttering such improbable words? Surely, even the low-browed girl would not be so easily deceived . . .

I—I—I l—love . . .

More plausibly N___ might say—*I care for you, too.*

Steering a careful course, as he thought it. Between his (outward) display of affection for the female specimen and his (inward) repugnance for the female specimen.

If the challenge was to overcome his (physical) revulsion for Mary Frances a yet greater challenge would be to overcome panic that for all his revulsion he was becoming (physically) attracted to her . . .

No! Not possible. The low forehead, the russet-red fringe of hair on the forehead, the matronly breasts and hips, the plain face with its simian cast—he could not be seriously attracted to *that.*

Yet, Mary Frances's soft limpid brown eyes were sometimes attractive. When love for N___, frank adoration for N___, shone so frankly in them.

When love for N___ glowed in her face like reflected candle-light. *Ohhh gosh, Nath'iel, you are so handsome.*

When it was not jocose and exaggerated and lipstick-smeared, her smile could be attractive. To a degree

When she refrained from grabbing his arm and speaking excitedly she could be, if not attractive, not (totally) unattractive.

Shame! You are falling in love.

N___ laughed, appalled—this was preposterous. Clueless Mary Frances joined in, giggling. Like a trained dog, eager to please its master and also to imitate its master. If she'd had a tail, N___ thought in disgust, she'd be wagging it, thumping it against his legs.

His lab colleagues had advised N___ to proceed cautiously. To behave like a (stereotypical) Asian male, courteous and deferential, warmly friendly, shyly affectionate, fascinated by the (white) girl's inane chatter. Above all, no threat to the (white) girl.

He, the Asian male, was too reserved to initiate sexual relations. If something should go wrong with *Project Galahad* it would be prudent if the girl, and not N___, had actually initiated the next, intimate stage of their relationship. N___ would behave as (in fact) he felt in the low-browed girl's presence—physically awkward, reticent. Not so comfortable with touching, and being touched.

It might be a matter of weeks before a sexual relationship could be established. Possibly months. Crucial not to hurry. Not to move prematurely. For the integrity of the experiment would depend upon the bond N___ established with the *experimental subject,* her unquestioning loyalty to the young man she knew as "Nathaniel Li." And yes, if necessary, this young man would enter upon an engagement with the *experimental subject*, during the pregnancy. If/when there was a pregnancy.

Marriage was a possibility. Though it would not be an actual, "legal" marriage of course but one arranged through the Professor's contacts.

By the last week in October a furnished apartment had been secured for N___'s use. (N___ would never bring the *experimental subject* to his own quarters of course. On principle, N___ never brought or invited anyone there.) The apartment was just far enough away from the University to assure some measure of privacy; its shelves had been hastily filled with books sloughed off from N___'s colleagues' libraries or picked up by N___ at sidewalk sales. The bed would be freshly made, towels and hand soap in the bathroom. It was N___'s responsibility to at least partly fill kitchen cupboards, bureau drawers, a closet or two, to suggest actual occupancy.

Reporting to the Professor weekly even when there was relatively little progress to report.

Stroking his stiff white goatee the Professor peered at pictures of the *experimental subject* on N___'s cell phone. Such an unattractive female! It was no wonder she was grateful for N___'s attention. The Professor evinced indifference to N___'s reports even as he insisted upon a voyeur's particularized account. In what ways had N___ touched the female specimen? Kissed her? And what sort of kisses? Light, glancing, casual or—impassioned? Had the female specimen signaled sexual receptivity, as a female chimpanzee might, in estrus? (But this was a joke: female chimps in estrus lifted their swollen genitals boldly to the male chimp's face.)

No? The *experimental subject* had not (yet) displayed this behavior? The Professor laughed as if suspecting that N___ was keeping something from him.

2.

Not a very aesthetic procedure. But at least not very difficult: procuring the first store of semen from Galahad.

Fortunately, Galahad was a lusty young animal in the prime of life and ripe for reproducing his kind—whether ejaculating into the vagina of a female chimp in the rabid heat of estrus or into a technician's rubber-gloved hand and a sterile glass beaker.

"Galahad, my friend! Hel-*lo*."

It was remarked in the Professor's primate lab: the chief technician N___ was not nearly so relaxed with his own kind as he was with certain of the experimental animals and especially with the young male Galahad, a beautiful chimpanzee specimen to whom he gave treats and even groomed with a bristle brush.

Galahad was nine years of age, four feet ten inches in height, one hundred lean-muscled sixty-six pounds. Emerging out of the black-haired pelt at his groin, an astonishing frequency of erections like living, writhing, tubular things—giant sea slugs with blunt blind heads of a bright-rosy hue, stiff with blood and translucent frothy liquid rife with the sperm of *Pan troglodytes verus*.

Nature's imperative to reproduce species, to replicate DNA into the next generation is never more evident than in chimpanzee sexual behavior. No romance to it, simply energy, zeal, application and repetition.

N___'s younger colleagues joked nervously about Galahad and other hot-blooded male chimps in the lab. If these near-human creatures could seize control of their jailers, if they could free themselves from their cages, they might imprison their jailers, or might just murder them where they overpowered them. In their place, that was what (murderous, vengeful) Homo sapiens would do.

Pan troglodytes verus (western Africa) were not carnivorous animals, essentially. Their preferred diet was fruit, nuts, vegetables, insects. If these were not available, small mammals. But out of meanness (just possibly) the rampaging males might mutilate and devour those human specimens who'd mistreated them and spare others who'd been kind to them. Ape memories were excellent, unforgiving, like the memories of certain corvids.

Apes were capable of humanlike behavior: rage, tantrums, vengeance. In the wild, ape communities were strictly hierarchical, with a strong alpha male dominating and all others chimpanzees subordinate to him; in captivity there was no community, only just (caged) specimens. You could argue that a caged specimen is sui generis, an aberration.

Older chimps in the Professor's lab, male and female, were not nearly so exciting or as readily aroused as young Galahad.

Lust had dimmed in their eyes—they'd endured too many experiments for the good of humankind, or rather for the good of Big Pharma. Since the Animal Welfare Act of 2010 these chimpanzees were no longer routinely subjected to the sort of painful experiments they'd endured when younger, but they had not forgotten their torturers . . .

One of the Professor's most famous experiments, however, hadn't involved electrodes in chimpanzee brains or injections of cancer, TB, AIDS into their blood but rather the discovery that chimpanzees could recognize themselves in mirrors. That is, individual chimpanzees were capable of recognizing themselves as individuals, in mirrors, and not simply as "chimpanzees." In a sequence of experiments now recognized as historic the Professor had drawn red dots on the foreheads of chimps who were then positioned before mirrors into which they gazed with great excitement and fascination, waving their arms wildly, grimacing and mugging; like Narcissus falling in love with his reflection the chimps came eventually to comprehend that they were in some unfathomable way seeing themselves, and not just another chimp on the farther side of a sheet of glass. This was a sight which they'd never seen before, and for which they had no neural imprint to guide them.

When the first chimp gingerly touched his forehead, leaning close to the mirror and rubbing the red dot with his fingers, everyone in the lab had burst into spontaneous applause.

N___ hadn't worked in the Professor's lab at that time. But almost, he could remember, he'd applauded the Professor's great discovery which would be replicated over the years in other laboratories.

Few other animal species can recognize themselves in mirrors. Certain apes, but not all monkeys and not marmosets. Asian elephants, Eurasian magpies. Dolphins, orcas. But not dogs or cats. Not horses. Not crows. And not brain-damaged, retarded or severely autistic human beings.

N___ was capable of seeing his reflection in a mirror or glass and not (immediately) recognizing himself. But this was only natural (he believed) since N___ resembled so many other young Asian men of his type, slender, cerebral, self-effacing, with glasses, glossy black hair, dark clothing, an air both earnest and stealthy.

Not visible, by design. Yet not (entirely) invisible.

In a variant of the classic mirror experiment the young chimp Galahad had recognized himself in record time. Waving arms, grimacing and mugging, in an expression of sheer animal joy, but in his manner something guarded, wary. Here was the quintessential (male) chimpanzee, tirelessly virile, fecund, whose copious sperm wanted only to populate the world in its own image. Out of Galahad's flat, low-browed hairless face innocently round eyes blinked and glistened with crafty intelligence, playfulness. His fingers were hairless, like his toes, the palms of his hands and the soles of his feet, as if in mimicry of his human jailers; his thumbs and big toes were opposable; his brain allowed him a cognitive map of a considerable range of territory, far greater than that of most human beings. (N___ had no doubt that, in tests involving spatial memorization and hand-eye coordination,

Galahad was superior to slower-witted individuals like Mary Frances.) He was not burdened with conscience, and he was not burdened with ambition. He did not dwell simultaneously in the present, the past, and the future, to his detriment. He could comport himself like a baby, for treats, he could "smile"—but if he wished, he could sink his sharp teeth in your face, and tear it off in a heartbeat. It seemed appropriate, N___ thought, that this fine specimen would be the father of the first *Humanzee* to survive—if all went well.

"Galahad! Hel-*lo*."

Slipping on the surgical gloves, a tight fit.

He brings her flowers. She is so touched that tears stream from her small squinting eyes. In turn, he is touched by her emotion. The gratitude the *experimental subject* feels reflects upon him—it's as if N___ sees himself for once in a mirror that flatters, not flattens.

She loves me. Therefore, I am worthy of love.

At last in early November breathless Mary Frances dares to stand on tiptoe to kiss N___'s cheek and then, as if impulsively, N___'s mouth; and to whisper in N___'s ear that (maybe) they might go to his apartment that night . . . . And N___ draws in a deep breath and says yes—"I've been thinking the same thing, Mary Frances."

Walking hand in hand then to the furnished apartment on Edgar Street which N___ has seen only once, and then hurriedly. At least, he has the key to open the door and does not fumble it.

Seeing, inside, on a coffee table, a much-annotated paperback copy of Darwin's *The Expression of the Emotions in Man and Animals* placed there deliberately, as a joke, presumably by a lab colleague. N___ wonders what other jokes may lie in store for him, in these several rooms that constitute an experimental laboratory of a unique kind.

Still gripping N___'s hand Mary Frances blinks and squints like one who is blinded by a sudden light. With a little cry saying, not very coherently, "Oh, this is where you live, Nath'iel! It's—like—a 'bachelor' place—I guess." Then, with awkward coquetry, "Could be a little more—*cozy* . . ."

"Well, it will be, Mary Frances. Cozy. Now that you're here."

Now that you're here. Forced, flat words. But Mary Frances seems not to notice, marveling at several shelves of the hodgepodge of used books as if they constituted an impressive library: "Gosh! All these books . . . I guess you've read all these books, Nath'iel?"

Hears himself murmur modestly. "Oh, well—some of them."

"Are you, like, a teacher? 'Assistant professor'—is that what you are called? And you teach these books?"

N___ has been vague in identifying himself to Mary Frances. So far as she knows he is someone attached to Rockefeller Life Sciences, a young colleague of the distinguished Professor; she has sighted N___ in the Professor's company, setting up the Professor's computer for his PowerPoint lectures. But N___ has been purposefully elusive in giving a title to his role, a subject attached to his work.

Chief lab technician. Peregrine hunter-falcon, sent out into the world to do the Professor's bidding.

Thinking: the seminal solution, in a syringe in a compartment of the refrigerator, carefully wrapped in gauze. Must be brought out, to be at room temperature, or near-room temperature, by the time of use. Twenty minutes?

Many times N___ has coolly rehearsed in his imagination the steps of the *insemination*. First, he must establish that the subject has ingested enough flunitrazepam to render her erotically stimulated and yet lethargic, dreamy; confused, yet not alarmed; trusting as a child is trusting.

"Mary Frances? I think you will like this. I—I chose this—for us . . . For this occasion."

Prominent as a prop in a play, a bottle of red wine on a counter in the kitchen. N___ has not purchased the wine but guesses that it is sweet, to appeal to the *experimental subject*'s probable taste for sweet things. N___ pours wine for each of them and in Mary Frances's glass surreptitiously dissolves the colorless and tasteless drug that will enter the girl's bloodstream within seconds.

"Oh! This is—kind of—going to my head . . ." Laughing as she trips on a carpet, and N___ catches her.

And, soon afterward: "It is getting kind of cozy here, I guess . . . But must be sad here, Nath'iel, isn't it?—to be alone so much . . ."

So wistfully she speaks, in her clumsy attempt to be coquettish, N___ understands that she is speaking about herself.

Neither is accustomed to drinking, it seems. Yet Mary Frances finishes the glass N___ has poured for her taking no notice that N___ only pretends to drink his glass. He cannot risk losing control of this situation which is quite unlike anything he has ever attempted in his life, and for which there would appear to be no precedent.

Unorthodox methods are but shortcuts to scientific advancement. But, being unorthodox, they cannot be shared with anyone outside the laboratory.

At last, after an appropriate number of minutes, leading the *experimental subject* into the bedroom. Switching on a light. Hoping that Mary Frances doesn't sense that this room isn't really a familiar place to N___, he'd had time only to cursorily glance around earlier that week, to bring over a few items, stock the refrigerator and a storage area with things essential to this step of the experiment . . . Even as N___ assures the girl that he will "be careful"—that is, he will use a condom—certainly, he will use a condom—he understands that Mary Frances is too excited/distracted to care what he might do, or even exactly to notice. As soon as N___ gently nudges her onto the bed, and they begin kissing, and running their hands over each other, and tugging at each other's clothing, Mary Frances is oblivious to all else.

Love love love you. Oh—Nath'iel . . .

A single glass of wine might have been sufficient to render the naive girl intoxicated, and Mary Frances has had two, in fairly rapid succession. And so the flunitrazepam will be doubly, even triply potent. N___ hopes he will be able to revive her—eventually.

It will not be an aesthetic experience but it should not be onerous: "making love"—"having sex"—with the *experimental subject*. Essentially a mechanical act like most physical processes that are quasi-involuntary, "instinctive"—in which N___'s body might participate while his mind looks on bemused. Or rather, his mind looks away, fastidiously repelled.

This is not actually me but another in my place—"Nathaniel."

It is difficult to tell if the *experimental subject* is drunk, or just wildly affectionate, or both. She is very demonstrative, sobbing with emotion. Many times moaning *Love you, Nath'iel. Love love love you* not seeming to notice that her lover remains (grimly) silent.

Does he dare to *see* the girl in the bed? The unclothed female body, so much larger, *fleshier* than he'd imagined? Heavy breasts corroded with faint bluish veins, nipples like copper coins, heated skin with myriad small blemishes and marks, coarser than his own. Wiry rust-colored pubic hair like underbrush sprouting at the pit of the protruding belly, far thicker than his own, or any he'd ever seen, or imagined. Yet it is touching, Mary Frances seems to have shaved her lower legs, that are hard with muscle; her thighs, slack and jiggly, are covered in coarse hairs. Touching too, the low-browed girl with simian features had taken time to apply mascara to her eyes, lipstick to her mouth.

Despite his reputation for aloofness among his scientist colleagues N___ has felt desire intermittently in his life.

Precarious and perishable as swirls of cloud in a windswept sky. Long ago—in another lifetime, and in another language—before he'd become N___—he'd been attracted to very young girls—(children his own age?)—with smooth, hairless, epicene bodies—and long silky (black) hair. These were not sisters of his but might have been sisters for all had been children together, lost and helpless and desperate to be saved by—whoever would save them . . . In his new lifetime no one matters to him, not as these young girls had mattered. And all of them vanished. He will not think of it, never thinks of it, for there is no purpose to such thinking in his new life as the chief technician of a renowned primate laboratory.

Wondering in subsequent years if it is a sort of sex-fetish—the female must have a full head of hair, preferably falling past her shoulders, yet the female must not have hair, hairs, on any other part of her body for such hairs are repulsive to the male eye . . .

Ugh!—having to touch the female *hairs*. That are springy and resilient to the touch, like Galahad's hairy pelt.

Yet N___ is discovering that despite his disdain he is "attracted" to Mary Frances—perhaps because of his disdain. (There are fine hairs even on her breasts!—disgusting.) It is somehow exciting to him, the girl has become so—passionate. Her skin is coarsely mottled, flushed. Her smeared lips are parted. She is panting, grunting. She is shameless, grasping at him with her hands as no one before has ever grasped at him. A descent into chaos, N___ thinks. Dissolution of a compound, hissing like acid. Fastidious N___ is falling into pieces, he is no longer *he*.

What springs out of the base of his flat belly, like the rosy-pink fleshy tube that springs out of Galahad's belly, is not *he*.

A crude stranger, suddenly frantic with desire. Grunting like a chimp.

Nothing aesthetic here. Only just raw appetite here.

No holding back, N___ must enter the female body as Galahad might have done. Shuts his eyes, ceases breathing. Immediately the female grips him, muscled arms, legs. Inside the heated flesh, muscle. He is thrusting, pumping. Involuntary. Helpless. The chief technician in the Professor's esteemed lab has become a wildly thrusting machine, brainless as a chimp.

Fleeting images of very young girl-children with long silky (black) hair pass through his brain like wraiths. But too quickly, he can't hold on to them and will forget them at once.

At last, it is over. Has ended.

Spent and exhausted on the sweat-slick body of the female. His spirit seems to have detached itself from the ordeal. Possibly N___ has died (he thinks): his soul floats above his lifeless body. He feels nothing—for air cannot feel.

The other, the low-browed girl, is barely conscious. She has been sobbing. Her face appears swollen, damp with tears, mucus. Her flesh has gone slack as if boneless. The drug has worked perfectly as the Professor has assured N___ it would.

How N___ would like to flee! Extricate himself from this smelly embrace, hurriedly dress and flee to his own apartment, step into a shower as hot as he can bear . . .

But no. Now comes the most delicate step of the procedure.

The syringe, filled with the frothy-clotty semen of *Pan troglodytes verus*, has been placed strategically beneath the bed, where N___'s groping fingers can locate it.

Very carefully, N___ raises himself on his elbow. He is still breathing hard, audibly. (When is the last time N___ has breathed audibly? Even when he jogs in the early morning, he does not pant; his heartbeat is only slightly accelerated, like the calm cascade of his thoughts.) With the most remarkable composure, under these awkward circumstances, N___ brings the tip of the syringe against the vagina of the *experimental subject*. Inside that nest of damp, sticky hair, as coarse as chimpanzee hair. N___ inserts the tip of the syringe as carefully as he can so as not to disturb Mary Frances who lies spread-eagled and sprawled in the damp bedclothes. (Though by this time very little could have disturbed the unconscious girl, who could not have been more deeply asleep if she'd been anesthetized.)

Within seconds the syringe is emptied of its cloudy liquid. N___ has succeeded in the first step of the experiment!

Unknowing, sprawled in a bliss of erotic satisfaction, Mary Frances slumbers on. Perhaps she will be impregnated this very night—it is not probable, but a possibility. The raw yearning with which she'd made love with him suggests that she is ovulating.

Ovulating! Disgusting thought.

Cautiously N___ climbs out of the rumpled bed and stands beside it, naked. With his iPhone he takes several quick pictures of the stuporous *experimental subject*, to email to the Professor who is sure to be waiting for the latest news.

Step one: completed.

Wondering whether, in fact, he might flee the premises and shower at his apartment, and sleep in his own, pristine bedsheets that night; or, for it is more in line with the romantic narrative in which N___ and the *experimental subject* each have roles, he should shower here, and try to spend the remainder of the night with Mary Frances who may, in the morning, need to be placated and assured that she is cherished by her lover.

No. Not possible that he can "sleep" with her. Someone will have to change those soiled sheets before he comes anywhere near them again.

The lab administrator can arrange for housekeeping. *He* will have nothing to do with it.

Deciding that he will shower in the apartment on Edgar Street. It would be distasteful to dress in his clothes, his body sticky and unclean.

It is the first time—he supposes, resigned, that it will not be the last time—that N___ showers in this apartment. At least, there is a good supply of towels, for which he has the lab administrator to thank. At least the shower is adequate—the water temperature is more responsive to calibration than the shower in his own small apartment.

N___ is still giddy—he is still mildly repelled—he feels a thrill of something like vanity. No one else in the Professor's laboratory could have executed the procedure so flawlessly. His colleagues will make crude jokes, out of envy. But not even the married men, seasoned in the routines of sex, experienced and adroit in feigning emotions they have long since ceased to feel, could have performed as convincingly as N____ performed with a female as unattractive as the *experimental subject.*

If the experiment comes to fruition, the Professor will single out his chief technician for special thanks though, given the unorthodox nature of the experiment, the details of N____'s contribution will not be divulged.

Previous experiments with creating a (forbidden) hybrid species, a *Humanzee*, have ended in failure. Insemination of female chimpanzees and other apes with the sperm of Homo sapiens have never resulted in fertilization, so far as reliable records show, though there are accounts of the efforts of the Russian biologist Ilya Ivanovich Ivanov attempting, in the 1920s, to create a hybrid species by impregnating a female ape, that ended with failure and the exile of Ivanov to Siberia.

There are (unverified) accounts too of human females impregnated with the semen of apes, whether voluntarily or otherwise, in laboratories in China, in more recent years; but no scientific data, no conclusive results. If there are rumors that a *Humanzee* was actually born, somewhere in China in the 1970s, it is usually the case that the *Humanzee* died soon after birth, and its remains were lost. No data, no photographic evidence.

Ideally, the *experimental subject* would be a human female voluntarily involved in the experiment, who would nurse and nurture the *Humanzee* after birth, as human females have occasionally nursed and nurtured chimpanzee infants; but overly restrictive "ethics" laws in the US and elsewhere make such an experiment impossible, and in any case, as the Professor has many times pointed out, no human female could be trusted to continue with the experiment if/when the *hybrid specimen* is taken from her by research scientists. If, for instance, for whatever reason, the *Humanzee* had to be euthanized and anatomized, like any experimental animal. Thus, ignorance on the part of the *experimental subject* is crucial to the project.

When N____ returns to the humid, smelly bedroom, revived from the shower, hair wetly combed, he sees with a small thrill of disgust that the girl is still unconscious, asprawl and oblivious. Hardly a *girl*, which suggests innocence, but a *young woman*, which suggests experience.

Softly the young woman moans in her sleep, her back teeth grind just audibly. Her eyelids flutter, he is panicked that she will wake up, but she continues to sleep. Has a forked sperm of Galahad's pierced an egg inside that slack, fattish belly yet? For N____'s sake, he hopes it will be soon.

Must keep in mind, they are a *couple*. He will leave a note for her on the bedside table—

Dear Mary Frances
    You are so beautiful.
    I will call you soon.
    Please lock door when you leave.
    Thank you.
—Nathaniel

It requires twenty minutes to compose the note. Each word is eked from him. Like squeezing leaden drops of blood out of his veins.

Realizing later that *thank you* was (probably) not the appropriate phrase.

In a turmoil of dismay, disgust like that sensation of diarrhea microbes simmering in the gut, about to explode through the intestines—N___ lies awake in his chaste bed in fresh-laundered sheets reliving the *sex-intercourse* with the *experimental subject*. A part of him is so appalled, it hovers in the air above his prone, motionless body like a wraith. Another part, more callow, careerist, beyond shame, is calculating that the Professor will be very impressed with him. Very.

No. He cannot do it again. *Cannot.*

But must. *One injection of semen will (surely) not be enough.*

In his insomniac misery N___ finds himself thinking of the mountains west of Red Bluff. Where with a college friend he'd hiked, backpacked and camped long ago in another lifetime it seemed.

In the mountains above Red Bluff they'd found an abandoned cabin overlooking a fast-moving stream, white-water rapids. Sleeping bags on the floor of the cabin, a birch-log fire in the fireplace. Even when pelting rain fell from the sky he'd been happy there with his friend as aloof and reticent as himself, and as smart.

N___ has long ago lost contact with his friend who'd failed to win a prestigious fellowship to Cal Tech as N___ had. But at the time of his thirtieth birthday N___ returned to hike and back-pack alone near Red Bluff wanting to give himself a gift and not knowing what to give himself, remembering he'd been happy on the trail there overlooking the white-water rapids, but the cabin had collapsed and he hadn't been able to sleep in his sleeping bag on the floor, or build a birch fire as he'd remembered . . . Yet still for a while he'd been happy there listening to the rushing, downward-plunging mountain stream. *So happy!*—he recalls.

"Was this person—'Mary Frances Bowes'—a *virgin*?" the Profes-sor inquires with an air of bemused disdain.

Taken by surprise N___ cannot think of a reply.

Was the *experimental subject* a virgin? Possibly. Or not. No? Is it important, belatedly? N___ tries to explain that he doesn't know, can't recall. In the height/depth of sexual urgency his consciousness was obliterated, he'd (virtually) ceased to exist.

Scrolling through the pictures on N___'s cell phone, strok-ing his stiff white goatee, the Professor seems distracted. At last glancing up at N___ as if he has forgotten that N___ is there.

"Good work, N___! *Project Galahad* is under way."

Nath'iel? Hi. Kind of missing you. Give a call . . .

He has given the *experimental subject* a cell phone number to call. It is not his cell phone and when he checks it, he sees that

Mary Frances has called several times. Maybe he will call back, or maybe he will wait for a day or two.

Even after they have become lovers it is N____'s stratagem to see the *experimental subject* intermittently and unpredictably. Not setting dates with the girl but promising to call her so that she is never sure of him, cannot take him for granted, and is grateful when he calls; often, practically sobbing with relief which she tries to hide, and N____ tries not to acknowledge. Neediness in the female is her disadvantage, and her disadvantage is their advantage. Keep her, the Professor has said, *on edge.*

"The crucial thing is, if and when the *experimental subject* becomes pregnant she must be led to believe that you will continue to love her, and that you and you alone will provide her medical care. She must not become desperate and tell someone. She must not arrange for an abortion."

N____ sees desperation in the small squinting eyes, and feels a thrill of guilt—*She is afraid of losing me. Me!* As if he were a rare treasure and not rather (as he often thinks of himself) an empty vessel waiting to be filled.

Clinging to N____'s arm when they walk together. Exasperating, and flattering! So desperate is the girl to establish that they are, not two individuals who see each other only occasionally, and who are obviously mismatched, but a *couple.*

N____ still tutors Mary Frances in biology at least once a week. This was the original pretext of their relationship and it is the (only) part of the relationship that N____ enjoys. It is satisfying to him when Mary Frances earns a decent grade on a quiz or, at midterm, a not-disgraceful grade of 74 which translates into a solid C—passing.

"Oh Nath'iel! *I love you.*"

Flinching from Mary Frances's exuberance as she throws her arms around his neck to hug, pressing her bosom against his narrow torso. Feeling a sharp current of desire, in the same instant rebuffed.

He has lost something of the acuity of the peregrine falcon. He must try to retrieve it!

N___ doesn't want to think that without him Mary Frances would soon forget everything he has taught her. Carefully memorized definitions of biological terms, processes—a synopsis of Darwinian evolutionary theory N___ had prepared for her in the simplest possible terms: in danger of evaporating overnight.

She might not get into nursing school, N___ thinks. How disappointed she will be!

For by then, N___ will out of her life. The *experimental subject* will be expelled from the experiment, of no further use.

Possibly, she could train to be a nurse's aide? A hospital attendant?

Elementary school teacher? No doubt, Mary Frances could make the right man a good wife.

Maybe, in some circuitous way unknown to her, the Professor could help her find work. N___ will inquire, in time.

N___ doesn't see Mary Frances for days. A week. It is part of the stratagem but he doesn't miss her and tries not to think of her—that is, of their frantic and convulsive couplings in the bed in the Edgar Street apartment which are followed by 1) Mary Frances's stupor, lasting for hours; and 2) the injection of chimpanzee semen, executed by the lab technician with unwavering skill if with unyielding disgust. When at last they meet for dinner at an obscure Chinese restaurant in the vicinity of Edgar Street N___ sees the wild anguish in the girl's eyes, the chapped lips that look as if she has been gnawing them, and the thought comes to him—*Is she pregnant?* He realizes that he is frightened of the possibility.

Mary Frances clutches at N___'s hand. It is her worry, she says, can't sleep at night worrying, that N___ does not "respect" her now. "I mean, now that we are, like, seeing each other—kind of—'seriously'. . . ." Her voice trails off weakly, she is deeply embarrassed and can't bring herself to say, *having sex.*

Quickly N___ says that his feelings for her have not changed at all—of course he "respects" her. But then his mind goes blank. He has no idea what to say next.

"I hope you mean it, Nath'iel, and aren't just saying it to—be nice . . ."

Still, N___ can't think what to say. He is supposed to say—*Of course I love you.*

Impulsively then, Mary Frances leans forward across the table, and kisses N___'s startled mouth. Her eyelids droop coquettishly, pathetically. "I think about you—us—all the time. Really hard to concentrate on my courses! Y'know—what I am thinking: do you? Darling?"

Darling. It is a word, an utterance, that sounds as if it has been many times rehearsed. N___ feels a trickle of icy sweat run into the small of his back.

A waitress arrives with sticky plastic menus. A Chinese-American girl of about twenty, child-sized, straight-cut black bangs, beautiful thick-lashed eyes, quizzical half-smile taking in N___ with the plain stocky white girl who appears to be in an emotional state, tears on her flushed cheeks.

N___ looks away, can't meet the waitress's skeptical eyes.

Can't acknowledge the waitress's mute query—*Why, you and her?*

3.

Each week reporting to the Professor: "Not yet."

Assiduously the chief technician will record in his (encrypted) notes for *Project Galahad*: eleven acts of *sexual intercourse* followed (within seconds) by injections of chimpanzee semen, intermittently through the month of November; each injection successfully executed without the suspicion of the *experimental subject* who'd been administered a powerful tranquilizer to render her lethargic, unaware of surroundings.

Prudently, N___ lessens the dosage of flunitrazepam dissolved into the subject's drink. The first dose left the female comatose for nearly ten hours.

And then, following the eleventh episode in early December, *insemination.*

That is, *impregnation.*

In the New Year, what a shock! But also relief. N___'s first thought is that he will no longer have to go through the motions of lovemaking with the *experimental subject* . . .

Shyly, hiding her face against his neck, on a sofa in the apartment on Edgar Street, on a cold windless evening in late January Mary Frances tells her lover that she is going to have his baby. N___'s thudding heart muffles his hearing but he does hear the emphatic—*your baby.*

Stammering apologetically, "I—I thought maybe—I might be p-pregnant—a while ago—but I wanted to be sure before I told you . . . I didn't want you to worry for no reason, Nath'iel."

This is touchingly considerate of Mary Frances, N___ would think, if N___ had the capacity to think at the moment.

N___ has been waiting for such a revelation for weeks—since the first heroic effort of sexual intercourse in November—yet is now not prepared. Oh, what is the *experimental subject* saying!

(He is thinking that he must get to a phone—he must contact the Professor. Or—maybe he should make sure that the *experimental subject* is really pregnant, and not imagining it? He does not dare misinform the Professor about something so crucial . . .)

Awkwardly N___ embraces and comforts Mary Frances who is wetting his shirt with her tears. Is the distraught young woman weeping out of joy, or fear? Apprehension, or excitement?

She'd taken a drugstore test, Mary Frances says. Twice. So far as she can calculate, she is about five weeks pregnant.

She'd thought she might be pregnant, at least two weeks before. No period for eight-nine weeks, and her breasts "sort of achy, sensitive." And a "real, queasy feeling in my tummy" in the mornings.

Period—awful term. *Achy, sensitive*—awful. N___ tries not to visibly recoil in revulsion.

Mary Frances is saying she hopes N___ isn't upset! She hopes . . .

"D'you still love me, Nath'iel? I love you—more than ever."

But N___ has not told her he loved her, at all!

Pleading with N___ as if the pregnancy were her fault alone: "Are you angry with me, Nath'iel? Please tell me you are not . . ."

N___ stammers: "Of course—not. I just can't understand how it happened, Mary Frances. I thought I was very careful, but . . ." Feebly his voice falters. He is perspiring, shivering.

This is such a private matter. So intimate. Physical.

Shameful! (And N___'s role in it, unspeakable.)

Innocent, trusting Mary Frances is *pregnant*. Mary Frances's womb has been *inseminated*. The numerous injections of chimpanzee semen have had the intended effect, a human female has been impregnated by a chimpanzee. It is no longer a theoretical experiment with a clueless *experimental subject* but is rapidly becoming—"real."

Yet it does not seem real to N___, just yet. He wonders if all "fathers" feel this way, having been told that a female with whom they have had sex is *pregnant*.

But it is only an experiment, N____ reminds himself. The fetus, the infant, the creature-to-be-born, is not *his*; does not bear his DNA. The experiment will be known in the history of science as *Project Galahad*.

Mary Frances's face is mottled with happiness like measles. Her usually coarse skin glows. She is mistaking N____'s silence for male dismay, perhaps.

"I hope this is not a terrible shock to you, Nath'iel. I know that you—you tried—to prevent what has happened. I've been praying for both of us, Nath'iel. I want us to do the right thing. It's like God found a way for us, without our knowing. It was meant to be."

Meant to be! But it was *not meant to be*. If Mary Frances knew what was beginning to germinate in her womb, she would be appalled, terrified . . .

"I have to pinch myself, to believe it's 'real.' Oh God—*me*. My parents would be *so ashamed*."

It is typical of Mary Frances to think aloud, in a sort of rambling exclamatory monologue. N____ has heard certain of his (white) colleagues in Life Sciences thinking aloud in this way, moving their lips, even grimacing and gesturing. *He* would never behave so riskily. *His* thoughts are meant for N____ alone.

N____ doesn't know what to do with his hands, shyly caresses Mary Frances's back as she presses against him, quivering with emotion. In the agitation of the moment N____ cannot think clearly. It is a profound fact—the *experimental subject* has become the *impregnated subject*.

The *impregnated subject* is likely to become one of the most famous/notorious female specimens in the history of science.

In a lowered voice Mary Frances tells N___ that she doesn't believe in abortion. Hesitating to speak the word, that sounds harsh and blunt in her breathy voice: *abor-tion*.

N___ stammers that he doesn't either. Does not believe in abortion.

Hears himself uttering such asinine words! Why would one *believe*, or *not believe*, in abortion?

"Oh Nath'iel darling! You don't? Really?"

"I—I don't. No . . ."

"Then—you want us to have the baby? Our baby?"

"Y-Yes . . ."

Our baby. N___'s head is swimming. He wonders if the agitation he feels is the agitation he would be feeling if indeed the inseminating sperm had been his.

Now Mary Frances is weeping in earnest. Her warm, fleshy body smells of perspiration and great joy. Already she seems motherly to him, matronly. Her sizable breasts, wide hips . . . Daringly she takes N___'s loose, limp hand and presses it against her soft belly, that bulges beneath the waistband of her slacks.

It seems that Mary Frances has been anguished about telling him. Worried that he wouldn't want her to have the baby—"It's, like, what most guys would want. Lots of girls I know. 'Get an abortion, I'll pay for it.' Like a baby is some kind of *accident*, and not God's plan."

"Yes. That—is so . . ."

"Lots of guys, they'd drop a girl cold. Maybe try to get out of paying for the abortion, even. Bastards!" Mary Frances shakes her head in disgust. How fortunate it is, N___ isn't one of *them*.

N___ hears himself say with numbed lips that of course he wants her to have the baby. Mary Frances is so naive, she doesn't question how she has come to be pregnant when, so far as she knows, N___ took precautions each time they'd grappled together on the bed; he supposes that to one who believes that God ordains all things, an improbable pregnancy has to be a part of a plan.

Ironic that, though indeed this pregnancy is a part of a plan, it is the Professor's plan, and not God's.

How thrilled the Professor will be! How pleased with his chief technician, another time.

N___ assures Mary Frances that she is so precious to him, their baby is so precious, he will oversee her medical care—entirely. She will not have to see any young, barely trained doctor provided by University Health Care—she will have a private doctor, the most distinguished obstetrician in the vicinity. Through his contacts in Life Sciences N___ will arrange for her prenatal care beginning with an examination within a day or two.

Seeing the wondering expression in Mary Frances's face N___ is inspired to tell her what the Professor has planned: "There's an excellent obstetrics clinic in Life Sciences Hall, on one of the high, 'restricted' floors. Not just a clinic for prenatal care but where you will have the baby. What isn't covered by my contract with the University, I will pay."

N___ is speaking extravagantly. Why is he saying such things? His heart beats rapidly and his face is flushed with the excitement of fatherhood. Almost N___ is thinking that indeed he would want to pay for the baby, for he is responsible.

How suddenly it has happened that Mary Frances Bowes, a plain-faced female to whom N___ would not have given a second glance under normal circumstances, has become a unique and priceless specimen. A female human successfully impregnated with the sperm of *Pan troglodytes verus*, possibly for the first time in history. Without her knowledge the female's fleshy/slatternly body has been transformed.

What is Mary Frances now *worth*? In terms of the scientific research the birth will spawn, many millions of dollars.

In terms of the scientific careers the *Humanzee* will enrich, yet more millions of dollars.

A Nobel Prize for the Professor. If all goes well.

Of course, the exact details of *Project Galahad* can never be revealed. The identity of the *experimental subject/birth mother*, the identity of the chief technician/surrogate father. The (unorthodox) means by which the impregnation was administered. Somehow, utilizing the genius for which he is known in the scientific research community, the Professor will find a way to present the lab's astonishing findings to the world that will protect the researchers from charges of ethics violations, and worse.

He will receive acknowledgment, if not the sort of fame that will accrue to the Professor.

Seeing how the *experimental subject* is gazing at him, with what adoration, awe, neediness, N___ wonders: will Mary Frances expect him to marry her? Once the euphoria of the hour wanes, marriage will certainly be an issue.

This too has been scripted beforehand. N___ is prepared.

Informing Mary Frances in a voice of regret that since he is in the United States on a special science-research visa he is not allowed to enter into any legal, contractual arrangement with any US citizen under penalty of expulsion—"It's a State Department regulation. So, Mary Frances, we could not be married, at least for the foreseeable future, until I become a US citizen."

"Oh! I—I guess so . . ."

Mary Frances absorbs the information with a glazed smile. Perhaps she is not quite hearing N___. Perhaps her brain is cranking out its elemental plan of childlike cunning—best to bide her time, not to appear upset, not to make demands on N___. God will work out things for the best.

N___ says, relenting: "We could become engaged. Would you like that? It would have to be a secret, though—like the pregnancy—for as long as you can keep it secret. And my identity, you would have to keep secret."

"Engaged! Do you mean it, Nath'iel?"

"My schedule can't be changed, unfortunately. I couldn't see you any more than I have been seeing you . . ."

"Oh no, I mean—I wouldn't expect it. 'Engaged'—that would be—wonderful . . ."

Mary Frances throws her arms around N___'s neck like a drowning person. She could not be more dazed than if N___ had given her flunitrazepam to dampen her cognitive abilities.

"As long as you understand, the engagement would have to be a secret from your family. The identity of the father of the baby would have to be a secret. Otherwise I could be deported. And then we would never marry."

Marry as a collective verb, in an utterance of N___'s. He is somewhat dazed himself, as if he has been drinking.

Mary Frances hugs him tight, tight. Confessing to him in a rush of words, that she is *very ashamed*—"Darling, I don't think that I can take you to meet my family anyway. They are—they are good Christians—but—they don't like people they call 'Japs' or 'Chinese'—'Orientals.' Or Mexicans. They don't like—well, anybody who doesn't look like them. (They are very biased about Negroes!) Even if I explained who you are, an 'Asian person' with an advanced science degree, a professor at the University, and nothing like what they might think—(they would probably think 'Communist')—they would not forgive me. I don't know that I could ever return home to them with our baby, or you. Please forgive me, Nath'iel—in this happy time, I am *so ashamed.*"

N___ is stunned by this revelation. He has so naturally assumed his superiority to the low-browed white girl, it's a shock to him that she might not share that conviction. In defying her racist parents Mary Frances is being bravely magnanimous in loving *him.*

N___ assures Mary Frances that he understands. Of course there are people who can't help their prejudices against other races. He doesn't doubt, he tells her—(though in fact N___ does doubt, vehemently)—that her relatives are "good Christians."

Thinking how fortunate he is, for the sake of *Project Galahad*, that Mary Frances doesn't want to introduce him to her family, and will keep her pregnancy a secret from them.

To celebrate the happy occasion (as an expectant father might plausibly wish to do) N___ opens a bottle of red wine with shaky fingers. Requires several tries to extricate the damned cork. Pours wine into two glasses but Mary Frances declines hers, eyes glowing and glazed with joy—"Oh Nathi'el, gosh! Now I'm 'expecting,' I can't drink."

But Mary Frances will sit close beside N___ on the sofa as he drinks from his glass, snuggling against him like a fevered, furry creature. Not drinking with him but it's as if the sweet red wine has gone to her head, or into the damp netherworld between her fleshy thighs. Her eyelids droop and her lips part, her head heavy upon his shoulder, stubby fingers tight-clasped through his, pulling his hand to rest on her soft stomach. A little sleepy-happy moan deep in her throat, of utter euphoria. N___ sits very still, neither yielding nor resisting.

He has not (yet) contacted the Professor with the good news. His thoughts swirl like a hive of aroused wasps even as the *experimental subject* sinks into a light doze.

Is the news good? For whom, good? N___ swallows a mouthful of wine. Thoughts continue to swirl, unresolved.

*   *   *

Soon then, N___ is instructed by the Professor to bring Mary Frances to the hastily constituted "Obstetrics Care Clinic" on the tenth floor of Rockefeller Life Sciences Hall where she is examined by an individual introduced to her as "Dr. Ellis"— gynecologist/obstetrician—middle-aged, male, Caucasian; in fact, N___ recognizes the man as an experimental embryologist and one of the Professor's collaborators.

After a thorough examination including highly detailed blood work kindly "Dr. Ellis" informs Mary Frances that, as she has suspected, she is approximately five weeks pregnant—"Which makes your due date approximately two hundred sixty days from now, my dear, in mid-September."

"Ellis" has been briefed on the unorthodox nature of the young woman's pregnancy; he has signed a confidentiality contract with the Professor, with whom he has worked on several projects in the past, of a sensitive nature involving the effects of experimental pharmaceuticals upon unborn fetuses (of black and Hispanic pregnant women patients at a city clinic). In calculating the expectant mother's due date he has shrewdly averaged the gestation periods—two hundred thirty-seven days for *Pan troglodytes verus*, two hundred eighty days for *Homo sapiens*.

Telling the young woman that the estimate is only approximate of course. "Some babies insist upon coming into the world earlier than they are expected, and some babies come later."

Mary Frances bursts into tears. Stammering to the doctor that she is so happy, God has blessed her at a younger age than she'd have imagined.

N___ has accompanied Mary Frances to the Obstetrics Care Clinic where he waits for her, for some time. N___ is the only person who waits in the small lounge. Fascinating to him, to see how an area of the tenth floor that was formerly office space for junior staff has been refashioned by the Professor's directive, virtually overnight, with the addition of stark white floor-to-ceiling partitions that give the space a clinical atmosphere. There is even a receptionist's desk, and a receptionist. There is a nurse named "Betty"—a mature woman in a white nylon pants suit, pale stockings and rubber-soled white shoes who has greeted the *experimental subject* warmly and will be an essential contact for Mary Frances through the months of the pregnancy. On the white walls are posters relating to women's health—diagrams of the female body with reproductive organs luridly highlighted, posters advertising essential foods for girls and women, photographs of Olympic women athletes bursting with health and strength. The receptionist, a younger woman, smiles at N___ as one might smile at an uneasy young father-to-be.

Against a floor-to-ceiling plate glass window, a large potted plant with shiny spear-leaves which N___ thinks he has seen before. In the Professor's outer office?

Fortunately N___ has brought along his laptop to the Clinic—the lightweight little computer is attached to N___ like a colonoscopy bag.

Mary Frances is with the doctor for more than an hour. Each of the *experimental subject*'s appointments in the Clinic will be thorough. Every aspect of the unorthodox pregnancy will be recorded. Unknown to the subject the examinations will be videotaped and studied by the members of the primate lab; these will include weekly pelvic exams, and an amniocentesis in the early second trimester of the pregnancy, for the progress of the *hybrid embryo* must be carefully monitored. Members of the primate lab are concerned that the hybrid fertilization will not "hold"—the Professor himself has cautioned against excessive optimism and not to be disappointed if *Project Galahad* ends in a miscarriage, for that is usually nature's way of correcting a genetic anomaly. But even a miscarriage will prove scientifically valuable, for the remains of the fetus, however rudimentary in development, will be eagerly and exhaustively studied.

Dr. Ellis has prescribed a restricted diet for Mary Frances, low in sodium and high in protein and calcium; daily exercise is "a must" and no bad habits—smoking, alcohol. Nurse Betty provides pamphlets for Mary Frances to take home and consult. If Mary Frances has any questions about the pregnancy, any questions at all, she is to call Nurse Betty at once on a private number—"Let's make that a promise, Mary Frances!"

All this attention is deeply moving and flattering to Mary Frances. Already her experience as an unwed expectant mother is totally unlike the dire predictions her mother and female relatives would have made for her; indeed, Mary Frances cannot believe *how nice* everyone is being, including dear, darling "Nath'iel" who has surprised her by being not disapproving and resentful since she's become pregnant, but supportive of her decision to have the baby.

Both Dr. Ellis and Nurse Betty caution Mary Frances, however, not to discuss her prenatal care with anyone. Not a roommate or a friend, not a family member or a relative. For the Life Sciences Obstetrics Care Clinic is a privately endowed health-care facility that can accept very few patients, and these are usually limited to the wives of tenured faculty. Other young female students at the University are eligible only for minimal prenatal care at the University infirmary but Mary Frances is "different"—"special"— because of N___'s appointment in Life Sciences.

Before Mary Frances leaves the Clinic she is asked to sign a "confidentiality contract," agreeing not to discuss any aspect of her prenatal health care. This includes the identity of her obstetrician and the location of the Clinic. Crucially, it includes the identity of N___ whose work-visa would be revoked by the State Department.

Seeing that Mary Frances is looking flushed and confused by so much happening to her within a small space of time N___ takes the contract from her to examine. He has seen a draft of the document previously, yet its contents are obscure even to him, who'd helped compose it: seven numbered paragraphs of tight-packed small print which grants to the Clinic certain prerogatives regarding the pregnancy and birth, including the surrendering of the infant at the time of birth or shortly thereafter, as well as the surrender of the fetus in the event of a miscarriage, at the "discretion" of the Clinic. Such an unorthodox document could have no legal binding of course but it is supposed that the naive *experimental subject* could be intimidated into accepting its terms if necessary.

N___ hesitates just a moment before telling Mary Frances to sign—"Go ahead, darling. It's just legalese. It's just *routine.*"

With a giddy smile and a flourish of a pen Mary Frances signs the document.

Has N___ called her—*darling?* The word slipped out, unbidden.

"Ideally, as soon as the hybrid is born, the mother should die. For in this case she can't be trusted to nurse it, and she can't be trusted not to reveal our secret."

The Professor speaks so thoughtfully, tugging at his stiff white goatee, others around the table are tugged in his wake, as a large speeding vehicle tugs smaller vehicles in its wake.

"Yes. That is—true. But to be realistic . . ."

"—we can't just kill her. Of course."

"Of course *not*. But in the event of her 'dying in childbirth'— being killed by an embolism, for instance—"

"—that would be very practical. An embolism is plausible. But—"

"—a hemorrhage, after a difficult birth. We'll schedule a caesarean, in any case. And the medical report would be that both mother and infant failed to survive a difficult birth. There'd be no problem about death certificates so that the *Humanzee* could be raised in seclusion, right on this floor, for its natural life."

"Yes, but—isn't it more likely that the embryo will self-destruct? A miscarriage . . ."

". . . *she* would never know. What was in her womb . . ."

". . . or a stillbirth. In which case she might see the body, and realize that . . ."

"No. She *would not,* necessarily. A premature infant *Humanzee* would probably resemble a human infant just enough that a drugged and distraught female wouldn't know the difference even if she did 'see' it."

"If it lives, the female can still be told that it has died. Just make sure that she's sufficiently groggy from the anesthetic . . ."

"But consider the possibility that she *can* nurse it—would want to nurse it. The strong maternal instinct to 'nurture' might overcome revulsion—"

". . . if she 'sees' the infant *Humanzee* but doesn't recognize it as something other than human . . ."

"The maternal instinct is so powerful, the female would wish to believe that her infant is normal, so she might actually see it as normal . . ."

". . . or a human infant with birth defects, a Down syndrome infant for instance, which she could certainly nurse and with which she might bond."

"That might work . . ."

"That is taking an enormous risk . . ."

"Except as the *Humanzee* matures wouldn't it become clear to even the most deluded female that her baby isn't—*human*?"

"But would it make a difference? If the female bonds with the infant, even a deformed or hybrid infant, isn't that enough for her to remain its chief nurturer? Isn't that the essence of the female *instinct*?"

"No, no! Wait—"

"Ridiculous—"

"Dangerous—"

"We can't have her 'nurturing' the hybrid as if it were hers. Bringing it up like a child! It's ours and belongs in our lab."

"She would never give it up, once she 'bonded' with it. No nursing!"

"Better to take it from her immediately after the birth, tell her it's dead. Show her—something. An infant corpse, an aborted embryo. I could easily acquire the remains of an embryo from an abortion clinic. She'd be so agitated she couldn't think straight . . ."

". . . maybe tell her it died, but we can harvest its organs. 'Give life to another baby.' Pay her off . . ."

"Tell her there's medical insurance at the Clinic. Five thousand dollars. That should do it."

"She won't be alone and grieving—N___ can take care of her . . ."

"What if she has a breakdown, is taken to an ER? They see she's had a baby, they ask what happened to the baby . . ."

"I told you: the ideal situation is that the mother dies as soon as the creature is born. We can provide nursing, nurture. What about Maude?"

Maude! A ripple of approval around the table.

During this discussion N___ sits in a state of suspended animation, numbed as if by Novocain. Taking notes on his laptop as usual. It is typical of N___ not to provide much commentary at the weekly meetings unless the Professor or another colleague asks his opinion; now, the Professor pointedly turns to N___ to ask what he thinks.

"'What do I *think*?"—N___ seems to be considering.

A long pause. A fleeting and indecipherable expression crosses N___'s face. His fingers have ceased typing on the laptop. The Professor and the others wait. Very straight-backed the chief technician sits, staring at the laptop screen as if searching for the answer there.

4.

Methodically N___ parcels out his time with the *experimental subject*.

Following the Professor's directive. *The female's disadvantage is the male's advantage. Keep her on edge.*

Keeping Mary Frances both dependent upon him and uncertain of him. Lonely for him and yet fearful of contacting him. "Crazy in love with him"—(she has said, embarrassingly)—yet fearful of annoying him. Just when the *experimental subject* thinks that she may have offended N___, and that N___ may have abandoned her, N___ will call her as if nothing is wrong; N___ will bring her flowers, take her to dinner and to the movies, bring her back to the apartment on Edgar Street to stay the night.

N___ will (clenching his teeth) call her *darling*. Acquiesce when the *experimental subject* seizes his hand to press against her alarmingly swelling belly.

Listen intently, nod, smile indulgently as Mary Frances chatters excitedly about names for Baby.

"Tiffany" is her first choice, if Baby is a girl. Runners-up: "Brooke"—"Emma"—"Sarah"—"Elizabeth" . . .

"Nathaniel, Jr." is her first choice, if Baby is a boy. Runners-up: "Joseph"—"Matthew"—"Jonathan" . . .

Asked what his favorite names are N___ says that he has no favorite names and will let Mary Frances choose.

"Oh, but—not even *one name*? Say it's a baby girl . . ."

N___ can't recall the names Mary Frances has suggested and so says, "Well—there's 'Mary Frances'—"

"Oh, gosh *no*. That's sweet of you, Nath'iel, but—not a good idea. 'Cause there's no 'Mary Frances, Jr.'—there'd have to be 'Big Mary Frances' and 'Little Mary Frances.'" Mary Frances shakes her head, laughing. "But 'Nath'iel, Jr.'—that would be nice. We could call him 'Nath-ie' . . ."

N___ shudders. His name attached to the hybrid *Humanzee*.

"'Galahad.' That's a distinctive name."

"'Gala-*had.*' Is that a well-known name? Not the Bible, is it?" Mary Frances frowns, considering.

N___ says, "It might be in the Bible. One of the obscure books. It's a traditional name."

"Yes, I like it, kind of—'Gala-*had.*' It's different. Like, high-class!"

N___ gazes at the *experimental subject* with something like affection. A weird, unwished-for rush of affection. To be so easily *made happy*! He who has no family, no siblings, feels their absence in his life now. If he'd had a sister like Mary Frances, relentlessly cheerful, optimistic . . . He will miss her, he thinks, when *Project Galahad* has no need for her.

Following her initial visit to the Obstetrics Care Clinic Mary Frances is issued an electronic ID card that allows her to enter the restricted tenth floor of Rockefeller Life Sciences unaccompanied by N___. (Mary Frances's card does not admit her to other restricted floors, but only to the Clinic on the tenth floor; she could not, for instance, wander about the eighth floor in search of her handsome Asian fiancé "Nathaniel Li.") Soon she comes to look forward to the weekly appointments with Dr. Ellis which are comforting and flattering to her, for she is treated "like a princess" by the kindly doctor; indeed, Mary Frances has never heard of any expectant mother who has been treated so well, and only wishes that she could boast a little to her relatives back home—"But no, I won't. I promised, and I *won't.*"

After the clinical examination with Dr. Ellis, Nurse Betty takes time to chat companionably with Mary Frances about how the expectant mother is feeling. Nothing is too trivial for Nurse Betty to inquire after: what are Mary Frances's moods, how is her appetite, does she have morning sickness, does she sleep through the night or get up to use the bathroom, and how many times; is she maintaining a good diet, getting exercise every day, is the baby starting to "move"—"kick"? Sometimes Nurse Betty invites Mary Frances to have coffee with her downstairs, to continue their conversation which veers onto other subjects: their respective astrological signs (Nurse Betty, Gemini; Mary Frances, Capricorn), their favorite foods, TV shows, celebrities.

It is wonderful, Mary Frances tells N____, how Nurse Betty has become her closest woman friend at the University. How Nurse Betty is just so *nice*, and so *kind*. How Nurse Betty *cares* about Mary Frances as her own mother definitely wouldn't— "Mom would just scold and say how ashamed they were that I was having a baby, and nag why I wasn't married."

Nag why I wasn't married. This has become a woeful refrain.

(N____ has not (yet) given Mary Frances an engagement ring. He has declared that they are "secretly engaged"—but it must be kept a secret from all of the world.)

Usually, N____ only half-listens to Mary Frances's chatter. His brain is elsewhere. If a brain could be encased in a laptop, N____'s brain is there encased, in the labyrinthine pathways of a thousand interests as remote from the *expectant experimental subject* as Jupiter is remote, and as unfathomable to her as that planet would be.

In fact N___ has no need to listen to Mary Frances's chatter for he knows far more about her pregnancy than Mary Frances herself knows. At the weekly primate meetings he and the others are briefed on the expectant mother's medical condition, in detail, by their embryologist colleague; if "Dr. Ellis" has videotaped the pelvic exam, it will be shown in ghastly magnification; the results of the amniocentesis will be of particular interest, indicating indeed that the developing fetus is genetically consistent with a "hybrid" species; ultrasound images of the maturing fetus (not obviously not-Homo sapiens initially, but definitely male) are displayed, and discussed. Every word however banal and irrelevant to *Project Galahad* that passes between Mary Frances and the kindly physician, and Mary Frances and the friendly nurse, is replayed for the team, and these words N___ must endure in dread of an impulsive outburst by the expectant mother—*Oh but gosh! He doesn't love me! The father of my baby doesn't love me! Doesn't even touch me now I am pregnant! Goes all stiff and cold if I touch him!*

"You must introduce me, N___! She will never suspect a thing."

So many pictures and more recently videos and ultrasound scans of the *experimental subject* has the Professor seen, so familiar has the elder scientist become with every square inch of the pregnant female's epidermis, still more the shadowy fecund interior of her uterus bearing its precious cargo, as well as her uterine canal and vagina, at last he decides that he must meet her in the "flesh"—in the fifth month of pregnancy when Mary Frances's belly is already round and heavy as a drum and her face is flushed with a rude sort of female health and vigor.

"My dear, hello! N___ has told me, he has been tutoring you in my undergraduate course . . ." The Professor seems surprised, the *experimental subject* is an actual person, not nearly so unattractive as her pictures have suggested; her pink-lipstick smile is childlike, trusting; her small mud-brown eyes shine. She is wearing colorful clothes, red shorts that reveal inches of her pudgy thighs, a sleeveless candy-striped blouse that exposes her fatty upper arms and billows over her belly. Her body, big-breasted, big-hipped, misshapen now with pregnancy, exudes its own attraction, like that of a large animal in the prime of its life.

Reluctantly N___ has brought Mary Frances to meet the Professor, seemingly by chance, in the first-floor lounge in Life Sciences. As if the distinguished Professor would be lingering here just waiting for them. It does not seem to occur to the *experimental subject* that it is odd, the Professor does not seem to think it is odd that his chief technician, an adult research scientist, seems to be romantically linked with a twenty-year-old female undergraduate in General Studies, low-browed and barely articulate.

"Oh yes, Nath'iel *did* . . . 'tutor' me. Saved my life, literally . . ."

"Did he! 'Literally.' That was kind of him."

Mary Frances murmurs, blushing, not very coherently that she "really loved" the Professor's lectures but had trouble remembering them afterward—"Even when Nath'iel explained what you were saying, and had me memorize, it was just so, so hard . . . Like 'Ontology repeats philology'—something like that . . ."

There is a pause. N___'s face flames, he cannot look at the Professor.

Of course, in his lecture, the Professor had spent some time ironically debunking the famous nineteenth-century formula *Ontogeny recapitulates phylogeny*—the (now discredited) theory that as the human fetus develops in the womb it recapitulates, in miniature, the stages of animal evolution itself, culminating in Homo sapiens. N___ had to instruct his easily confused student in the original meaning of the catchphrase, in order to discredit it; but this turned out to be too complicated for Mary Frances who soon reversed the point of the Professor's lecture, and seems to have scrambled the formula itself.

The Professor laughs, delighted. "Ontology repeats philology'—that is a novel idea, my dear. Thank you!"

N___ dreads the Professor telling this anecdote to his colleagues in the primate lab. Teasing a subordinate, sometimes mercilessly, to rouse the others to laughter, is one of the Professor's less admirable traits; yet few fail to laugh when he does.

(Except N___ refuses to laugh when the Professor is being witty at the expense of another. His impassive face, downturned eyes, stiff posture give no hint that he is even aware of his mentor's playful cruelty.)

N___ has not been tutoring Mary Frances recently. One semester of Intro to Biology was more than enough for the struggling first-year student who'd managed to pass the course, through N___'s valiant effort, with a C–.

(Did N___ cheat on behalf of the *experimental subject,* preparing her lab reports for her? Providing her with exam questions before the final?) At N___'s suggestion Mary Frances has concentrated on General Studies courses in elementary school education, public health, "communication arts," in which she has managed to earn B's and C's without making herself anxious and exhausted. Her hope of nursing school has been deferred.

And now the spring semester has ended also, and most undergraduates have departed the campus. Except Mary Frances of course, who will remain over the summer months, ever more pregnant with the hybrid *Humanzee,* living now in the apartment on Edgar Street and seeing "Dr. Ellis" and "Nurse Betty" each Monday morning without fail. (N___ has moved out of the Edgar Street apartment, or rather has pretended to move out, since he'd never lived there, explaining to Mary Frances his need for greater privacy and quiet in which to do his work. It is Mary Frances's assumption, if she thinks of it at all, that N___ pays the rent on the apartment.)

Eyeing her closely, greedily, the Professor shakes the warm fleshy hand of the *experimental subject,* and inveigles her into an awkward sort of banter—an older, white-bearded gentleman asking questions of a stout flush-faced girl clearly in awe of him; squinting at him, smiling nervously, leaning back so that her weight is on her heels, one hand absently resting on the swell of her belly. *Oh!*—she is provoked to laugh, the gentlemanly Professor is so witty.

In sulky silence N___ listens to the exchange, standing a little apart from the two, as if he were not the Professor's chief and most trusted technician, and the girl's most intimate acquaintance, indeed, in the girl's fevered imagination, the father of her baby-to-be.

N___ is relieved that the Professor has let drop *Ontology repeats philology*. And notices that in his enigmatic way the older man seems rather in awe of Mary Frances. (Is he reconsidering his chilling strategy of deleting her from *Project Galahad* by allowing her to die, or rather arranging for her to die after giving birth?) N___ feels a stab of something like sexual jealousy as the Professor's playful remarks provoke the pregnant girl to blushing, and to giggling foolishly.

In reply to his queries Mary Frances tells the Professor that she is staying on campus that summer and not returning home— "I love it here! I have my own apartment here. The wonderful maternity clinic, I could not get anywhere else." Glancing at N___ as if waiting for him to concur. Waiting for N___ to declare proudly to the white-haired gentleman—*We are having this baby together, Professor.*

N___ says nothing of the sort. Stiffly N___ stands several feet away from Mary Frances and the smirking Professor as if disdainful of listening to their conversation.

Though wincing when the Professor asks, "Have you selected a name for your baby-boy-to-be, my dear?"

"Oh! How did you know it would be a *baby boy*?"—Mary Frances asks, wide-eyed.

"Why, I—I did not *know*—it was a guess." Adroitly the Professor smooths over his blunder saying he has a sort of "second sight" about such matters, an intuition based upon how far back on her heels an expectant mother balances herself. "Male fetuses tend to be heavier, on the whole, than female. The mother's posture corrects for this."

"His name is maybe going to be—well, we don't know. Yet." Mary Frances's face turns rosy; she'd come close to revealing her favored name, "Nath'iel, Jr."

Soon then the Professor goads Mary Frances into stammering that yes, she and N___ are engaged, kind of—"Nath'iel doesn't want people to know but well—we *are*."

Clapping her hand over her mouth in the realization that she has revealed a secret! Mary Frances is chagrined.

N___ smiles grimly. He is certainly not going to chide Mary Frances in front of the Professor who has been glancing at him bemused.

Of course, the Professor knows that N___ and the *experimental subject* are "engaged." And the Professor knows that the "engagement" is supposed to be a secret. It is mischievous of him, like a naughty grandfather, to have pried the secret out of credulous Mary Frances.

"Well, then. Congratulations are due to you both! But I will keep your secret, of course." Pausing then, before saying, with an amused glance at N__, "And why does your fiancé want to keep the engagement secret, Mary Frances? I am just curious."

"Because"—Mary Frances casts a dismayed look at N___, "Nath'iel might be deported by the US government if he 'enters into a contract' . . ."

"Yes. I see. That is so—'Nathaniel' is not an American citizen quite yet."

Is there a veiled threat here? But why? The Professor has always favored N___ and has assured him that, under his protection, N___ will be granted citizenship soon.

Unexpectedly, as if he were addressing a child, the Professor asks Mary Frances if she likes animals?—of course, Mary Frances says yes. The Professor asks if Mary Frances would like to visit the animal lab on the eighth floor of Life Sciences?—of course, Mary Frances says *yes*.

N___ hears a humming in his ears. N___ feels faint. A strong desire to strike the smirking Professor on his right temple where a pale-blue vein throbs like a writhing worm. Strike, smite. Cast the white-haired Professor down dead.

The humming in N___'s ears is just air-conditioning. By now N___ should be accustomed to the climate control of Rockefeller Life Sciences Hall where currents of cool air buffet heads like malicious spirits. Outside, a premature heat wave has come in early June.

N___ says there isn't time for them to visit the eighth floor even as the Professor slides his arm through Mary Frances's arm with startling familiarity and leads her to an elevator. With his ID card the Professor accesses the (restricted) floor where experimental animals are kept in air-conditioned isolation.

On the eighth floor the Professor leads Mary Frances through another security door into the animal quarters where the air is both cold and stale-smelling. Though the Professor has not exactly invited N___ to accompany them N___ has clearance to enter the animal quarters at any time he wishes, and it would be awkward for the Professor to exclude him.

So many animals! Rats, mice in small wire cages. Chattering monkeys, marmosets in larger cages. Mary Frances is amazed, wide-eyed. The circulating air is so chilly, Mary Frances hugs herself, shivering. Oh but the *smell.*

Against a farther wall, in large cages, are several chimpanzees. Like prisoners in solitary confinement sighting their jailers, and suddenly aroused to attention. Is it mealtime? Too soon for mealtime? Most excited and garrulous is the handsome young specimen Galahad, screeching and flinging his arms about eagerly to draw the attention of the stocky rust-haired girl in red shorts and billowing striped blouse whom he has never seen before.

Galahad recognizes the men, coolly ignores the men. Though in Galahad's crafty shiny eyes the thought that, if the Professor comes near enough to his cage, Galahad will seize the Professor's wrist and sink his teeth in it to the bone.

N___ isn't sure how Galahad regards him. Seemingly, Galahad "likes" him, for N___ often gives Galahad treats. Yet, N___ knows better than to trust the crafty wild animal whose semen he'd been milking for weeks.

"Ohhh is this a *chimpanzee*?"—Mary Frances is thrilled. She pronounces the word carefully. "Gosh! He's *big*. What's your name, Mr. Chimpanzee?"

The Professor tells her: "His name is 'Galahad.' "

"Oh hi there—'Galahad.' That's a nice kind of high-class name somebody gave you . . . Wow, you *are big*, and you are *handsome*." Brightly Mary Frances smiles at the chimpanzee, to N___'s relief not seeming to recall having heard the name "Galahad" recently. "You kind of *smell*, though. I guess you can't help it."

Galahad extends his forearm through the bars, hairless palm up and fingers extended in an urgent appeal. Though pared short his nails are sharp-looking. So curious, Mary Frances must be thinking, the chimpanzee's palm is as hairless as the palm of a human being, and as pale as her own. The chimpanzee's face is hairless, and his shiny-black eyes resemble her own. The chimpanzee's coarse hair covering most of his body is dark russet-red-brown, the approximate hue of her own hair.

Playfully Mary Frances waves her hand, sticks out her tongue, and Galahad immediately mimics her by waving both hands, sticking his tongue far out, to her delight—"Monkey see, monkey do. That's just what it is!"

Mary Frances asks the Professor what the animals are doing in the lab, and the Professor says they all do their work, humans and animals alike—"Furthering the cause of science. Shining a beacon into the deep, bleak cave of ignorance."

"Do you, like, do 'experiments' with them? Like make them run through mazes, to get bananas?"

The Professor laughs. "Bananas are the favored reward, yes."

With a genial smile the Professor turns to N___. "D'you have your cell phone, N___? Please take a picture of your friend Mary Frances with Galahad."

N___ is offended by this command and pretends to pat his pockets, searching for his phone. Tells the Professor that he doesn't have his (damned) phone. With the same genial smile the Professor instructs N___ to look more thoroughly, of course he has his phone, a chief technician is never without his phone, and so N___ discovers the cell phone in a deep pocket of his khaki shorts.

Pictures of the smiling *experimental subject* standing in front of the caged Galahad who smiles in his own devious-chimp way, baring saliva-wet teeth.

N___ is furious with the Professor for so manipulating Mary Frances and him. N___ has no choice but to obey the Professor. He will mail to the Professor several colorful and unnervingly sexual pictures of Mary Frances posing in front of the chimpanzee's cage which (N___ supposes) will long outlive them all—human mother of the first hybrid *Humanzee,* chimpanzee father of the first hybrid *Humanzee.*

Even if the hybrid doesn't survive, even if the pregnancy ends in a miscarriage, prints of these images will survive as priceless collector's items. As an amateur historian of his field N___ has to wonder what names, what findings, will accrue to them. The Professor's name, surely. But his own? Very likely not.

Galahad has begun leaping about inside his cage, so far as Galahad can leap about inside his cage, frantic to keep the wavering interest of his human visitors. Putting all dignity aside the handsome chimp emits a heart-piercing cry, repeatedly bumping his flat forehead against the bars of his cage with a lovelorn expression. "Oh—you are *something!*" Mary Frances cries. There is something like a fever between them, an electric spark of mutual recognition, N___ can't help but notice.

Naively Mary Frances approaches the chimpanzee's cage to pet his head through the bars as N___ deftly intervenes: "No. Stay back. He might bite."

Indeed, Galahad clicks his sharp glistening teeth, angry at being thwarted. Mary Frances backs away cringing. Galahad has begun to shriek, baring his teeth in a savage expression, furious with the *experimental subject* as if she has personally wronged him. He spits, reaches his forearms through the bars, claws at her, rubs his (suddenly swollen, bright pink) penis against the bars. Quickly N___ ushers stunned Mary Frances away as the Professor chides the chimpanzee: "You are a naughty boy, Galahad. Such bad manners, you never learned from *us.*"

In another cage a smaller, more somber chimpanzee with a thinner pelt crouches in a posture of dread. N___ sees that poor Maude's scalp has been shaved recently, that electrodes have been inserted in her brain in a battery of neurological tests. She shrinks from both the Professor and N___. She is less lively than usual though gazing fascinated at Mary Frances with mournful brown eyes. Mary Frances says cheerfully: "Oh, *hi.* I bet you're a female, are you? Looks like you had babies—lots of babies." N___ sees that it isn't just the chimpanzee's scalp that has been shaved but her bruised upper arms where IV lines have been inserted.

Mary Frances asks what the chimpanzee's name is and the Professor says her name is Maude.

"That's a nice name—'Maude.' Did you have baby monkeys, Maude? What'd they do with your babies?" But Mary Frances becomes contrite, the female chimpanzee is looking so sad. "Gosh! D'you think I could feed her and the other ones? Like, bananas? Would that make them happy?"

Unfortunately no, Mary Frances is told that the animals are fed only on schedule, and given treats only during trials. Otherwise they would be clamoring for food continually and would be unmanageable.

Before the tour ends the Professor has one more request of N___: would he please take pictures on his cell phone of Mary Frances and him together, in front of the chimp cages. But N___ dares to say no, can't, his cell phone has lost its charge.

The Professor gazes at N___ for a long moment, bemused. Or is the Professor alarmed. Saying then, in a tone that will not be contradicted, that N___ can use his cell phone, in that case.

N___ has no choice but to concur. His usual stoic-Asian demeanor has become jaundiced, sullen. Taking several pictures of the smiling white-haired Professor and the smiling *experimental subject* in front of the captive chimpanzee's cage and noting only belatedly, scrolling through the images hours later, that the Professor's right hand is cupped casually, yet unmistakably, at Mary Frances's waist; and that the two are standing closer together in the image than N___ would have sworn they'd been in life.

Maybe he will have mercy on her, then. Won't arrange for her to die of an "embolism."

5.

"Oh! Feel Nath'iel, Jr. *kick*."

Reluctantly N___ allows Mary Frances to seize his chill hand in his, to press against her alarmingly swollen belly where in fact N___ does feel, with a tremor, a distinctive *kick*.

"That's for-sure a boy baby! You can tell."

On a baby calendar Mary Frances is marking off days in a bright-red crayon. It is midsummer, and then it is late summer, and soon it will be September and the fall term at the University where Mary Frances has decided not to enroll until (maybe) the spring term since Nath'iel, Jr. is due near the end of September.

Or maybe she won't enroll then. Maybe (Mary Frances is thinking) she will be a full-time mother for as long as she can be. As long as God advises. (N___ has not tried to dissuade her.) She has made no mention of nursing school for months.

Dr. Ellis's estimate of two hundred sixty days is weeks away. Yet N___ is uneasily aware of the fact that the gestation period for *Pan troglodytes verus* is only two hundred thirty-seven days, and so the hybrid baby could come "early" while at the same time, since the gestation period for Homo sapiens is two hundred eighty days, the hybrid baby could come "late."

Mary Frances has struck up conversations with other expectant mothers casually encountered in town. In their exchanges it doesn't seem to have come up that Mary Frances's due date is earlier than the average, nor has Mary Frances betrayed the trust of Dr. Ellis and confided in these other expectant mothers that she has a "special" maternity care under the auspices of Rockefeller Life Sciences.

There has been one upsetting incident: after months of estrangement Mary Frances receives a call from her home, and a series of text messages from an older sister named Rhonda, informing her that their mother has been ill with an "undiagnosed condition"—"some kind of bad arthritis," and "depression, maybe." The messages are reproachful, chiding. Mary Frances is panicked that she will be expected to return home, and she cannot possibly return home, not in the (pregnant) state she is in, and not if she has to leave N____ behind . . .

N____ is relieved to see how devoted Mary Frances is to him, and how adamantly she insists that she certainly will not return home—"Not for a long time, maybe never. They would never accept Baby, and they would never accept *you*."

N____'s pride is bruised just slightly, that Mary Frances has to insist upon her allegiance to him over her racist family.

In midsummer heat in the Edgar Street apartment with its barely functioning window air conditioners the very pregnant *experimental subject* lies contentedly on a sofa for hours watching TV, or half-watching TV, surrounded by baby books, women's health books, baby clothes ordered online, bibs, diapers, rattles, small stuffed animals; nibbling handfuls of raisins and Cheese Bits, Rice Krispies, stale pizza slices, broken doughnuts, syrupy-sweet fruit yogurts in four-ounce containers—"As long as it isn't ice cream, Nurse Betty says it's OK." Her favorite *weird foods* are swaths of peanut butter on Count Chocula cereal and sushi swathed with mustard.

Despite Dr. Ellis and Nurse Betty who have cautioned her not to gain more than twenty pounds, by the first of August the *primigravida* has gained thirty-four pounds and has become so large, at times she can barely heave herself to her feet, and must clutch at furniture, or N___, to keep her balance.

How large is the hybrid fetus?—eight pounds, five ounces.

Eight pounds, eleven ounces.

Nine pounds . . .

During the soporific summer months when even some of the research faculty are away from their laboratories, and the Professor himself retires to Lake Tahoe with his family, N___ tries to maintain the Professor's directive to keep the *experimental subject* on edge; to thwart her expectations of his behavior and resist any sort of domestic routine. *The female's disadvantage is our advantage.* But it has several times happened, away from Mary Frances, in the chill of the lab in Life Sciences, or in his own apartment some blocks from Edgar Street, N___ begins to feel—is it *alone? Lonely?* It is not an existential condition

N___ has felt often in his previous life, and he is surprised and resentful to be feeling it now.

Calling Mary Frances on her cell phone and vexed when she doesn't answer at once. Doesn't return his calls within minutes. Hours?

Though he'd set aside an evening to be alone with crucial reading in his field, catching up on scientific papers, N___ becomes restless, decides to join Mary Frances for supper after all. Stops by the Chinese restaurant for her favorite takeout—greasy/oily sauces with lumpy chicken nuggets on mounds of sticky white rice or noodles. To counter these large portions Mary Frances will restrict herself to two six-ounce containers of fruit yogurt, and not ice cream.

So happy to see N___ in the doorway her eyes fill with tears. Declaring to him that she and Baby were missing him badly. "Like, we just prayed to God, 'Please let Nath'iel come over,' and thirty minutes later—here you are."

Despite the faulty air-conditioning at the Edgar Street apartment Mary Frances seems to be enjoying the third trimester of her pregnancy. Not only are her thick ankles swollen, her entire legs are swollen; the lard-colored skin of her belly is stretched tight; her breasts have become half again as large as they were. Her face appears swollen, even the eyelids; her eyes have become slits, out of which her adoring eyes shine. The pregnancy is a great cocoon inside which something is growing, thriving, eager to burst free. Even the expectant mother's "tummy troubles"—(N___ guesses this means constipation, doesn't inquire further)—don't upset her greatly, for Dr. Ellis has prescribed a battery of drugs for her to take if natural remedies fail.

N____ glances away not wanting to see Mary Frances unclothed—her pregnancy is so *enormous*. But sometimes plaintively she asks him to help her rise from bed, or from a chair; to help her step out of the bathtub, where she takes long steamy-hot soaking baths, exulting in the contentment of late pregnancy; whispering and singing lullabies to the feisty Nath'iel, Jr. in her womb. N____ stands outside the door, his cheek against the door, listening. Feeling just slightly excluded.

Until Mary Frances senses him on the other side of the door and calls out, "Nath'iel? C'mon in! Nath'iel, Jr. and me are lonely missing you!"

Not likely that N____ will enter the smelly steamy bathroom, stare appalled at the enormous belly floating in soap-scummy water like a great fish belly-up, and at the floating balloon-breasts with their rude bold ruddy nipples like copper coins, and the cheery flushed face oozing oil from every pore, not damned likely N____ tells himself and yet—sees his hand push the door open, and draws a deep breath stepping inside.

Casually he mentions to the *experimental subject* that a "certain percent" of babies are born with birth defects. These are usually, but not necessarily, the result of genetic abnormalities. Often, the result of premature birth.

Mary Frances is immediately stricken. Pressing her hand against her belly as if with sudden pain.

"Gosh! I know. 'Preemies'—so little, their hearts are not strong. Or something is wrong with their little lungs, or they are deaf." Mary Frances pauses, her voice quavering. "But that won't happen to Nath'iel, Jr., he's going to be a big strong baby, Dr. Ellis says. *He* won't be premature."

As if this were an utterly ordinary conversation N___ asks Mary Frances how she would feel if their baby had something wrong with him? If he was disfigured somehow, or—disabled?

"How would I *feel*? Oh, sad—real sad. Like if it was a Mongoloid baby, and looked funny—poor things."

"I think you mean 'Down's' babies. Not 'Mongoloid.'" N___ speaks stiffly, the outdated Western racism offensive to his Asian ears.

"'Down's'—is that the same thing? But they are so *sweet*, like angels. An aunt of mine had one of—them. Our mother would tell us, she wished we were more like Timmy, she could love us more. I never blamed her—Timmy was so sweet, never acted up like other boys, liked to be hugged and kissed and have you feed him, even when he got to be kind of big—ten, eleven. He couldn't go to school, I guess." Mary Frances pauses, considering. "Well, I would love one of them, if my baby turned out that way. I would be sad but I would be grateful too, that my baby was special, and that Jesus had a plan for him."

"You would think—'Jesus had a plan for him.'"

"Well, God does. I guess it would be God, who creates things. Jesus helps you with your attitude, but God is the creator. I think that's it."

N___ lets this pass. A flush comes over him, of pure annoyance, embarrassment, hearing Mary Frances speak matter-of-factly of her religion, a rural-based branch of Protestant Christianity. In the past she has said such preposterous things, and N___ has not challenged her.

"If a baby was disfigured somehow, or didn't look 'normal'— you would love him just the same, Mary Frances?"

"Oh I think I would love him *more*." Mary Frances speaks passionately, both hands now resting on her belly.

"Really? Why?" N___ regards the *experimental subject* with something like wonder.

"Because he would be ours—*yours*, and *mine*. Because he would have no one else but us to love him. That's why!"

Mary Frances seems both agitated by N___'s close questioning and thrilled and excited by it as if such an interrogation, uncharacteristic of N___, were a kind of intimacy; and N___ is not very intimate with Mary Frances, usually; affection between them is one-sided.

"Oh gosh yes, I would love him *to death*. I mean—I would!"

Has to admire her, such conviction. Optimism. Perhaps it is only naivete and ignorance but there is something noble in it, N___ thinks. Every other girl he'd known would have been frantic to have an abortion, to rid herself of even the possibility of such a burden, but here is Mary Frances claiming tearfully that she would love the *hybrid specimen* no matter what it looks like, and no matter what, in scientific terms, it might be called.

Mongoloid! A *Humanzee* might be mistaken for a "Mongoloid" baby, N___ thinks, depending upon the degree to which chimpanzee features were dominant, and depending upon the degree of wishful naivete in the mother.

"In approximately seven weeks it should be born. If it is going to be 'born' at all."

Hearing these clinical words uttered by the embryologist N___ thinks reprovingly—*Not it. He.*

Shadowy ultrasound images of the maturing fetus are being passed about the oak table, marveled-at. No one has seen such images in the history of science!—the astonishing fact ripples about them like a crashing surf.

Coiled in the mother's womb in the birth sac is a small creature with a large head and flat puckered face, tight-shut eyes, tiny clenched fists, that could be mistaken for a purely human fetus, or, from another angle, a chimpanzee baby with somewhat human features. It is normal for a chimpanzee mother to have a single baby, as it is normal for a human mother to have a single baby. The shadowy fetus has a slightly rounder head than one might expect in a human baby, and the face seems flatter and broader; the miniature nose flatter, with wider nostrils. The mouth is wider, the area of the chin more pronounced. The arms are just slightly longer. The miniature ears are slightly larger, and rounder. Except for the small puckered face, the tiny palms of the hands and the soles of the feet the epidermis appears to be covered in a very fine down that is thicker and darker on the scalp than elsewhere. The fetal heartbeat is "strong." The expectant mother has reported that the fetus kicks intermittently through the day and night but whether the activity is more or less than that of the average (male) fetus at this point in the pregnancy, the embryologist can't say.

The embryologist reports that the hybrid fetus weighs nine pounds, six ounces. It will continue to grow and will likely weigh more than ten pounds by the time it is born—"A large baby, that may present 'complications' for the mother."

With much excitement N___'s colleagues peer at the pictures. These unique documents! When N___ holds one in his fingers, his fingers shake. His mouth has gone dry, his brain feels numb, obliterated. *His!*—the hybrid baby is *his.*

With the passage of weeks at these (classified, confidential) meetings on the eighth floor of Rockefeller Life Sciences it has come to seem, strangely, inexplicably, that N___'s colleagues are starting not to associate the chief technician with the pregnancy; without N___'s noticing, his role is being usurped by the Professor, and by the embryologist, who do most of the talking and answer most of the questions at the meetings. It's as the *experimental subject* who was N___'s discovery has been appropriated by them. As if the *experimental subject* has been impregnated by their agency, and not his. N___ wants to drum his fingers on the oak table—*Wait! Look at me. I am the father.*

It makes N___ uneasy to hear the Professor reiterate another time that the primary, indeed the sole purpose of *Project Galahad* is to create a *hybrid specimen*; once the creature draws breath and utters its first cry, the mother's role will have ended—"Maude will do as well as any human mother and if not, we will find other means."

The embryologist concurs: "The *primigravida* has put on more weight than I'd advised, thus risking her health. If something happens to her in the delivery it might be argued that it's her own fault."

"Certainly, yes. She has received the very best prenatal care."

"It would hardly be our fault, if . . ."

Hemorrhage. Embolism. Heart failure. Rapid drop in blood pressure. Allergic reaction to the anesthetic.

Any of these. All of these.

It is rare now for anyone at the table to object, even mildly. Without N____ seeming to realize, the possibility of the *experimental subject's* being given the opportunity to nurse the hybrid specimen seems to have been dropped.

"She isn't very bright, poor thing. That has been her disadvantage, and it is our advantage. We would be very foolish not to seize that advantage." The Professor smiles wryly even as he continues to stare at his trophy, the shadowy ultrasound image.

N____ takes notes on his laptop. N____ is a pair of hands, remarkably adept fingers. Though he feels as if he has been shot full of Novocain.

N____ has sensed the senior members of the Professor's team exchanging glances at times. Not only are they forgetting what N____'s role has been in *Project Galahad*, N____ is certain he has heard them alluding to lab meetings of which he hasn't been aware. Are they meeting without him? Is the Professor grooming a replacement, among the technician's own young assistants? Is the Professor who has always seemed to favor N___ going to cut N___ out of this historic project, exploit his heroic work, betray him?

(Of course it is hardly the first time that a distinguished research scientist has exploited a younger associate, passed his work off as his own, terminated the younger scientist and banished him from the laboratory. And N___ is more vulnerable than most for he is not (yet) a US citizen.)

"If there's a miscarriage?"—N___ hears himself ask.

"Well. If a miscarriage, we get to keep the remains."

"*She* will never see the remains. We'll send her home."

What N___ has dreaded has come to pass, at last.

It is a poor recording, on Nurse Betty's iPhone. In the background are voices, a clatter of spoons, cups. All around the oak table N___'s colleagues listen bemusedly while the Professor's chief technician sits very still and his face stiff as a papier-mâché mask.

A plaintive female voice, that of the *experimental subject*:

Ohh I guess—I don't know—sometimes I just—wonder—(unintelligible)—Nath'iel doesn't, like, *love me?*—

I mean—it's embarrassing, gosh!—he's, like, if he has to like touch me, with my belly so big, he doesn't seem to—it's like he is—wishing he was somewhere else . . .

A more forceful, mature voice, that of Nurse Betty:

Oh no—he loves you, Mary Frances! I know he does. It's just that a man has more trouble than we do connecting with his emotions. That's all it is, hon—he's, like, when I saw you with him, Mary Frances, I could see—he's shy, he's awkward with women, one of those scientist-types like there are in this building, and Asian too, who are like geniuses almost, but you can't talk to them and they can't talk to you . . . (Laughter)

Aggrieved-child voice of Mary Frances:

. . . all I know is, I love him like crazy, but I can see, like, he doesn't love *me*—much. All the time I am praying for our baby to be born healthy, I am praying for Nath'iel to love him and me—I mean, as much as he can. Like maybe, being Asian like he is, and coming from someplace where (I guess) there was war and famine, maybe he can't "love" people the way we can—like, if he was wounded in his soul? Sometimes in his eyes I can see (unintelligible) . . . And so I am praying for that too, that I can help him. And I am feeling the love from Jesus, and I think it will happen, and will be strong enough, we will be a family and he will come to love *me*.

At the conclusion of the recording there is an embarrassed silence. N___ cannot lift his eyes to the faces of his colleagues. His face is a mask of humiliation. Scarcely can he breathe. A wispy female voice hovers in the room distracting as a moth fluttering about—*will come to love me.*

Shuffling papers the Professor says in a voice of disdain, "Well. No scientific content there. Recommend *delete.*"

6.

. . .will come to love me.

In his cubbyhole of an office on the eighth floor of Rockefeller Life Sciences not far from the Professor's large office N___ sits at his desk computer, fingers poised.

So large is the computer, it blocks N___'s view of an obscure corner of the University campus. Rarely in his many years at this desk and facing this window (a narrow column of green-tinted glass from floor to ceiling, soundproof) amid a constant churning of cooled air against his face and hair has N___ troubled to lean around the computer to gaze out the window.

Nor does N___ now. Sitting numbed, vacantly staring at the computer screen. What does it hold? Is the screen a way into the future, a way into N___'s own, elusive soul? Or is the screen but a thin plastic scrim over nothingness?—N___'s soul?

Fingers poised at the keyboard. Waiting.

While in the apartment on Edgar Street the *experimental subject* is waiting.

Is she lying hugely pregnant, part-naked slovenly-sumptuous as an odalisque on the familiar sofa sagging beneath her weight, eating cereal in handfuls, chewing on broken cinnamon doughnuts, her favorites; is she frowning over a pamphlet given to her by Nurse Betty, *My Baby & Me: Our First Month*, like a methodical schoolgirl underlining crucial phrases in yellow Magic Marker? N___ squints but N___ cannot see: is the frizzed rust-colored hair brushed back from the low, earnest brow? Are the bare swollen legs spread, that have not been shaved in weeks, and sprout distinctive dark hairs? Inside the belly swollen tight as a drum the baby-to-be gives a *kick.* "Hey!—That hurt!"—Mary Frances laughs in delight. *So happy, God has blessed her.*

Or is she, as N___ has more than once discovered her, busily engaged in cleaning the kitchen? *Wiping down* she calls it, paper towels and Windex.

And the linoleum floor, with a sponge mop. Other rooms, *tidying up.* Who would have guessed, the *experimental subject* enjoys housekeeping, even hugely pregnant? To N___'s astonishment one day seeing that Mary Frances had started alphabetizing haphazardly arranged books in several bookcases as if these were actual books in an actual library carefully selected by "Nathaniel Li."

Yet more unexpectedly N___ one day discovered that Mary Frances was reading, or trying to read, Darwin's *The Expression of the Emotions in Man and Animals;* another day, a neuroscience textbook titled *Brain, Body, and Behavior* which she'd shut quickly with an embarrassed laugh when N___ came in. "Oh gosh! Hope nobody's gonna quiz me."

As a graduate student N___ had annotated virtually every page in this classic textbook. Out of curiosity when Mary

Frances was out of the room N____ leafed through the first chapter to see that Mary Frances had been annotating as well, in yellow Magic Marker; she'd gotten only to page nineteen before being interrupted. The last highlighting was *Microglia function like astrocytes, digesting parts of dead neurons. Oligodendroglia provide the insulation (myelin) to neurons in the central nervous system.*

How totally obscure this information must have been, to an undergraduate who'd barely passed Introduction to Biology! N____ was touched by the effort. Guiltily wondering if Mary Frances was making the effort in order to relate to *him.*

Not knowing that, very soon, as soon as the *hybrid specimen* is born, N____ will disappear from her life.

N____ wakes from his trance. Fingers briskly typing on the computer keyboard.

How will *Project Galahad* proceed?—N____ speculates.

1. Most likely: spontaneous miscarriage. The *hybrid specimen* is genetically unstable and not capable of living outside the mother's womb. In the last weeks of the third trimester a miscarriage will be physically traumatic for the *primigravida* but if she is strong, and receives good medical care, she will survive. What will be issued from her body will be *fetal remains*, not an "infant"—not a "baby." Yet, these remains will be precious to researchers, particularly immunohistochemists who will prepare photomicrographic slides of the specimen's brain and

other organs. The chief technician will help, and will be crucial to the research.

2. Another possibility: induced miscarriage. N___ has access to lab drugs including an abortifacient used to induce miscarriages in chimpanzees which he could dissolve into Mary Frances's food, inducing violent contractions and hemorrhaging; he would have to ensure that she wasn't taken to the local ER but to the Clinic in Life Sciences, where the fetal remains could be salvaged, with results identical to those of 1).

In this way (N___ reasons) less is left to chance, he would be in control and no one (including the Professor) would ever know why the *hybrid specimen* was a miscarriage. And the *experimental subject*'s life would (probably) be spared.

3. Possible: the *hybrid specimen* is born in the Clinic on the tenth floor of Life Sciences. Very likely it will be a caesarean birth. The *Humanzee* is immediately taken away from the mother who is heavily sedated. When the mother is wakened she is informed that her baby died at birth—it was a *stillbirth*. The *Humanzee* will be confined to a highly secure area of Life Sciences, or to an equally secure, restricted space elsewhere, to live out its (his) natural life as one of the most remarkable *experimental subjects* in the history of science. (Eventually, if he dares to publish his findings without being

charged with grievous scientific misconduct, and proof that a *Humanzee* was born in the Professor's laboratory can be established, it is very likely that the Professor will receive a Nobel Prize.)

A. Possible: the (physically traumatized) mother receives excellent medical treatment in the Clinic and is soon released. She receives financial compensation in exchange for "confidentiality." She departs the University without a degree. In sorrow but not in rancor.

B. Possible: the (physically traumatized) mother does not survive the ordeal of giving birth to a *hybrid specimen* weighing in excess of ten pounds. In the *Project Galahad* official (classified) report it will be noted *In the difficult labor, which lasted for __ hours, the mother died suddenly of what an autopsy revealed as an embolism in the heart. Died suddenly of what an autopsy revealed as an allergic reaction to the anesthetic. Died suddenly of what an autopsy revealed as cardiac failure. The infant* Humanzee *survived and was given to a mature female chimpanzee on the premises, to be nursed.*

Beyond this N____ can't imagine. Though if he continues as the Professor's chief technician he will be involved in the battery of experiments that will define the *Humanzee*'s life.

Especially, the Professor is eager to establish whether language can be taught to the *Humanzee* as it is routinely taught to Homo sapiens but has failed to be taught to apes despite countless experiments over decades.

In time, it will be established whether the *Humanzee* can mate with any female specimen, human or chimpanzee, or whether the *Humanzee*, like the donkey, hybrid offspring of horse and mule, is sterile.

How lonely the *Humanzee* will be, isolated in its (his) clinical quarters on the eighth floor of Rockefeller Life Sciences! Though possibly, sooner rather than later, another *Humanzee* specimen will be created by the Professor's lab team, a sibling that might (if it is female) be a mate for the *Humanzee* . . .

In his state of trance N___ sits at the computer, thinking. Or rather, thoughts move through his brain as through a convoluted and contorted maze.

. . . *we will be a family and he will come to love me.*

Hurriedly N___ clears out his office in Rockefeller Life Sciences Hall taking computer files on memory sticks, documents, papers, a selection of books that are essential to him.

Returns to the apartment on Edgar Street. Tells the astonished Mary Frances that they must leave at once: the State Department has learned of N___'s engagement with her and that she is bearing his son and so a warrant has been issued for N___'s arrest and without being allowed a legal hearing N___ will be deported to a "hellish" part of the world he has not seen in more than thirty years and their baby, when it is born, will be taken into detention by the US government under the Illegal Alien Act of 1971 . . .

Hurriedly they must pack. Must pack!

No time to waste, no time for explanations other than the bare stark terrifying fact that Mary Frances will lose not only her fiancé but her baby as well if she does not flee with N___ that very day. If she stays behind it is highly probable that she will be arrested and charged with "aiding and abetting" an individual arrested under the Illegal Alien Act and in any case, the baby will be taken from her and she will never see it again.

Wide-eyed Mary Frances never doubts these fantastical words of N___'s uttered in a voice of heightened calm. Mary Frances has not ever doubted N___, and will not doubt him. When she stammers asking where can they go N___ tells her that eventually they can cross into Canada—"There are relatives of mine in Vancouver, they will take us in and protect us"—but in the meantime they can hide in the Sierra Nevada Mountains where no one would ever think to look for them.

It is true, N___ has saved a good deal of money over the years. Few expenses, a frugal bachelor life. As if for such an occasion: a sudden disappearance, fleeing federal authorities, exile. Fleeing the Professor. Perhaps N___ has been on the run, an illegal alien, for most of his life.

As they pack suitcases and cardboard boxes N___ tells Mary Frances about the beautiful scarcely populated mountains west of Red Bluff. They can rent a cabin easily, he recalls a trailer village beside a lake, yes and the small town Red Bluff, no one would know where they'd gone, no one would have the slightest idea, cleverly he'd consulted several websites about hotels in Costa Rica and if/when his office computer is examined in an effort to track him these sites will be discovered and it will be believed he'd gone to Costa Rica . . . With tearful but trusting eyes Mary Frances listens to her fiancé, she has never seen N____ so fiercely animated, so certain of what must be done, the two of them together, a *couple*. N____ pauses to take her warm moist hand tenderly and squeeze it in the way that one might squeeze the hand of a frightened child to comfort her, a gesture he has never made before.

"Oh but, Nath'iel—what about the baby? How will he be born—safe?"

"We can do it. I can help you. Our ancestors knew how. We don't need the Clinic. 'Natural childbirth.' The hell with them."

"The hell with *them*! Good." Mary Frances laughs wildly, her eyes are shining with tears of wonder, devotion. "God will protect us."

"God *will* protect us. I know it."

Elated N____ runs to his apartment to load the van (armloads of books, it is his books N____ most values, which he will bring with him into exile) and to bring it around to Edgar Street. By this time N____ has convinced himself that they must leave at once, he must not be detained, they are both in grave danger, their baby is in grave danger, at any moment government gestapo will be knocking at their door, they are equal to the challenge of natural childbirth in the mountains, there will be no need for a medical doctor, a hospital or a clinic. For how can N___ explain to Mary Frances that if she gives birth successfully, her baby will be taken from her and her life will be snuffed out? How can N___ explain to Mary Frances that it is he, her fiancé "Nath'iel," who has herded her, like a heifer into a chute leading to the slaughterhouse, to this fate? Telling himself the crucial thing is the prevention of infection of the mother's birth canal. N___ will boil water, sterilize surfaces. N___ will wear latex gloves. (Must remember to purchase gloves and other items needed for the home birth, en route to Red Bluff.) Something in the refugee N___, primitive, defiant, gives a little lurch, this will be the challenge of his life.

Mary Frances is not likely to panic when contractions begin, as another woman might in such circumstances. Mary Frances is solidly built to give birth, wide-hipped, a wide pelvis, heavy breasts bursting with milk. Mary Frances will pray for courage, and her God will give her courage. Mary Frances will deliver her baby by instinct, grunting and heaving as her female ancestors delivered their babies, managing to survive against the odds.

And whatever is issued from between Mary Frances's great straining thighs streaked with blood and sweat, she will honor as a gift of God.

By four-twenty P.M. they are prepared to leave. Breathless, exhilarated! It is strange, N___ has not wanted Mary Frances in his van before, had not even told her that he owns a vehicle; he has not (he'd thought) wanted the female presence to linger in it, her scent, the impression of her body, the dampness of her perspiring thighs, yet now he has not the slightest concern but is deeply grateful that he owns a vehicle, that they can flee together. Indeed N___ adjusts the sun visor so that the afternoon sun won't glare into Mary Frances's eyes.

Boxes of books, hundreds of books gathered from both apartments, fill the van. In his fever of anticipation N___ imagines long idyllic evenings of reading aloud to Mary Frances from such texts as the great works of Charles Darwin beside a birch-wood fire, Nathaniel, Jr. in a cradle, or in a crib, in a shadowy alcove, features blurred in the innocence of sleep.

On the interstate they should get to the Sierras by sunset and in the morning to Red Bluff. That night they can rent a motel room or, maybe, sleep in the van in sleeping bags within earshot of the white-water rapids cascading down the mountainside.

Walking Wounded

1.

Late morning but there's a heaviness to it like dusk. Bruised sky like an eye swollen shut. Smell of sulfur in the warm wind from the lake shallow at this end, rotted with cattails, tall reeds and rushes and something floating just beneath the surface.

He has returned to our small town on Lake Cattaraugus. He has returned eviscerated.

He is forty-one years old. His youth has been lost to him.

Torn away like clothes cut off a stricken man by EMTs wielding shears in an emergency.

He has learned respect for the astonishing swiftness of (young, vigorous) emergency workers. As soon as you lose control of your body in a faint, in a public place, your body is theirs.

Why think of this?—he isn't. Hell no. *Not.*

* * *

At the southernmost edge of the lake he sees her.

A luminous figure in the mist that lifts from the lake on this mild, overcast June morning.

She is standing at a railing of the esplanade, very still.

He is very still, a little distance away.

Her back is to him yet he is certain that she is a stranger.

Her hair is loose, curly and tangled partway down her back. Her shoulders are narrow, she is delicate-boned, a young woman, a girl who is (he is sure) a stranger to him. She leans forward against the wrought-iron railing, gazing out at the lake in utter stillness.

Light glimmering on the rippled slate-colored water, which seems almost to encase the woman. Or is it moisture in his eyes as he stares, he is so deeply moved . . .

Is it—her?

Like a clapper inside a bell his heart clamors.

Am I terminal? he'd asked.

Should I have hope? Or—is that ridiculous? Selfish?

Early that morning he'd been awakened by a sharp cramp in the calf muscles of his left leg. Jolted from the comfort of sleep that is his only solace.

When this happens he is stricken with pain in his leg. Furious at being wakened so early.

He has learned to get quickly out of bed, stamp his bare foot on the floor to soothe the cramp. Whimpering to himself like a child; the pain is excruciating.

Lightning-swift pain in his leg that clamps tight. Toes in his foot rigid as claws.

"Jesus!"—rendered helpless, staggering about trying to overcome the cramp.

Within a minute or two the worst of the pain usually fades. Like a rueful afterthought the muscle ache will remain for hours.

Since his *evisceration* L___ has longed for sleep—it is his only refuge. Insomniac nights he'd resisted drugs, alcohol. He knows how easy that would be: stepping into the dark water that rises to his knees, his mutilated lower body, over his mouth, nose, eyes. No.

Sleep is L___'s happiest time even when it's riddled with turbulent and senseless dreams.

As a boy he'd been a runner. He'd been on the track team of the (local) high school. His leg muscles had cramped then, sometimes. But that was different. A different kind of pain. A shared pain—the other boys on the team had had cramps in their calves too.

Only vaguely he can recall, as you'd recall a dream told to you by another.

If amid the detritus in this house he encounters photographs of that boy—skinny, yearning face; dark, hopeful eyes—he turns quickly away.

"That was my life then. When I had a life." But there is no woman. But he is lucky.

No one sharing his bed to be a witness to the way such stabbing pain unmans him, renders him helpless as a child.

What's a man without pride? Unmanned.

Fact is, he could not bear another knowing of his condition. He'd told no one. He'd avoided the telling.

Bluntly he'd said to her, *No. I don't love you. It was a misunderstanding.*

Doesn't recall the look on her face; he'd turned away.

And now he has returned to the house of his childhood at Lake Cattaraugus, New York. Even if she knew she would not have dared follow.

Just go away. Leave me. And don't touch me!—your touch makes me sick.

He has confided in no one—of course. For there is no one. "Just tell me, Doctor: Am I 'terminal'?"

He'd been blunt, brave. It had seemed a kind of braveness— bravado. Or possibly he'd been rude.

In fact he had not asked about *hope*. He had not even thought of *hope* at that time.

Seething with anger, even as he was shivering in the chilled examination room. He could not bear the indignity, it was the indignity that maddened him, more than the other.

The doctor's answer was an unhesitating *No. You are not "terminal"—not inevitably.*

What the doctor meant was that with the proper medical treatment, of course, life is prolonged. Some sort of life is prolonged. After five years (he was told) there is a 65 percent survival rate for individuals in his age group afflicted with this particular cancer.

If the cancer has not metastasized to lymph nodes, other organs, bone. If surgery removes the malignancies. If treatment can be tolerated, which sometimes, even in seemingly healthy and "fit" individuals in his age group, it is not.

Nine months of chemotherapy following the radical surgery— the *evisceration*.

He does not recall the surgery clearly. Days, weeks immediately following. The relief of being alone, not having to speak of the *considerable physical trauma*, see its reflection in another's (concerned, pitying) (repelled?) face.

Grateful then that he hadn't been married. To *be wed* to another is to *be welded* to another and when you are mad to be alone, you do not wish to be either.

So, L___ is alone with his body. If he is *wed, welded* to anything it is to this body.

If he examines the ravaged body, still he does not clearly recall. The partially healed shiny-white scar tissue like the configurations of frost on a windowpane, the disfigurement of his lower belly and groin that suggests a playful distortion. A mist has settled over his brain. Very easy to forget, or to misremember. There is mercy in such drifting patches of amnesia.

By day he has become brisk, matter-of-fact. In his dealings with others he is hearty-seeming, quick to laugh, and quick to cease laughing, inclined to impatience if cashiers, service workers, waiters don't move fast enough for him.

On the phone he is assertive, his laughter is a kind of barking punctuation. Though he does not—ever—lift the receiver of a ringing phone unless he sees that it is a professional contact who is calling, an editor perhaps. Not *the personal* but *the impersonal* is his solace.

By day, when his clothes conceal the mutilation. Very quickly you learn to adjust to the new contours of the body, disguised by ordinary (loose-fitting) clothing. As a person afflicted by joint pain learns to walk with his weight distributed *just so*—no limp is detected. (Except by the unnaturally sharp-eyed or the suspicious. Whom L___ avoids.)

He is somewhat proud of such adjustments. By day. Deals with himself briskly and matter-of-factly as another might deal with him.

The body he has become.

Shields the colostomy pouch close against his (flat, flaccid) belly beneath his clothes. It is hidden there, it is protected. It has become the most intimate connection of his life like an umbilical cord and this attached to the tiny hole in his stomach, the stoma. An external (plastic) gut, a practical measure, in fact an ingenious solution to having no rectum and only a few meager inches of some five feet of large bowel remaining.

The pouch has to be changed at regular intervals depending upon the uses to which he puts it. (How much he ingests, digests.) If leaking, more often. Carefully remove the old pouch, empty contents into toilet, attach the new. Dispose of the old pouch in an opaque white plastic bag placed carefully inside the dark green trash container to be wheeled out to Road's End Lane under cover of darkness Thursday nights, for Friday morning pickup by Cattaraugus County sanitation.

His task. He is his own nurse's aide. He is indentured to himself. His fingers should have grown deft by now but remain clumsy, shaky, as if shy.

He would laugh, it *is* funny.

And what is most funny, how L___'s teenaged self would have recoiled in disbelief and loathing foreseeing such a fate. How once with a ninth-grade friend watching a TV documentary of wounded and disabled Vietnam veterans in wheelchairs L___ had said with the vehemence of youth if anything like that ever happened to him he would "blow out my brains with a shotgun."

You don't, though.

Abashed watchword of the walking wounded—*You don't.*

And so it has been a shock to L___ this morning. Having seen the young woman at the lake.

Having felt for her—something . . .

She is a stranger, he is certain. No one who has known L___ or L___'s family.

The luminous figure. So still!

Elsewhere in the park were teenagers, adults with young children, even a boy with a model airplane droning overhead like a maddened wasp. Their noises did not seem to penetrate the silence that enveloped the young woman; she stood apart from them as if invisible. Curly, tangled hair partway down her back—very fine, very pale, silvery pale, with a mineral sheen. And wearing what appeared to be a sweater or a wrap of some pale-gray cobwebby material. And her white (linen?) skirt long, nearly to her slender ankles, and her bare feet in open-toed sandals, white-skinned.

From a little—safe—distance he regarded her.

He was almost waiting to be disillusioned—to see that, yes, this was not a young woman but someone he knew, had gone to school with long ago. Worse yet, the daughter of an old Cattaraugus classmate.

But he did not know her, he was certain. *She is new to this place also.*

Feeling so strange! Light-headed, dry-mouthed . . .

That stab of excitement, recognition. It can leave you shaken, faint. An electric current running through the torso to the groin—the vagus nerve.

If the shock is severe, the vagus nerve shuts off blood to the brain; you fall at once in a faint.

Hello—he might (plausibly) have called to her.

Excuse me—he might (plausibly) have approached her. His heart beats strangely, just to think so!

A shock to him, at his age and in his condition, who has expected to see nothing at Lake Cattaraugus, and to feel nothing.

Hello. Don't think I have seen you here before . . .

I used to live in Cattaraugus. Now I've returned . . .

Ridiculous! Such words, faltering, stale, hopeless, and contemptible as deflated party balloons, or stray condoms in the mud at the lakeshore caught amid broken cattails.

Flung after him the cruel female taunt *Go away. You are not even a man. Why would I want to speak to* you?

Chloroform is the most pragmatic. Swift, clean, leaves no trace and he knows where to purchase it without being questioned.

Other methods are cruder, clumsier. Within the past several years he has perfected his method.

The primary element is surprise. And, of course, no witnesses.

He has grown deceitful. It is a rare pleasure.

Returning to the family home at Lake Cattaraugus and telling no one who knows him, not relatives in the area, not family friends, old friends from school, long-ago acquaintances.

Returning wounded, and wise in deception. Armed with a "project"—a manuscript of more than one thousand pages that requires his deepest concentration.

The great effort of L___'s life. L___'s remaining life.

In the cobblestone house on Road's End Lane amid a tangle of tall old oak trees he plans (he thinks) to be happy.

For happiness is not fixed but alterable. For some, happiness is the ability to draw a deep breath without recoiling in pain. Happiness is the little stoma that is not reddened and infected but functioning perfectly. In our small town, however, it is not possible to remain secluded for long. The more you wish to hide from us, the more we wish to seek you out.

Hello? Sorry can't talk right now.

Yes it's been years . . . Will call you back. Busy time can I call you back.

Yes just for the summer. Thanks but—Work. No. Don't think so. Work. Deadline. September first. Sorry! Somebody at the door.

Signaling in the very jauntiness of his voice and the vagueness of his words *God damn you let me alone will you! I have not returned to my childhood home at the bottom of a fetid lake to squander a moment of my remaining life with any of you.*

He is not hiding. He is not one to *hide.*

Eventually whoever is ringing the bell will go away.

In the wake of the mysterious visitor a scribbled note stuck beneath the door knocker, or a US postal form shoved into the crack of the door, or an advertising flyer, or—nothing.

Not a trace! No one.

He is safe from prying eyes. In fact, he is in an upstairs bathroom. In the midst of changing the plastic pouch attached to the stoma—the little surgical hole in his stomach that bleeds easily, thinly.

Very careful washing hands, sanitizing hands, shaky hands. Very careful positioning the plastic pouch that is soft, malleable as an intestine. And very careful disposing of waste in toilet and used pouch in secure opaque white plastic bag.

His forty-second birthday is rapidly approaching.

Swiftly and deftly the chloroform-soaked cloth is pressed over her mouth, nose. She fights him bravely, desperately. He will see her eyelids flutter. He will see the light go out in her eyes. But she will not have seen his face.

Within seconds her limbs grow limp.

Surprising heaviness of the limp, slender body as if death is an icy lava flowing into her bones.

Unwittingly, he has trapped several small birds in the garage. Shutting the slow-sliding overhead door, not realizing the birds are inside.

Cumbersome sliding door that moves—so—very—slowly— you hold your breath expecting it to stop midway.

Frantic birds! He hears their panicked cheeping, the flutter of their small wings. A scrambling sound like mice amid stacks of cardboard cartons piled to the ceiling.

Birds have built nests in the garage. In the rafters.

Quickly he presses the switch to reverse the slow-sliding overhead door but even when it is fully open the panicked birds continue to flutter their wings, throw themselves against unyielding objects, make their cheeping sounds. He can see them overhead, shadowy little shapes, blinded in terror.

"Go on! It's open! *Go.*"

Claps his hands. Impatient with the birds too frightened to locate the opened door, and so save themselves.

The garage has three sliding doors. In theory the garage will hold three vehicles.

In fact, the garage is crammed with things. Too many things. L___ can barely fit his station wagon inside and from now on he won't bother shutting the door.

The birds have fallen silent but L___ knows that they haven't escaped. He presses the switch to cause another of the slow-moving doors to rise, rumbling overhead.

Presses the switch to open the third door.

All three garage doors are open now. Still the interior of the garage feels airless, trapped.

He claps his hands again: "Now *go*."

The interior of the garage is crammed with the detritus of his parents' lives. He has not wanted to see. He has not wanted to feel this sensation of dread, vertigo.

His parents have been dead for seven years (father), and for three years (mother). There is a *deadness beyond dead* that is pure peace and it is this L___ wishes for them. He feels grateful that they've been spared knowing how their only son has been *eviscerated*.

They had loved him, he supposes. But love is not enough to keep us from harm.

Now their lives have been stored in the old garage, which had once been a carriage house. In the corners, stacked to the very rafters. Taped-up cardboard boxes, cartons and files of financial records, legal documents, IRS records. Household furnishings—a swivel chair, a floor lamp, an upended mattress. A tall oval mirror shrouded in a gauzy cloth. Neatly folded curtains and drapes, covered in dust. Stacks of books, magazines bound with twine. And there are myriad forgotten things of L___'s own—bicycles with flat tires, broken wagon, toys. Weights he'd lifted in high school. Tennis rackets. Old skis, snowshoes. Boots. Mud-stiffened running shoes. L___ feels a twinge of guilt, and a stronger twinge of resentment.

No he will not. *He will not sort through these things.*

It is too late. The detritus of the past means nothing to him now. He stumbles away, back into the empty house. Leaving the small fluttering birds to find their own way out.

Hello! Please come inside.

We won't stay long. I will just show you—the inside of my life.

The house is locally famous; in fact, it is "historic"—a "landmark" in Cattaraugus County. An architectural oddity composed of cobblestones and mortar, built in 1898 with a low, sloping shingled roof above windows like recessed and hooded eyes.

Though Mura House looks large from Road's End Lane behind a scrim of ravaged trees, the interior is divided into small rooms with small windows emitting a grudging demi-light. Upstate New York with its savage protracted winters, driving snow, subzero temperatures had not been hospitable to a wish for larger windows, scenic views. Low beamed ceilings, wood-paneled walls, hardwood floors. Heavy leather furniture, brass andirons.

And oddly named—"Mura House."

"Why does our house have a name? Nobody else's house has a stupid name."

Growing up in Mura House he'd been embarrassed, resentful. At the same time he'd felt a twinge of pride, that the L___ family house was locally recognized as something out of the ordinary, distinguished by a small oval marker at the stately front door.

He'd asked his parents about the name. He can remember only his mother's vague explanation—*We were told "Mura" might have been the builder's name. We've made inquiries at the historical society* . . .

Except for a glassed-in porch at the rear of the house, constructed in such a way that it is not visible from Road's End Lane, and except for renovations in kitchen and bathrooms, Mura House has not been substantially altered since 1898. If L___ wished to remodel the house he could not, restricted by New York State law protecting "historic" properties.

L___ has no interest in remodeling, rebuilding. He has said to several intrusive persons who've made inquiries about his plans in Cattaraugus, that he didn't plan to live in Mura House "much beyond the summer."

He has not been seeking her.

He has avoided the lakeside park. The esplanade along the lake. He has been avoiding even thinking of her and in this he has become slack, careless, negligent, like one who has let his guard down prematurely.

And so when he isn't prepared he sees her for the second time: entering the Cattaraugus Public Library.

A glimmering figure in white, at dusk. In the heat of summer of upstate New York there is a moist heaviness to the air that seems to gather like an electric charge with the waning of the light in the sky and it is at this time he sees her, not certain at first if it is *her* . . .

A tall, pale gliding figure. And her tangled silvery hair partway down her back.

Without a backward glance at L____ , who stands stunned and breathless on the flagstone walk outside the library, staring after her. Should he follow her into the library? *As if he were entering by chance?*

(But of course it is chance.)

(L____ has not been following her. L____ had not even been aware of her being nearby.)

Or (he is thinking) he should continue past the library as if he has no business in the library after all.

(No one will notice! He is sure that no one is watching.)

The Cattaraugus Public Library is a small library housed in the first floor of a gaunt, faded-redbrick colonial on Courthouse Square; it shares the house with the headquarters of the Cattaraugus County Historical Society at the rear. The historical society is darkened but the library is still open at seven P.M., though most of the staff has gone home and there are few patrons in the library.

This is the first time since his return to Cattaraugus that L____ has revisited the library and it is both gratifying to him and a little disturbing that the library has changed so minimally over the years. Obviously, the library budget for Cattaraugus County isn't generous. All of central upstate New York has been locked in a "recession" for years—decades. (When does a "recession" become a permanent state of being? Who is there to formally acknowledge such transformations?) Still, the Cattaraugus Public Library retains the power to excite L___ with the prospect of a new adventure—a book he has not read yet, an author of whom he hasn't heard. L___ experienced his first sense of *the forbidden* in the rear of the library, where, as a boy, he'd been looking through novels in the section marked *Adult Fiction* and a frowning librarian had surprised him skimming impenetrable pages of James Joyce's *Ulysses*—"Excuse me? What is your age?"

His age! He'd been twelve or thirteen at the time. The prim-faced middle-aged woman with staring eyes had known very well that the trembling boy she'd apprehended was hardly eighteen.

She'd taken the forbidden book from him, shut it, and replaced it on the shelf. Abashed, he'd fled.

L___ smiles, recalling. *That* was a long time ago, when anything in any library could possibly be "forbidden" to him.

Now, L___ is standing on the walk outside the library, uncertain. It is near dark. The gaunt old brick house is lighted from within and so he can see a few figures, a wall of bookshelves, a display of books—but he can't see *her*.

Out of restlessness he'd been walking in the early evening. Down the mile-long hill at Juniper Avenue, from Road's End Lane to

Lake View Avenue; avoiding the lake, he'd decided to visit the historic quarter—a town square bounded by the Cattaraugus County Courthouse and post office, the YM-YWCA and the library. Here there's a small park with a World War II memorial, a Revolutionary War cannon, a rain-worn American flag, a few benches. Near deserted, which is a relief.

The library is one of those small-town public libraries of the kind scattered across America, often housed in a "historic" building. L___ feels a tug of nostalgia, seeing it.

The Cattaraugus library has very few books in which L___ is interested, and none helpful for his current project. Yet L___ is drawn to the library, as a haven of sorts. The welcome of warm lights within, which seem to beckon to him. He recalls how he was sent here by his grandmother to take out books for her, slender mysteries with little black skulls-and-crossbones on the spine of the plastic covers, and the black letter M. (Mystery? Or Murder?) Strange that his genteel grandmother had devoured murder mysteries!—as if death were some sort of entertainment.

She'd given him her card for this purpose, not to be confused with L___'s own (child's) card.

In a trance of indecision L___ has been debating whether to enter the library. He thinks: he can simply ignore the woman with the tangled silvery hair—she's a stranger to him, she will not "recognize" him. And truly she is nothing to him.

Still, he feels some hesitation. A part of his brain cautions him against behaving recklessly.

The library is small, cramped. It is not really possible to avoid other patrons if they are in the front area, at the checkout desk, as you enter. L___ feels a visceral dread of getting too close to the woman with the shimmering silvery hair for fear that he will (unwittingly) call attention to himself and she will see him staring at her and if she sees him *she will know.*

Oh but what will she know?—something. Something she will see in his face?

A premonition of something that will happen, or something that will never happen?

Something that *has already happened?*

He decides not to enter the library. Yet not—quite—to leave.

Finds himself walking along a darkened pathway beside the library. Staring up into the windows as he passes—sees several figures—a man with a fleshy flushed face—a middle-aged woman—but not the silvery-haired woman.

Then at the rear window he sees her: her back to the window.

She is leaning over an oversized book, like an atlas. Probably it is, as L___ recalls, *The American Gazetteer*, a nineteenth-century book of maps kept with other, similar atlases in a corner of the reference section of the library.

He sees the woman's slender arm, her fingers turning the oversized parchment-like page. He sees silver filaments in her hair, which falls in tangled waves over her shoulders. He can see the side of her face, just barely: the curve of her cheek, her parted lips.

The scene is brightly lit from within. Only a few yards away he is standing in darkness, invisible. The sharpness of Vermeer, he thinks. He feels a yearning in the region of his heart so powerful he is almost faint.

Why is the young woman interested in that old book? Why *The American Gazetteer*? As a boy, he'd paged through atlases in that library, examined the Rand McNally globe that spun with geriatric slowness; its carefully outlined countries were defined by faded colors, outdated thirty years ago. Perhaps it was a collector's item, a novelty of history like Mura House.

How erotic, the sight of the silvery-haired woman's arm as her sleeve slips down to her elbow. And the faint shimmer of her hair. Every movement of the woman is exciting to L___, the more that she's unaware of him watching her so intently.

She must never know. She must be protected from—whatever is happening.

L___ rouses himself, and passes quickly by the window. He has not meant to linger, and stare.

His heart is beating rapidly. How absurd! He is ashamed of himself but he is very excited.

At the rear of the library he pauses. Here is a shadowy alcove, a little distance from the street. A grassy patch, not well lighted. A pedestrian pathway that functions as a shortcut to the next street and it is quite reasonable that L___ might take this pathway, close beside the library. You might think that he'd parked his car nearby. A library patron, like others.

He has positioned himself in such a way that he can see, not the front entrance of the library, but much of the front walk, which leads to the street. No one can leave the library without being seen by L___—he is certain.

From his vantage place in the shadows he observes a heavy-hipped woman leaving the library, picked up at the street by someone in a station wagon. A solitary man in shorts, trotting across the street to his parked car. It must be closing time: 7:30 P.M. on a weeknight in summer. L___ can't see anyone else inside except the librarian, an older white-haired woman whose name he should know.

Still, the silvery-haired woman must still be there. He seems to be waiting for her to leave the library after all. *But he will not follow her.*

Under a hypnotic spell, time passes slowly for L___. In fact, it is a pleat in time; L___ is neither here entirely in the shadows at the rear of the Cattaraugus Public Library nor is he elsewhere. He is *suspended in time.*

Earlier that evening he'd had to walk out of his parents' house, where the air of late afternoon becomes thick as suet and where it is difficult to breathe.

He wants to plead with the silvery-haired woman—*There has been some mistake. The person you see is not really me. What was done to me and what I have become . . .*

And the woman will turn to him, and she will touch his arm, gently. All of his senses are alert, to the point of pain: he can scarcely breathe, in anticipation of what she will tell him.

Why she has entered his life, what she has been meant to tell him . . .

There is a jolt. Time has passed. L___ rouses himself to realize: the library is empty except for the librarian, who is switching off lights.

How is this possible? Where is the silvery-haired woman? He wants to protest: he could not have missed her. Not for a moment has he turned his gaze away from the front walk. He has scarcely dared to blink.

(Is it possible she left the library by another door?)

(But there is no other door for library patrons, he is sure. Only an emergency door at the rear, which would sound an alarm if opened.) Admonishes himself: It is not possible that she left by the front door, and he didn't see her. *He could not have missed her.*

In a state of agitation he approaches the front entrance of the library. How familiar the doorway is, the truncated view into the library, as if he has never left his childhood home, and his adult life has been a delusion . . .

He peers inside—as one would; a husband, for instance, or a father, waiting for someone inside to emerge from the library, who has (unaccountably) not emerged.

Must happen all the time. Nothing to alarm anyone.

However, there is no one visible except the librarian, Mrs. McGarry. "Hello! Can I help you? I'm afraid we're closing just now . . ." Doesn't Mrs. McGarry recognize L___ ? He is older than she has ever seen him, of course; his face is lined, his once thick, dark hair is scanty, thin like the feathers of very young birds not yet fledged. Perhaps he is unnaturally pale. And perhaps he is grimacing impatiently, irritably, his face so contorted that Mrs. McGarry can't seem to recognize the boy who used to come into the library so often, a lifetime ago.

"Oh! Is it—"

The light of recognition comes into the white-haired woman's face. Now L___ cannot escape.

Mrs. McGarry speaks his name. Mrs. McGarry greets him warmly. She is just locking up the library, she explains. Switching off lights and the ceiling fans. Would he wait a moment? Of course! How can L___ possibly say no?

"I was a friend of your dear mother for many years . . ."

"Yes. I know."

L___ shakes her hand, or would shake it. But Mrs. McGarry extends her hand to clasp his, in commiseration, perhaps, not merely to be shaken.

L___ is eager to escape. L___ is eager to drift away into the night in chagrin and shame and a kind of fury except Mrs. McGarry retains him. "The last time I saw you, I think—Margaret and I had just returned from visiting Chloe Sanderson in the hospital— poor Chloe!—your mother brought her flowers from her garden, an armful of the most fragrant flowers—white carnations—" A bittersweet memory. A memory to be shared. A memory not to be avoided and so L___ endures it with a stoic smile.

"Are you living in your parents' beautiful house now? I thought I'd heard this. Are you returned to us?"

Mrs. McGarry clutches at his hand. Her eyes search his with a discomforting intensity and he sees that it is Mrs. McGarry (perhaps) who has been awaiting him in this place, not the other.

L___ wants to ask the librarian about the shimmering-silvery-haired woman who'd leaned over the old atlas: Who is she? Did Mrs. McGarry see her too? He wants to ask her what she recalled of the boy he'd been. What his mother might have told her, of him. But the words choke in his throat, he can only smile and allow his hand to be clasped and stroked, in consolation for his loss.

Are you returned to us? He has no idea.

No. *Ridiculous! Yes. Ridiculous.*

He is very tired. "Drained."

His energy drains from him like the slow drip, seep, ooze of excrement. His life.

Wouldn't have had the energy to follow the silvery-haired woman if he'd seen her. That is the sobering fact.

He has his eye on the farther edge of the lake, along the east shore. On one of his restless walks he has scrutinized the area. The possibilities. His mind is always working. Swift, sharp like flashing scissors. He'd recalled from years ago and has reacquainted himself now: that fetid stretch of rotted cattails, fish floating belly-up, broken Styrofoam. Since he has no boat to row out onto the lake, no motorboat, no way of assuring that the body will be far enough from shore that the body will sink to a depth of more than six feet to lie against the mucky bottom of the lake, he will have to dump the body in a more convenient place.

* * *

"A highly challenging, very ambitious project for which I need seclusion here in Cattaraugus."

So he said. There was pleasure in such a statement made to the inquisitive. Saliva gathered in his mouth as with a delicious taste.

A shock to L___, yet deeply flattering, that he'd been named executor of the literary estate of the distinguished writer-historian V___ S___, who'd died, at eighty-four, the previous December.

Obviously there had been a mistake on someone's part: for L had not been contacted beforehand. Nor would L___ have expected to be singled out for this honor, which carries with it a good deal of responsibility.

A call from a lawyer, congratulations from friends, his name in the very last paragraph of S___'s obituary in *The New York Times*—all so sudden, unexpected.

He had just begun chemotherapy. Every two weeks for four hours in succession, poisons dripping into his veins and coursing through his heart, so lethal the infusion-room nurses had to wear protective clothing, gloves. Yet when S___'s lawyer called, L___ heard his voice crack with emotion.

"Yes, of course! Though I knew, it's still a—surprise . . . and a great honor."

Flushed with this honor like a transfusion of fresh blood, L agreed to help S___'s editor prepare S___'s final book for publication in January of the new year.

A Biography of Biographies will be a "magisterial" work—no doubt. The manuscript, or manuscripts, runs to thirteen hundred pages.

S____'s editor, upset and aggrieved that the prominent elderly author had died before his book was quite ready for press, assured L____ that the book was all but finished: it needed only "minimal reshaping, reorganization, some revision and rewriting, and an index."

L____ had agreed without hesitation. Like a drowning man clutching at a lifeline, which will haul him out of a turbulent sea, allow him to breathe for a while longer, to *endure.*

"Thank you! This is an honor."

And: "I'm a longtime admirer of S____. I think that I've read everything he has written . . ."

And, somberly: "We were never exactly friends. There was a generation between us. But I felt a kind of kinship with S____, and only wish now that I had known him better."

Is this true? Perhaps not entirely. L____ has certainly not read all of S____'s work, which consists of a dozen or more substantial books. Nor had S____ sought him out, though S____ had always been perfectly friendly, kind, and behaved as if he was interested in L____'s work. It is true that L____ initially is grateful for the assignment. Or was. Fact is, after his *evisceration* L____ has no energy to undertake original work of his own nor can he foresee a time when he will regain his energy.

(Possibly this was the case even before the *evisceration.* But L____ doesn't care to consider that.)

Some days L___ is enthusiastic and hopeful about the project; other days L___ is rueful and chagrined that he'd made such a blunder in a craven gesture of attaching himself to a famous and respected name in the hope that some of the glory would rub off on him, like the faint iridescence of a broken moth's wing.

He has been working with at least three manuscripts written at different periods of time, derived from several computer files; he has been trying to give structure to an essentially structure-less book. There is much to admire in S___'s eloquent prose but there are many passages that are haphazardly written, and uninspired; there are sections that have been left blank—glibly marked *material TK.* (With a sinking heart L___ wonders who is expected to provide this missing material.) Chapters have been many times revised, with much overlapping and repetitive material. Footnotes are overlong, pedantic. Other footnotes are just numerals, with no information at all. At the time of his death S___ hadn't even begun an index. Most upsetting, *A Biography of Biographies* seems to be based upon numerous other books on the subject, and to contain virtually nothing that is original or inventive. Like every other historian of the subject, S___ begins with Plutarch's *Lives* but he ends (arbitrarily) in the early 1980s with Leon Edel's *Henry James* and Richard Ellmann's *James Joyce,* as if these are the most recent major biographies S___ had troubled to read.

What a joke! A cruel joke.

L___ had hoped to attach himself to a work of substance, even of genius. *A work of literature that mattered.*

A (posthumous) collaboration with S____ would have lifted L____'s sodden spirits even as it would have lifted his reputation. Not that L____ cares so much any longer for a "reputation"—at nearly forty-two, he has lived long enough without one.

What had he hoped for then? To live again, through another?—through the elderly S____?

He thinks: He could give up. He could admit defeat. But he will not admit defeat. *He is still alive.*

There is much more work to do on the book than L____ anticipated but perhaps (he tells himself) this is good—good for him in his depressed and morbid state of mind . . .

He is not so happy with S____'s editor. A prominent New York editor, much respected.

L____ has patiently explained to S____'s editor that he prefers email exchanges to telephone conversations yet the man continues to call him, never less than once a week. This is a particular sort of harassment, L____ thinks. Oblique but unmistakable.

When the other day the editor called to ask L____ how his work on the book was "progressing," L____ replied with a sardonic laugh, "Well. I'm hoping to stay alive long enough to finish it."

S____'s editor was stunned into silence for a long moment, unsure how to respond to this remark.

"I—I don't understand . . . Are you ill?"

"No! That was a joke."

(Not a very witty joke. Immediately L____ regretted having made it.)

"Well. If you need an extension . . ."

"Not at all. I will get the revised manuscript to you by"—he named the September first deadline he'd been given.

Thinking—*Are they hoping I will give up? Do they know that I am a terminal case?*

Thinking—*They don't really want to publish this book. A posthumous author is a lost cause.*

Since the library, he avoids the library.

Since the lakeside esplanade, he avoids the lakeside esplanade.

He has become an ascetic. He is scrupulous in denial. *He is not a fool to wish to approach a woman he doesn't know in a public place, who would be repelled by him.*

That particular area of Cattaraugus Park near the bandstand, near playground swings, the children's wading pool, popular on hot summer afternoons and early evenings. He has a fear of encountering people whom he knows, and who might know him.

"I will not. I *will*."

And, "Ridiculous. You are risible."

Risible not a word one commonly uses. Rhymes with *visible*.

In any case there are other places to walk in our small town. The thick-wooded dead end of Road's End Lane where dirt paths once made by children (including L___ and his friends) have mostly grown over. The neatly mowed Lutheran churchyard and the lake itself—the farther, eastern shore of Lake Cattaraugus that is usually deserted.

The grassy stretch along Catamount Road that ends in a marshy field. A dirt lane with narrow dirt paths leading down to the mucky water. Thinking how, when he was a boy, the eastern shore of Lake Cattaraugus had been a place to fish. Somehow it has happened that, in recent years, the lake water here has become clotted with algae, broken and rotted marsh reeds, cattails, discarded trash; the black bass population has been decimated as the water level of the lake has steadily lowered.

And there are times for walking that are not so dangerous as others. Of course.

In the early evening when (you might suppose) the young silvery-haired woman would be preparing dinner for her family, assuming the young woman is married, and has a family, including children, perhaps a young baby.

Places where a man might walk when he can't bear his life. When he can't fathom his life.

Thinking in derision—*Just forget. Oblivion.*

He never shuts the slow-moving garage doors any longer. Never troubles to drive his vehicle inside the garage only just to park it at the rear of the house so that no one can see, from the road, whether anyone is home.

Avoids the garage. Detritus of the *lost self.*

Except once or twice, out of curiosity. (He discovers a beautifully executed birds' nest of twigs and dried grasses amid the dusty folded curtains.) Wondering if the panicked little birds had found their way out and deciding, yes, they had.

Smiling, he thinks—*At least, they've escaped and saved themselves.*

He knows that he will see the silvery-haired woman again. It is inevitable, for him and for her. But he wishes it would not be inevitable for *her.*

He does not want to hurt her. He does not even want to frighten her.

He does want her to acknowledge *him.*

She owes him (he thinks) that much. A beggarly gesture, for which he will be absurdly, abjectly grateful.

He has taken to hiking out to the lake via Catamount Road, he is so restless. Even with his cramping legs.

We have observed him, at a distance.

Some of us have outboard motorboats, rowboats. Some of us have canoes though we don't "canoe" so much in the muggy summer heat of the Finger Lakes region, now that we've grown up and become adults.

L___ limps slightly. You almost wouldn't notice. (She will not notice. L___ is determined.) But he can limp quickly like a dog with three practiced legs.

It is the largest and (by tradition) the most beautiful of the eleven Finger Lakes of central New York State—Lake Cattaraugus. Indeed it is oddly shaped like a finger, a beckoning finger, forty miles long (south/north), four miles at its widest. The village of Cattaraugus is the only populated area on the lake though there are cottages and cabins scattered around it, some of them difficult of access, and some abandoned. Much of the eastern shore has reverted to the wild.

It is good to see this, L___ thinks. How quickly wilderness moves in, suffocating the merely *cultivated*.

Occasionally there are boats on the lake. For the lake is quite deep at its center. Outboard motorboats. Sailboats. L___ is intrigued to see, to think that he sees, a shimmering flash of silvery hair—in one of the blinding-white sailboats drifting past. She is with one or two others. A man, two men. A woman. He shades his eyes but the figures fade in a haze of sunshine.

Sees, thinks he sees, the young woman in a bathing suit, on a deserted stretch of beach, later that day. Not so slender as he'd imagined but lanky-limbed and hard-muscled like a high school girl athlete. Her hair has been pulled back into a ponytail and seems to be lighter, wheat-colored. Distasteful to L___ that the beautiful girl is in the company of other, cruder individuals her age, all of them in bathing suits, barefoot.

He is shocked, repelled: one of the loutish boys tugs at her ponytail, teases her.

If he'd brought a rifle with him . . .

(Why has he thought of a rifle? There is no rifle in his parents' house. He had not been brought up to use firearms.)

But no: that girl is not *her*. He is fully sane. He is not sick-minded. He knows this.

Before the teenagers can see the white-skinned middle-aged man spying on them from behind a bank of cattails he withdraws shrewdly.

* * *

He can drink all he wants.

He can drink until he has forgotten why he is drinking.

Several old whiskey bottles of his father's left behind in a sideboard in the dining room. Scotch whiskey, bourbon, gin. Why not?

In the upstairs bathroom, stripping himself bare. Hearing his breath catch.

Though he'd showered early that morning before dawn, after a violent leg cramp had awakened him, he feels the need, the compulsion to shower again by late afternoon.

Beneath his (loose-fitting, ordinary and not-unattractive) clothes he is a marvel of male ruin, scarred and pallid, like wax that has partly melted and then hardened. He has learned to avoid contemplating the genitals between his legs, which are both swollen and shrunken, like small tumors in sacks of very thin ripe-plum-colored skin.

His mouth tastes like chemicals, still. Poisons that have dripped into his veins to "kill" cancerous cells and have not been totally flushed out of his body even after months.

If he were to kiss a woman. The silver-haired woman, turning to him, lifting her face to his in a gesture of trust.

Idly he wonders—*Am I radioactive? Can I kill on contact?*

God help me.
I cannot help myself.

Today she has brought a book with her. She is seated on a bench overlooking the lake and engrossed in her book as a young girl might be engrossed in a book in a long-ago time.

She is not in the place he'd seen her initially. For L___ has avoided that place.

In another part of the park that is much less popular where (L___ has thought) he would be safe.

Immediately he recognizes her. With a gut-sick sensation of certainty his eye swerves upon *her*.

He sees her from behind, and then he sees her in profile from approximately twenty feet away. He is shaky-legged suddenly.

He will not see her face fully unless he approaches her and positions himself in front of her, to her (left) side. It is quite natural that a visitor to the park might stand at the lakeside rail in this way to look out at, to toss bread crusts at, an excited little flotilla of mallards and geese bobbing in the water. No need to defend himself from accusers!

But doing so would (probably) draw the attention of the young woman, which he must avoid.

How beautiful she is! How solitary.

Speckled sunlight falls upon her like gold coins. He dreads violating that stillness.

She is wearing a long skirt of some thin, silky fabric, slit to the thigh—a startling sight. It is a provocative way of dressing and yet (L___ thinks) it is a classic Asian style, an elegantly long skirt, unexpectedly slit to the thigh. (What he can see of her leg, her thigh, is an expanse of very pale flesh, not muscular, but very lean. The tight, taut flesh of a young person.) Her hair is less silvery than he recalls, more likely faded blond, ash blond, threaded with glinting hairs. Not so wavy—curly today and falling straight past her shoulders.

L___ feels his heart missing beats. He has had few cardiac problems, his doctors have been impressed. Such physical trauma to a man's body, such incisions, eviscerations, are more profound than simply physical injuries, and he has prevailed nonetheless, his heart has rarely failed him. And now, his heart is hurting.

He sees: the book in which the young woman is engrossed is covered in transparent plastic, a book borrowed from the local library, no doubt, not a purchase of her own.

He is just slightly disappointed that the young woman hasn't bought the book for herself. That it is only a library withdrawal suggests that her commitment to it is ephemeral.

He wonders what the title is. At the same time, he believes that it would be better for him not to know.

Knowing curtails *desire*. From his former life, when he'd been alive, he recalls.

Still, he is excited to have discovered the woman. Until this moment his day had been tortuous, beginning with painful leg cramps at an hour before dawn, the dismay of being awakened so early, with the prospect of the long, interminable day ahead.

He has had to confront the fact: His work is stalled. He sees himself in a vehicle stalled on railroad tracks, paralyzed as a locomotive rushes at him.

He'd spent that day, he has spent several days—in fact, weeks—in a trance of frustration so extreme it borders upon wonderment. Each morning he hauls himself to his writing table in the glassed-in porch as you might haul a lifeless body—he works for lengthy hours, becoming increasingly fretful as the morning hours wane, and he has little to show for his effort; but with the appalling movement of the clock downward, in the afternoon, he becomes ever more agitated, and it is very difficult for him to keep his mind from fastening on to—*her*.

His thoughts are both roiling and "flat"—thoughts at a boil that nonetheless go nowhere. Like chapters in S___'s book so many times revised, and rewritten, the momentum of their prose has wound down. And the more L___ rewrites S___'s prose, the deeper he sinks into a bottomless sand that will soon cover his mouth.

Indeed his lips have gone numb as if all sensation has drained from them.

He keeps his distance from the woman, who sits very still, almost unnaturally still. He tells himself this is all very casual. There is nothing *urgent*, *fated* about discovering her. There is nothing *doomed*.

This is a "good" side of the lake where the water is relatively clear of the algae that grows elsewhere in thick metastasizing slime clumps. All is calm today. Calmer. The lake's surface reflects the sky dully like hammered tin.

What *is* she reading?—L___'s heart contracts with yearning; he wants badly to know.

(It is not a heavy book—not a long novel. Nor does the slate-gray cover, with calm pale letters, suggest a popular best seller.)

From time to time the young woman glances up from the book as if it reminds her of something—a moment of tenderness, a private thought.

He will not approach her, he thinks.

He will respect her privacy. Her beauty.

For he feels inadequate, of course. He is wearing his loose-fitting clothes that have been chosen to disguise his body and not in any way to reveal it. A T-shirt, khaki shorts. Running shoes and no socks. He launders his clothes in the washer in the house. He does not trouble to iron them.

He will say—*Excuse me. I happened to have seen . . . The other day, I think I saw you sailing . . .*

Here is a rude surprise: Children are approaching. First, middle school–age boys on bicycles, loudly calling to one another. Then a young couple with small children.

The calm of the lakeside has been shattered. The father in T-shirt and rumpled shorts is chiding one of the children, who has displeased him in some trivial way, and the mother is trying to placate the father in a soft, pleading voice. *Please. He didn't mean it.*

L___ tries not to stare at these intruders with a look of rage. Thinking how much more beautiful it would be, and more merciful, if human beings did not utter words out of their contorted mouths but "signed" them as the deaf do, with precision and grace. He has frequently been impressed—indeed, fascinated—by observing a deaf interpreter sign to an audience at a public event. It occurs to him that the silvery-haired woman whose voice he has never heard is a kind of "sign"—her beautiful averted face, her shimmering hair, her slender and very still body.

Yes, L___ is weary of those dull, banal, predictable and de-meaning words that are uttered aloud, that abrade the ear. How he yearns for the beauty that is directed to the eye in silence.

So absorbed in her book, the young woman seems scarcely aware of the intrusive family who have, to L___'s dismay, set down their picnic things on a nearby table. L___ wonders if they are aware that there is a much more attractive picnic area elsewhere in the park, in a shaded grove.

Only mildly annoyed, it seems, the young woman glances around at the bickering family, and for a dazzling, heart-stopping moment, at *him*—but without quite seeing him, L___ thinks.

(Yet: He has seen her. The impact of that face, those eyes, will remain with L___ for a long time.)

It is time to leave! On his shaky legs L___ retreats.

That night as he drifts into sleep he realizes—the silvery-haired woman had been reading *his book*.

Vividly now he recalls the slate-gray cover, the pale, pearlescent letters—he is sure it was *his book*.

His first book, a little-read novel titled *Jubilation*. Into which L___ had opened his veins and never quite recovered.

It was L___'s first published novel, though it had not been the first novel he'd written. He had not ever written another.

Of course, I've done other things. I've published other books. I am a "literary figure"—of a kind. I have even published poetry—poems. Not yet a book of poems.

He is explaining to the silver-haired young woman, who listens intently. He is captivated by the way she brushes her hair out of her face with both hands, like one parting a curtain of some fine, shimmering material like silk.

Of course, the Cattaraugus Public Library has *Jubilation* in its fiction collection. L___ has checked. At the time of its publication (in 1999), Mrs. McGarry or another librarian would have been sure to order it—unless L___'s mother donated a copy.

It comes to L___ in a flash, he can learn the name of the silvery-haired woman if he visits the library and determines who has withdrawn the single copy of *Jubilation* in the past week . . . The possibility leaves him too excited to sleep.

Chloroform makes of the most resistant body a very bride. The struggling hands, the clawing nails, the convulsive flailings of the limbs—all surrender within seconds.

Her lover tells her: Please understand. I am providing a happy ending for you, who will be protected from the terrible erosion of time. In my arms you will always be young—you will always be my bride.

You will always be worthy of love, and loved.

In a dead faint he has fallen. *Dead faint* is exact for the brain is extinguished in an instant.

Fallen heavily onto the ground in some public place, a chatter of excited voices, deafening sound of a siren, a siren too close, and strangers bending over him to "revive" him . . .

The first he knows how very sick he is.

Must've known. Fastidiously averting your eyes from the blood traces in the toilet.

How ridiculous you are, how pathetic thinking you can deceive . . .

Later in the hospital he will discover that his clothes have been expertly sheared by the EMTs to allow access to his body. Deft hands of strangers touching his body. Blood-pressure band tightening around his upper arm, forefinger pressed against the carotid artery in his throat, an unresponsive eyelid lifted, small light ray piercing the (sightless, unfocused) eyeball. A defibrillator on hand, which, fortunately, they don't have to use.

The patient knows nothing of this at the time, nor does he realize he has wet his underwear and trousers.

Internal bleeding. Brackish-black blood. You never know. Until you know.

2.

"'Evangeline.'"

It is a beautiful name, an archaic name. He knew a girl with this name long ago in grade school, the daughter of a local minister who'd died, or moved away—all he can recall of Evangeline is the girl's curly red-gold hair, silver barrettes in the hair, and the girl's profile, the curve of her cheek. L___ had sat behind her in fifth grade and also in sixth grade, an accident of the alphabet.

He does not think that the silvery-haired woman is Evangeline—for the minister's daughter would be much older than this woman. (She would be L___'s age. Would L___ be interested in a woman in her early forties?) That Evangeline's life would be much different than the life L___ can imagine for the silvery-haired woman. And perhaps she is not even alive now.

So often L___ finds himself thinking that persons of his generation, his age, whom he has not seen in some time, are probably *not even alive now.*

She tells him, *We are all forgetting each other, constantly. Life is a shimmering stream. The light plays on the stream through the trees for just a measured distance, then it is gone—but the stream continues. We bask in the sunshine, then the sunshine is gone. But when the sunshine is gone, we are gone. So we don't feel the loss. We don't feel pain.*

Doomed love. Unrequited love.

L___ recalls having read an appalling news item years ago. "Sinkholes" in a township in the Chautauqua Mountains, not far from Cattaraugus. Scudder Mills, a mining town. The local product was gypsum. A man, a homeowner, stepped into his backyard on the morning after a severe rainstorm and, in bright sunshine, the earth beneath his feet fell away.

A gaping hole beneath, thirty feet, possibly fifty feet, the man fell, helpless to save himself, and was smothered, horribly—calling, screaming for help—but there was no help.

Earth filled his mouth, and he was silenced.

This horror happened in Scudder Mills when L___ was a boy. In all, there were several sinkholes in the mining town, but no one else was trapped in this way and no one else died. At Lake Cattaraugus everyone talked of it. At home, at school. He tastes something sour and deathly in his mouth, recalling.

Scudder Mills had been abandoned, the mining town declared a disaster area. L___ had forgotten about it until now.

Thinking how doomed love is a sinkhole. He will fall, and fall, and never come to the bottom of the sinkhole. And if he cries for help, no one will hear. There is no one.

"Not possible. *No.*"

L___ has made a discovery in S___'s manuscript. Or, rather, in one of the variants of S___'s manuscript, written several years before S___'s death.

It is shocking to him but seems unmistakable: The distinguished scholar-critic-historian S___, twice winner of the Pulitzer Prize and a member of the American Academy of Arts and Letters for forty years, seems to have plagiarized a part of a chapter on medieval "saints' lives" from a scholarly article available online through Google Scholar. The plagiarism is almost verbatim, though S___ made of several paragraphs one single-length paragraph and substituted arcane words for plainer words—*exsiccation, thrawart, immergence, adnate.*

L___ tells himself that S___ intended to delete these passages at a later time; at least a skilled writer like S___ would recast them more thoroughly, so that their origins in the work of another scholar would not be so obvious. (L___ has checked: there is no footnote attributing the source.) L___ decides that the wisest strategy for him is simply to delete the passages as if they'd never existed. (S___'s editor has these files also, but L___ doubts that S___'s editor will ever read through the massive manuscript, still less detect plagiarized passages.) It is urgent for L___ to protect S___, at least S___'s reputation.

Problem is, deleting passages means that L___ will have to provide a transition of some kind. He fears that he will be incapable of doing this, replicating S___'s elegant prose. And he can't help but wonder if S___ has plagiarized elsewhere in the manuscript.

His work as an indentured servant for the dead man will never end. He sees that now. Another, even more shocking discovery after L___ has been away from the manuscript for forty-eight hours, and returns to take up another, later section: Mixed in with S___'s scholarly writing is a kind of journal, or diary. It is a very different kind of writing altogether and (L___ thinks) it must have been inserted in the manuscript by mistake.

Chloroform is the most pragmatic. Swift, clean, leaves no (visible) trace and he knows where to purchase it without being questioned . . .

And,

Swiftly and deftly the chloroform-soaked cloth is pressed over her mouth, nose. She fights him bravely, desperately. He will see her eyelids flutter. He will see the light go out in her eyes. But she will not have seen his face . . .

L___ is appalled by what he reads. But he is excited as well.

He has discovered approximately forty pages of prose charting the stalking and murder of an unidentified woman. The prose is intense, intimate, obscenely poetic. It is possible that S___ was writing a darkly erotic novel or a quasi-journal tracking the obsession/disintegration of a personality resembling his own, but not himself; but in all of his career S___ had never published fiction, so far as L___ knew.

What is particularly upsetting to L___ is that the "erotic" material is in a section of the manuscript that S___'s editor was supposed to have read. Yet clearly he had not.

L___ will have to delete these pages also. He won't allow himself to keep reading but will delete without reading.

He must protect the elder writer, who cannot protect himself. *All must be hidden! Erased. No one must know.*

He flees the house. He is scarcely able to breathe; the air has turned thick and porous.

It is the brackish odor of the rotting lake. Dead things in hot sunshine. Ripe, rank smells. He is terrified that the body is partly exposed, there in the marsh. An outflung arm, a satiny-smooth pale leg. It has occurred to him too late, turkey vultures will circle in the sky. The ungainly wide-winged black-feathered scavengers will draw attention, out in the marshes . . .

Then he realizes that none of this has happened yet—"We are safe."

He shudders with relief. Tears streak his cheeks; he has not cried like this in years.

He has not glimpsed the silvery-haired woman in many days.

He has deleted the offensive passages in S___'s manuscript—the plagiarized material and the obscene material.

He has concentrated on another part of *A Biography of Biographies*. He is determined to salvage what he can of the remainder of his life.

He has even succumbed to an invitation from family friends, to come to dinner one night the following week. He will bring the older couple a bottle of good red wine and a bouquet of flowers from his mother's garden—white carnations, daisies, roses growing wild behind the house.

His hand will be shaken vigorously by his host. He will be hugged, kissed by his hostess.

We have missed you here in Cattaraugus! Have you returned to us for good?

He shudders at the prospect. Yet, he will prevail.

He will manage not to show surprise at how old the couple has become, whom he has not seen in fifteen years; as they will manage not to show surprise at how old L___ has become, whom they have not seen in fifteen years.

Several mornings in succession he is wakened by the sound of a woman or a girl sobbing.

"Hello? Is someone there?"—quickly he rises from bed to investigate, his heart pounding in dread.

Of course it is no one, nothing. The wind in the trees surrounding the house. Strange muffled cries of birds in the eaves.

He listens. The mysterious sound has faded.

Through the day at wayward times he thinks he hears this sound but doesn't allow himself to be distracted. He concentrates on his work. He has begun the index. This is a daunting task but it signals the beginning of the end of the project, and about this L___ feels hopeful!

And then, to his chagrin, L___ discovers more of the offensive material he'd believed he had deleted.

> *Chloroform makes of the most resistant body a very bride. The struggling hands, the clawing nails, the convulsive flailings of the limbs—all surrender within seconds. . . .*

In exasperation L___ deletes this. How disgusting! He is left shaken, bewildered. He is plagued by the (absurd yet appalling) possibility that offensive material of this nature will remain in S___'s manuscript, hidden in the file, to be (horribly, irremediably) printed and published in book form, embedded in the chaste scholarly prose of *A Biography of Biographies*. What a scandal, if this should happen! L___ can't trust S___'s editor, certainly. He can't trust the publisher's copy editors and proofreaders, who are strangers to him; the fact is, L___ will have to trust himself, to make sure that all remnants of the offensive material, and of the plagiarized material, have been detected and deleted from the manuscript file. Yet he is terribly worried: can he trust himself?

"Hello? Is someone there?"—he hears the sound of sobbing, somewhere close by.

He has just emerged from a wine store, where he has bought a bottle of wine to bring to his parents' old friends that evening. Out of restlessness he's been walking, and, happening to see the wine store (it has a familiar name but seems to be in an unfamiliar setting), he'd decided to make the purchase now, rather than later, though it means carrying the wine bottle back up the long hill to Road's End Lane. Now in the parking lot beside the wine store he hears, he thinks he hears, the sound of sobbing, but when he turns to look he sees no one, nothing.

L___ is perplexed but not especially frightened. For this is not happening *inside his head* as he has (sometimes) feared when he hears the sound in the early morning, in his house. It is not at all unlikely that a woman, a girl, a young boy, might be sitting inside a vehicle in the parking lot, sobbing. And that L___ has happened to overhear.

But there are only a few vehicles parked in the lot, and no one is visible inside any of them.

He listens closely. The sobbing seems to have faded.

He walks on. He is feeling hopeful. The bottle has an attractive label: it is a Chilean chardonnay, new to him. He will enjoy himself that evening, he is determined. It has been too long since L___ has spent time with friends. He needs to engage in conversation, he needs to laugh. He needs to forget about S___ and he needs to forget about E___. He will deflect questions that seem to him too private, too personal—about his health, his circumstances, the precise nature of the work he has brought with him to Cattaraugus—but he will do this in a discreet way; he will try to be gracious.

Are you returned to us?

We have been waiting for you—for years . . .

He has left the wine-store parking lot and will return to Road's End Lane. But by a circuitous route.

Already it is late afternoon—past five o'clock. He must return home, he must shower and cleanse himself thoroughly before going out to dinner. He has a fear of offending the nostrils of others, who know nothing of his secret and must not guess it.

He is walking in a neighborhood in Cattaraugus that is not familiar to him. As a boy he'd bicycled along some of these streets—narrow, hilly potholed streets—past shabby row houses and vacant lots, and yet all seems different to him. No one is out on the sidewalks, no one is in the streets. He has taken a wrong turn, it seems, though no turn in Cattaraugus will take L___ far out of his way, it is such a small town; and if there is danger, he is armed with the bottle of chardonnay.

He finds himself crossing a pedestrian bridge. It is a very old bridge—miniature maple trees, no more than an inch high, are growing in the cracks between planks and in the plank railings!

To his left, just visible through a maze of wood-frame houses and scrubby foliage, is a stretch of slate-colored Lake Cattaraugus. To his right is the sprawling New York Central railroad yard, desolate at this hour. Beneath the bridge is a marshy area, an inlet of the lake that has become shallow and mucky and infested with buzzing insects.

Ahead he sees a young woman at the bridge railing, leaning her elbows on the railing as if she is very tired. Her long, tangled hair falls forward, hiding her face, which seems to him an aggrieved face, though he cannot see it clearly.

It is this woman who has been sobbing—(is it?). L___ stops dead in his tracks at the sight of her.

He will recall afterward he'd had no choice but to approach her to ask if anything was wrong.

"Excuse me—? Hello?"

The young woman doesn't seem to have heard L___ Already she has turned distractedly away, she is walking away, a stricken creature, wounded, wincing with pain (he thinks); she does not want him to see her face.

Is she crying? Is she ashamed that she is crying? He sees that she is wiping at her face with both hands as she hurries away.

He thinks—*But I have no choice!*

The woman is wraithlike, very thin. She seems scarcely to be walking or running but rather gliding. She wears a long, dark skirt of some flimsy material like muslin. She wears a shawl wrapped about her shoulders. He can't see her face and so has no idea how old she is but her movements suggest that she is young, lithe. Her hair is a shimmer of hues—blond, ash blond, wheat, silver—that flies about her head as if galvanized by electricity.

L___ doesn't quicken his pace, he will not overtake the woman. If the woman needs help, if she needs protection, L___ will be close behind her, but he does not want to frighten her.

He keeps a fixed distance between them: thirty feet perhaps. "I am here if you need me. I am always here. That is all."

L___ follows the woman across a street of badly broken pavement. He follows her into a vacant lot behind a block of brownstone row houses, which look as if they have been scorched by flame. Here there is underbrush, discarded and rotted lumber, broken glass sparkling in the late-afternoon sun. Broken clay pots—why so many? And empty bottles, gutted tin cans. L___ has become confused, for what is this fetid place? *Where is the young woman leading him?*

"Hey. You."

Out of the rubble an angry man approaches L___. He is fast and springy on the balls of his feet. He is belligerent and menacing as a pit bull.

L___ is taken totally by surprise. Naively he glances over his shoulder to see if the angry man is addressing someone behind him but it is L___ at whom the angry man is staring with stark, protuberant eyes. It is L___ at whom he is speaking in disgust.

"I said you! What d'you want?"—the flush-faced man, a decade younger than L___, not taller than L___ but thicker bodied, obviously stronger, is bearing down upon L___ with a look of fury.

L___ would turn away and flee. But L___ doesn't want to retreat in the face of the other's irrational anger for (he is thinking) that will violate his integrity; also, he dares not turn his back on such anger.

The angry man spits at him: "You sick fuck! What the fuck d'you think you're doing following her?!"

Now it is clear. It is clearer. The man is in alliance with the unhappy young woman.

L___ would explain that he meant no harm, he was only seeing if the woman needed help, he did not mean to upset her, he is sorry if he has been misunderstood; but the angry man isn't interested in anything L___ has to say. He has stepped boldly close to L___, and he continues cursing L___. To his chagrin L___ sees that the young woman has taken a position behind the man, as if L___ presents such a threat to her that she has to hide behind the angry man; at the same time, the woman has become defiant herself, flushed with indignation. Her face is radiant not with tears but with intense emotion.

This is certainly not Evangeline: L___ sees now.

She is no one he has seen before. She has small, crushed-together features but she is not at all delicate-boned. Her hair has a coarse, metallic sheen. The shirt or blouse she wears has a low neckline, her bony upper chest is exposed, her pallid skin.

In an incensed and infantile voice she tells the angry man that this is the person who has been following her, scaring her. "The son of a bitch is always following me. This is him!"

Before L___ can protect himself, the angry man rushes at him and strikes him in the face. It is a powerful, stunning blow—L___ feels his left eye socket crack.

He staggers backward. The angry man has wrenched the wine bottle out of L___'s hand, and threatens to strike him with it.

"Hey! Don't break this for Christ's sake"—deftly the young woman detaches the wine bottle from her companion's fingers.

L___ would retreat but the angry man won't allow him. L___ dares not turn his back for fear he will be murdered. He tries to defend his bleeding face as a child might, with his elbows, uplifted arms, bending at the waist, cowering, but the angry man continues to pursue him, not so hurriedly now, almost randomly striking him with sharp blows, his chest, his shoulder, his left temple. L___ can barely see, both his eyes have been struck, his vision blotched by pinpoint hemorrhages.

"No—please—*don't*"—L___ tries to protest but his mouth has been wounded. His teeth are loose and bleeding. His lower lip has been savagely slashed. He would stagger away in desperation—he would crawl away—but the angry man refuses to let him. The wrath of this stranger seems to be building, like that of a vengeful god. The more he punishes his victim, the more furious he is with his victim. L___'s very blood on his hands, splattering his clothing, is a goad to him, a provocation.

A forlorn thought comes to L___, belatedly—*Your mistake was leaving Mura House today, on foot.*

L___ is knocked to the ground by the angry man's pounding fists. It is a mistake too to fall to the ground for now the angry man is even angrier, and is kicking L___. Grunting, cursing, kicking at L___—the angry man is a flame that cannot be quenched, that must burn itself out. Kicking the fallen L___ in the ribs, without mercy. L___ feels the bones which protect his heart and lungs cracking. He is writhing in pain, he is pierced with pain as with a steel blade. The tangle-haired woman is taunting him, she is not trying to save him from the angry man but has become his assailant too, bent upon vengeance. L___ wants to ask—*Why?*

And now it is worse, it is unbearable, L___ is being kicked in the stomach, in the terrible wound in his lower belly that has not yet healed, in the stoma that bleeds so easily, a mere touch can start it bleeding and the terror is of bleeding to death. L___ can't draw breath to explain, he is unable to speak, the angry man will not let him speak and the angry young woman will show him no mercy.

They have confused L___ with someone else—is that it? He wants to protest, to plead with them it is the wrong man they are punishing. But in his agony he can't draw breath to speak.

L___ hears the angry man grunting as he kicks his final blows, each blow is a final blow, a death's blow. His grunting is a righteous sound. Such punishment is work. Such punishment is justice. Between L____'s legs pain escalates so powerfully it can't be contained but explodes from him like a geyser.

And then suddenly he is alone, his assailants have departed. It is very quiet except for L____'s gasping breaths.

One of them has taken his wallet, torn it from inside his blood-soaked trousers.

L____ is alone, flat on the ground, and the tin-colored sky close overhead like something that is shutting. The pain continues to build. Behind his blinded eyes the flame grows in intensity until there is nothing but the hot, blinding, searing flame that envelops him, and is him.

No ID? Who is this? Jesus!—looks like somebody was real mad at the poor bastard.

3.

Hello!

Her eyes lift to his. He can't see her face clearly. But he can see that she is smiling at him, shyly. He believes that she is smiling at him. They are in a secluded place that smells of the lake. Rotted algae, carcasses of fish mummified in the summer sun. He sees a fleeting shadow on the ground, the shadow of a large bird, a predator, or rather a scavenger, with wide, dark, comically awkward wings. He does not know if this is a turkey vulture. He knows that there are turkey vultures in Cattaraugus County.

The bird is too large to be a crow or a raven. It is too large to be a blackbird. It is not flying but rather walking, with ungainly steps. It is walking toward him. Its eyes are bronze, unwinking. Its beak looks sharp and it is long enough to reach his heart.

The silvery-haired woman is close by. This is Evangeline, he is certain: but perhaps she does not want to be called by that name, by L____. Perhaps that is a secret name, not to be uttered. She is not so close that he can reach out to touch her, to clutch at her hand as he wants to do. For if he could clutch her hand, if she would grip his hand firmly, she might pull him up onto his feet—badly, he wants to be raised to his feet, he is in despair of what has happened to him, and it will be the first step in making things right, in returning to his normal life, if the young woman will help him to his feet, if she will offer him her hand. She is not so close that he can see her face clearly, or her eyes. He senses that her eyes are veiled. But he sees that she is there. She has not abandoned him.

Gently she says to the fallen man—*O love. Give me your hand.*

Night-Gaunts

1. The Sighting

In a high, small, octagonal window of the (vacant) house he sees the face he is not prepared to see.

Stops dead in his tracks. Climbing steep cobbled Charity Hill where (once) the Cornish family had lived. *He* had lived.

It is gaunt, narrow, grave as a face carved in granite. Very pale, impassive. The eyes are sunken yet alive and alert—*gleeful*.

A face not quite *pressed against* the glass, which would have distorted the features. Hovering just behind the windowpane and so almost out of sight so you must look closely to determine— *yes. A face.*

The Cornish House, as it is called, at 33 Charity Street, Providence, Rhode Island. A graceless foursquare mansion of sandstone, brick and iron (originally built 1828), in a lot of approximately two acres behind a twelve-foot wrought-iron gate and wrought-iron fence.

So then, if Cornish House is vacant, as he has reason to believe it has been vacant for years, that cannot be a face in the octagonal window on the third floor. More likely what appears so uncannily to be a face is a reflection in the glass, possibly the moon, for there is a quarter-moon on this gusty March evening, paper-thin and elusive behind a bank of gauzy stratus clouds.

And then he hears—*Son? Come to me.*

He is eleven years old. Or, he is seventeen. Or—he is much older, an adult. His father has been dead for many years.

You know, son—I have been waiting.

It had seemed like the start of his life. His *new life*.

That day, or rather that hour. When his father's death was revealed to him.

He'd been alone. So abruptly they'd been called away, summoned to the hospital, his Scots nanny had accompanied his mother who was distraught with emotion.

In the lower hall of the house on Charity Street he'd heard the women's urgent voices. Wanting to stop up his ears for the words of adults had often been terrifying to him when overheard by chance.

Chance means *you cannot control. Cannot even anticipate.*

Chance means a leakage of the universe, that might trickle into your brain.

And so the two women were gone, and had forgotten him. In the excitement and dread of their departure for the hospital neither had given any thought to *him*.

This, he realized with a sensation of hurt, alarm and grim satisfaction spreading like the quick damp warmth of *wetting the bed* which was a very bad thing to do and which since his fifth birthday he was resolved never to do, not ever not again.

Since he'd come into consciousness as a very young child the greatest dread had been that his father would be displeased with him. Already in the cradle he'd seemed to know. An affable sort of mockery—*Is that my son?—that?*

You could see (the son could see) that the father had once been a handsome man, a fit man, now thick-bodied, with shadowed jowls, suspicious eyes, yet still the old boyish grin, laughter intended to mask cruelty and impatience beneath.

If the Scots nanny complained to his mother of the child *wetting the bed* and his mother complained to his father it was not (he knew) to punish *him* (for his mother loved him very much, with a desperate smothering love) but rather to express reproach to the father who in those years had often been gone from the household, away in his own mysterious life.

Our son has become anxious, Horace. He rarely sleeps through the night.

Please try to be gentler with him, to seem to love him even if you do not.

(Had the child heard these astonishing words? How possibly could he have heard, when the words were uttered in the master bedroom in the mother's faint tremulous pleading voice scarcely audible to the father?)

But all that was over. The pleading. The hurt.

No *wetting the bed* any longer, since his father had been "hospitalized."

No need to cringe in apprehension that Father would stare at him with a mocking smile and screw up his face as if smelling a bad smell. *Jesus! Get him away from me.*

Even after he'd been bathed by the nanny, and certainly did *not smell.*

However, he had ceased to think of his father. No need to think of his father. So long his father had been *gone away*—(as his mother told him with her tight-stitched smile)—*in a place where he is resting, and getting well again.*

Not thinking of Father, and not counting the days since Father had been carried from the house. (One hundred nineteen.)

Not recalling the last time he had seen Father living. Not recalling the strangulated cry Father had flung at him, managing with much effort to lift his head from the stretcher upon which he was strapped, being borne away by husky white-clad strangers, that had sounded like *Son! Don't let them take me! Help me!*

Too young, he had not heard. Hadn't been anywhere near.

Had not seen the frenzied eyes. Ravaged jaundiced gaunt face and saliva-glittering lips out of which the desperate cry escaped.

On his father's right cheek, a small coin-sized birthmark of the hue of dried blood, with a suggestion of miniature fingers, or tendrils. An opened hand? But very small.

Almost you might miss it if you didn't know it was there.

A dozen times a day, the child touched his right cheek. Peered at his reflection in the mirror with relief, *there was no birthmark on his cheek.*

It was strange, the child seemed to recall a time when the birthmark on his father's cheek had seemed of little consequence, scarcely noticeable, like a freckle. But then, in the year or so preceding the hospitalization, the birthmark had seemed to grow, to become inflamed-looking. Often, the father had scratched at it, unconsciously. Often, the father's breath was fierce as a combustible gas, terrible to smell.

A clattering of bottles, "empties." (The word "empties" fascinated the child, as commonplace words often did, that suggested obscure and surreptitious meanings.)

Cut-glass tumblers containing a fraction of an inch of amber liquid. These were scattered in the downstairs rooms, sometimes even on the carpeted steps leading to the second floor. Once, the child discovered a near-empty tumbler on a windowsill in what had once been his grandfather's library, clumsily hidden behind a drape. Daringly the child lifted the tumbler to inhale the fumes, and would have swallowed the amber liquid except his throat shut tight, in sudden fear of being poisoned.

For the whiskey was a *poison*, he seemed to know. No one had needed to warn him.

He'd come to associate the sharp-smelling liquid with alterations of mood in his father but he could not invariably predict his father's mood—affable, irritable; quick to laugh, quick to sneer. A brisk hug, a brusque shove. Uplifted voice—*What the hell, are you afraid of me? Of your own God damned father, afraid? I'll teach you to be afraid! Little freak.*

Painful to realize that his father was provoked to cruelty by the very sight of him, the spindly limbs, puny body, sallow skin and doggish-damp eyes, a way of cringing that suggested curvature of the spine—and so it was wisest for the child to avoid the father as much as he could, like any kicked dog; though like any kicked dog eager to be summoned by the master to have his hair tousled, shoulder fondly cuffed, if the mood shifted sufficiently.

Then there was likely to be Father stumbling up the stairs, muttering and laughing to himself, to fall across the immense canopied bed of the master bedroom, at any hour of the day.

Quickly then, Mother would shut the door to the master bedroom, from the outside.

Mother, too, had learned to stay out of the father's way at crucial times. Warning the child—*Try not to provoke your father, he has much on his mind.*

So young at the time of his father's hospitalization yet already the child had learned essential stratagems of survival. The creature that can best camouflage itself amid its surroundings, and does not call attention to itself, is the one that will elude the predator, while other, more naive and trusting creatures become prey.

His mother held him, and comforted him, but chided him as well—*You see, dear, your father works very hard, he is distracted by many worries.*

One day the child would learn to his surprise that his father had scarcely worked at all in those years. Once he'd been a traveling salesman (orthopedics, medical supplies) but no longer. Often he'd been away from the house on Charity Street, possibly traveling, or staying somewhere else in Providence, in the Grand Whittier Hotel, for instance, where he met with his poker-playing (male) companions and other companions (female) about which the mother knew very little but more than she wished to know. Having married a rich Providence banker's spinster-daughter who would adore him to the day of his death, and who would be the principal heiress of his estate, why should Horace Love *work*?

Of *aristocrats* and *riffraff* the world was comprised. It was a very clear world which vulgar persons hoped to muddy with arguments in favor of increased taxation, increased "suffrage," increased budgets for public education, public works. The father, Horace Phineas Love, had liked to joke that he'd "jumped ship"—leaving behind his *riffraff* origins—and had landed on his feet, very happily, on Charity Hill.

Much of this the child would piece together, in time. A taciturn child, but very alert, vigilant to the seemingly random remarks of his elders. As, with uncanny patience, of a kind rarely found in a child so young, he might spend hours piecing together jigsaw puzzles whose pictures were replicas of brooding-dark nineteenth-century landscapes by Corot, Rembrandt, Constable, Courbet.

Why, look! The boy has almost finished the puzzle already.

No! That doesn't seem possible . . .

Other predilections of the child, of which the mother and the Scots nanny might not have approved, the shrewd child kept to himself.

Late that night when his mother and the Scots nanny returned home with their grim news it was to discover the child hunched over a near-completed jigsaw puzzle in the drawing room, a replica of Gericault's *The Raft of the Medusa.* He had known at once that something was terribly wrong since neither woman praised him or seemed to notice the highly challenging puzzle at all.

Indeed, the child's mother turned away from him, her face very white and her mouth twisting as if she were determined not to burst into sobs. "Take him to bed, Adelaide; he will make himself sick, staying up so late."

But when the frowning Scots nanny tried to lift the child in her strong arms, as she'd done since he'd been a baby, the child squirmed from her lithe as a snake. "Why, Horace! What is wrong with you?"

Wrong with *him?* What was wrong with *them?*—these words caught in the child's mouth, he could not speak.

"Adelaide, take him away please. I can't bear him right now. Tell him what has happened, and when the funeral will be. I—I'm exhausted, and am going to bed."

"But, ma'am—"

"Take him away! Please."

As he was borne off struggling the child managed to catch a glimpse of the mother's face, so contorted with grief, or with rage, that he could have barely recognized it; her reddened eyes, glancing at his, suggested no compassion for him, no sympathy or pity, only just the rawness of animal misery.

And so it was, the night of the day of *the miraculous death.*

Such relief! To know that the father would not ever return from the hospital but had *died.*

A sobbing sort of happiness like something writhing in his chest, seeking release.

But of course such happiness had to be kept secret. No one would understand and all would chide him, as a coldhearted child. *Freak.*

A succession of grave-faced adults offered the child *condolences.* Some of the females actually dared to stoop, to grasp the stiff-limbed child in their arms before he could wriggle away.

"Horace! Behave now, please"—so his mother instructed, with trembling lips.

Horace! That was the father's name, too.

The father was *Horace Phineas Love, Sr.* And he, the son— *Horace Phineas Love, Jr.*

The Scots nanny had dressed Horace, Jr. in dark woolen clothing that fitted him loosely and made his sensitive skin itch. Against his tender throat, the stiff-starched collar of his shirt chafed.

The child had been led to believe that he would not ever see his father again, and yet!—there in a chapel smelling of sickish-sweet lilies was the father, formally dressed in a dark pinstripe suit and waistcoat, unnaturally lying on his back, flat on his back as the child had never seen him, in a shining mahogany coffin the size of a small boat. How could this be! The once proud father, smaller than the child remembered him even as the birthmark on his right cheek appeared larger, seemingly asleep in a brightly lit public place? How mortified Father would be, and how furious! A sensation of paralysis suffused the child's small body even as his eyes stared fixedly at this astonishing sight.

"Horace, come here"—the Scots nanny urged him closer to the coffin.

Father's skin had coarsened during his illness, and was poorly disguised with (peach-colored) makeup; deep creases around his mouth and at the corners of his eyes made him appear much older than he was. (How old was Father at the time of his death? In his early forties?) The birthmark had become an inflamed-looking boil that no amount of makeup and powder could disguise.

What was most distressing, Father's eyes were not peacefully shut as in an ordinary sleep but tensely shut, with a grimace, as if he was steeling himself for some fresh insult, worse than death. His hair that had once been dark and thick had thinned so that small bumps and protuberances in his skull were perceptible and even his mustache, that had once been so dapper, had become sparse as if with mange. Forced to come closer to this hellish sight the child could not escape seeing a scattering of small inflamed sores on the father's forehead and the lurid-pink tip of his tongue protruding between thickish lips; and these lips also covered in small blister-like sores.

"Horace, come kiss your father goodbye. You know he loved you . . ."

The sickly-sweet fragrance of the lilies was making the child queasy. Under ordinary circumstances his stomach was easily upset.

His heart clattered and clanged and came to an abrupt halt like a clock stopping—but then, after a terrifying moment, began again, rapidly and painfully. Paralyzed to the tips of his toes the child could move neither forward nor back. The Scots nanny expressed impatience with her young charge, whom other mourners were observing with concern, trying at last to lift him forcibly toward the coffin, hands beneath his arms, that he might kiss his father a final time . . .

The eyelids flickered. About the sore-stippled lips, a faint greenish froth.

"No! No!"—the child began screaming and kicking, breathless, and fell to the floor in a faint.

Quickly then he was lifted, and carried to an open window, where fresh air partly revived him. (But where was Mother? In her distress and distraction had Mother no time for him?) *Poor boy! He loved his father very much. The father and son were very close. He has the father's features, you can see—the eyes . . .*

Observers believed that the child should be taken home, and spared the emotional strain of the funeral service to follow, but the mother insisted that the Scots nanny bring him, as they'd planned—"Horace would not have wanted it any other way. They were so very close."

And, "The Cornishes do not shrink from their duty. The boy is far more *Cornish* than *Love*."

In a trance of horror the child was made to attend the funeral in the family pew in St. John's Episcopal Church of Providence, from which the father would now be permanently absent; and afterward the lengthy church service, barely able to walk, tugged forward by the nanny, he was a terrified witness to another, briefer ceremony in the cemetery behind the church, that ended with the most remarkable of all sights: the shining mahogany coffin, now mercifully shut, was lowered into a fresh-dug rectangular hole in the grass, and earth was shoveled onto it even as the priest continued to recite his mysterious words, drowned out in the child's head by a roaring of blood in his ears.

And then, it was ended. Clearly now, Father was *gone*.

So strangely, a kind of party followed—food, drink, lighted candles, hordes of guests in the downstairs rooms of the Cornish house. The child was given food to eat—"You must keep up your strength, Horace!"—though he had no appetite, and wanted only to crawl away upstairs and hide in his room. Again, he was subjected to embraces, unwanted kisses, *condolences*. And the assurance that, as some visitors were claiming with a forced air of conviction, his father *had gone to Heaven*.

(Did anyone believe that? What exactly was *Heaven*? The child knew of Hell for he'd seen the most terrifying engravings of Hell in certain books in his grandfather's study, and these were utterly convincing; but illustrations of Heaven, which were rarer, did not seem convincing at all.)

Another time, the child grew faint. At last he was led away by the nanny, and allowed to go to bed early. Through the night buffeted by thoughts like gusts of wind rattling the leaded windows of the austere old house long after the many guests had gone home—*And now you are free. Never will that terrible man hurt you again.*

Little freak.

Soon then, the *night-gaunts* began to appear.

Never by day. Rarely outside the house. Though the child was uncomfortable at school yet no *night-gaunt* had ever appeared to him at the Providence Academy for Boys where he was to excel in English composition, science, mathematics. (Already in sixth grade, while his eleven-year-old classmates were struggling with simple arithmetic, Horace Love, Jr. would be allowed to take high school algebra and geometry in which he also excelled, to the resentment of his adolescent classmates at the high school.)

A *night-gaunt* was a creature of seeming substance, that might appear suddenly, within an eye-blink—as if (indeed!) the thing was a sort of optical imprint in the child's brain, resembling an animated dust mote, or a living molecule, that quivered, and shimmered, and if it did not fade at once (which sometimes, if the child held his breath and willed it to fade, it did) seemed to enlarge, into three dimensions, as a protoplasmic life-form might enlarge, horribly, yet exuding an uncanny fascination to an alert and imaginative prepubescent boy who spent a good deal of time entirely alone.

With the passage of time the *night-gaunts* acquired more definition as if, rooted in the child's brain, like actual roots, or rapacious parasites, they had now the power to grow.

Though their natural habitat was the darkness close about the child's bed yet a *night-gaunt* might be discovered in a mildly shadowed corner of the child's room, or reflected behind the child in a mirror; on the narrow, steep stairs leading to the third floor of the house: a shimmering figure transparent as a jellyfish, with limbs resembling the tendrils of a jellyfish, deep-embedded eyes, an odor of damp rot from which the child shrank in terror, heart beating so hard his legs buckled beneath him and he had to crawl to safety along the carpeted floor . . .

"Horace? What is it?"—anxiously the Scots nanny spoke, discovering the half-conscious boy lying on the floor in the upstairs corridor curled upon himself like an invertebrate that has been trod upon.

Managing to stammer to the nanny that he'd only just tripped and fallen.

In such haphazard ways, Horace, Jr. was spared annihilation. For the time being at least.

What he most feared was, kept home from school with a bad chest cold, or bronchitis, he was made to remain in bed, waited upon by a servant and dangerously vulnerable, when alone, to a *night-gaunt* drifting across the ceiling of his room, to descend in a fine greenish toxic froth into his nostrils, like the froth that had shone about his father's lips in the coffin, if his eyelids drooped shut; or, yet more insidiously, a *night-gaunt* of the size of a rat might flatten itself like a playing card, to slip beneath his pillow, quietly biding its time matching its breathing with his until he let down his guard and fell asleep, at which time the *night-gaunt* would slip out from beneath the pillow and begin to gnaw at his exposed throat . . .

Greatly agitated, coughing and choking, Horace, Jr. would be wakened in a trance of horror, on the brink of suffocation.

Help! Help me!—someone . . .

Another manifestation of the *night-gaunt* was a buzzing rattling sound, initially like the sound of a wasp, that caused the boy to lean over the edge of his bed in tremulous wonderment, and to see, or to imagine he saw, something like a ball, a living ball, a ball of . . . was it loathsome, coiled serpents?—writhing together in an obscene struggle, beneath a table or a chair.

Help! Help me!—please . . .

The Scots nanny now spent much of her time in the mother's company, where she was badly needed; for the mother had become a "bundle of nerves" in her deep mourning for the father and could not bear to be alone. And so, it was not often that the Scots nanny could hurry to the boy's bedside as she might once have done.

If a servant overheard the boy's cries and came to his aid, the boy did not dare name the *night-gaunts* to another person; for he understood that no one else had quite the eye to see them, as human beings cannot see certain light rays, gamma rays or X-rays, or hear high-pitched sounds that are audible to animals.

You must not reveal to anyone, how you are a freak.

That you are a freak is your curse but may one day be your blessing.

Eventually, if the boy shut his eyes tightly, and hid beneath the bedclothes, and distracted his agitated mind with inwardly multiplying numbers, or envisioning the periodic table, or counting the steps of the several staircases in the house which he could perfectly envision, the danger would fade; he might even fall asleep; and when he dared to look again, the *night-gaunt* would have vanished, as if it had never been.

2. "Infectious"

Soon then the boy was shocked to discover, in one of the antiquarian volumes in his grandfather's library, which he perused without the permission of his mother or the awareness of the vigilant Scots nanny, an extraordinary likeness of a *night-gaunt* in an illustration by a nineteenth-century Belgian artist named Felicien Rops: an obscene naked creature, a (female?) skeleton upon which translucent skin had been tightly stretched; with a skull for a head sparsely covered in savage tufts of hair, and a terrifying grin that seemed somehow, as Horace, Jr. stared, in flirtatious acknowledgment of *him*.

Quickly he shut the volume. Yet, after a few minutes, unable to resist he opened it again, turning the thick parchment pages until, horribly, the skeletal *night-gaunt* grinned up at him again.

Little freak! You know you are one of us.

By degrees Horace, Jr. became morbidly drawn to certain tall volumes on obscure shelves in the austere wood-paneled room that was called the "library"—"your dear grandfather's library"—(though the grandfather, his mother's father Obadiah Cornish, the founder of the Bank of Providence, had long been deceased by the time of his birth)—in which he was *not welcome,* as a child; for it was claimed that Obadiah Cornish had accumulated a collection of rare, priceless books and manuscripts dating back to medieval times, including antique copies of horrific but luridly beautiful drawings by such great masters of the transcendental macabre as Hieronymus Bosch, Goya, Durer, and the anonymous illustrator of the *Necronomicon,* and it was not "safe" for a child to peruse such materials, as it was not safe for the materials to be perused by a mere child.

As if *he* were but a mere child! An ordinary boy, crude and ignorant, willfully stupid, who might tear pages out of books or soil them, out of sheer idiocy.

Strange how, though the adults could see clearly that Horace, Jr. was hardly the son of Horace, Sr., who'd so often behaved roughly, carelessly, destructively with precious things (cut-glass goblets, Wedgwood china, antique chairs that shuddered and sometimes collapsed beneath his weight), that Horace, Sr. had often expressed his contempt for the very delicacy, hesitation, *feminization* of the son, yet the pretense in the household was that Horace, Jr., being a child, could not be trusted in the grandfather's library.

(In fact, as his mysterious illness worsened, and attacks of ill will and temper came almost daily, the father had threatened to "clear out"—"auction"—the grandfather's library; and only his total collapse had spared the precious books.)

Yet, in his shy, stubborn way, Horace, Jr. had learned to insinu-
ate himself into the library so very stealthily, as a cat is stealthy,
with eyes that can see in the dark, when no adult was likely to be
observing; in the high-ceilinged room turning on only a single
desk lamp with a green glass globe like an inverted bowl, so that
no sliver of light would be visible through the crack beneath the
shut door if anyone walked by.

How happy the boy felt, what excitement mounting almost
to fever, and a dread that such happiness might be taken from
him at any time, in Obadiah Cornish's library!—though the
library was not impervious to *night-gaunts,* any more than the
boy's bedroom or other desolate parts of the house.

In time, Horace, Jr. would make his way through an illustrated eighteenth-century English translation of Dante's *Inferno,*
with fine-ink illustrations of the tortures and sorrows of Hell;
Ovid's *Metamorphoses,* magnificently bound in a sort of chestnut-
colored hide, that caused the boy to wonder uneasily if it were
human skin, for it was so very soft, and warm to the touch,
and seemed to invite stroking. Also, volumes of Homer's *Iliad*
and *Odyssey,* lavishly illustrated: a muscular, armor-clad warrior
(Achilles?) piercing another (Hector?) with a lance; a giant with
a single glaring eye in the center of his forehead, devouring a
screaming man. How was it possible, such horrors existed! Yet
each was so finely drawn, it was the beauty in suffering that
most riveted the boy.

Secrets of the adult universe, forbidden for children to know:
how beauty and suffering are intertwined.

Long would Horace, Jr. remember the rainy afternoon in his grandfather's library when he discovered, in the *Necronomicon*, a crouching figure in an engraving depicting the interior of a sepulchre, that struck him so powerfully that the breath was knocked from him; for here was a gargoyle-like creature resembling a *night-gaunt*, with a face uncannily like the face of Horace Love, Sr. Horrified, yet fascinated, the boy held a magnifying glass he'd discovered in his grandfather's desk to the page, to see, on the gargoyle's right cheek, an unmistakable birthmark, a miniature hand with extended fingers, unless perhaps they were tendrils.

A small cry leapt from his lips, of alarm and wonder. His fingers sought his own face, where the skin was (yet) smooth and unblemished.

Hurriedly he shut up the *Necronomicon*, and shoved it back on the shelf.

Oh, he had to flee the library!—for that day, at least.

Climbing the stairs to the second floor. But not to *his* room as an observer might have supposed.

Instead his feet followed the long carpet where a beam of sunshine shone through a leaded window, a flurry of dust motes in the air like the chaos of thoughts that sweeps through a stunned brain.

Finding himself outside the room that was, or had been, his parents' room. There, his feet paused.

His mother no longer slept in this room. She had not slept in what was called the "master bed" since the day of the father's death and on the day following the father's funeral she'd directed the servants to move her things into another room, elsewhere in the house, leaving most of the furniture behind and the father's closet untouched. Horace, Jr. had somehow assumed that the door to the room was locked for (he reasoned) in his mother's place he would certainly have locked it.

Should anyone happen to notice him, Horace, Jr. was carrying a book. Rare was Horace, Jr. not glimpsed carrying a book, like a shield.

It was not a book from his grandfather's library of course, but rather an innocuous textbook (geometry, Latin) or a boy's adventure book of the sort his mother and relatives often gave him for birthdays and Christmas, having not the slightest idea what the precocious boy's (secret) interests were. With a forced smile he thanked them. *The Adventures of Tom Sawyer, Penrod Jasper*—just what he'd wanted, he assured them. (What a charade! *He* was not a child.)

Exciting to Horace, Jr., and intimidating, to see that he stood outside the *master bedroom*. Of course, he would not open the door, for that was forbidden.

Yet: No one was near. No one would witness.

How long since his father had *passed away* by this time, he could not easily recall. Four years? Five? It did not seem that long but rather, in weak moments, scarcely a year.

You know that I have not gone anywhere, you little freak. You know that I am on the other side of this door.

The passing of time was like water dripping into water, deep in a well or cistern. Horace, Jr. had not glimpsed his father for many months before the father's death and during that time, his mother had assured him that his father would be home again "soon"—always it was "soon, just not now." Horace had never dared ask what sort of illness his father had, and his mother had never told him; he'd heard relatives whispering, sighing and shaking their heads, but—what did they know? Tuberculosis had been mentioned: did that mean *lungs?* Or—some sort of paralysis, like polio? No one spoke of *alcohol*. No doubt, the adults were as ignorant as the child.

Chronological time had come to be confusing to Horace, Jr. For while his father was hospitalized he'd had difficulty remembering the person his father had once been before the hospitalization, when he'd been "well." The nature of the father's illness (if indeed it was a single illness) had been gradual, and erratic, in this way particularly insidious, for no one could have told when the father began to be seriously and irrevocably ill, and not just "unwell." The father himself had no idea—often, he'd denied that he was "unwell"—entirely. For the child it was like peering into a mirror facing another mirror—a terrifying vertigo of mirrors disappearing into infinity.

There had been that time, unreachable now as a place in a forest that has reverted to wilderness, when his mother might have casually said to him *Your father—. Your father is—.* For Horace, Sr. had existed in the world at that time, as fathers normally "exist";

it was only afterward that a shadow fell upon that time as well, like the shadow of a thundercloud, threatening to obliterate it.

Butler Hope Hospital. Was that the name?

He'd forgotten the name until now. The shock of his father's death had clotted the words in his brain.

Butler Hope Psychiatric Hospital. That was the full, shameful name.

When first he'd heard of the hospital he'd smiled inanely. His mother, seeing, had been upset with him—*Oh, Horace! Why are you smiling? That is where your poor father is.*

He had not meant to smile. Such a smile was a betrayal, like a hiccup at the wrong time, a fit of sneezing or coughing.

He could not tell his dear mother, that was why he was smiling. For it suffused his heart with relief, to know that there was somewhere his father *was* that was *not here.*

We will take you to see Father, soon. He has been asking for you, he misses you. Oh, you know—he loves you . . .

In a paroxysm of fear the child held himself very still until the mother released him. Not daring to speak, nor to attempt any sort of smile of acquiescence.

Now, in the corridor outside the master bedroom, Horace, Jr. saw with alarm that his (chilled, wary) fingers were daring to turn the doorknob. How had this happened?—he had not the slightest desire to open the door.

Still, he could not imagine that the door was not locked: he was sure that his mother would keep it locked for what danger, if it were not!

Keeping you out.

Keeping whatever is inside, in.

His heart was beating so quickly, he feared he would begin to hyperventilate and lose consciousness . . .

Yet, the door was opening. The door was opening *easily.*

Inside, the room was cloaked in shadow. A large room, with a separate sitting area, several closets, windows with drawn drapes. All was shadowy except for a single thin swordlike beam of light from a window, that penetrated the gloom and illuminated, atop the canopied bed, a figure in repose like a figure on a tombstone, too large to be a *night-gaunt* but suggesting the shimmering and insubstantial property of a *night-gaunt*, at the very edge of the spectrum of visibility.

Quickly Horace, Jr. moved to shut the door but it was too late.

Son! Come here at once! You know that I have been waiting.

It had happened so long ago, the child's tears had long dried and turned to salt.

Slowly, with deliberation, as one might slip a serpent through rungs, Father removed his leather belt. The waistband of his trousers looked unnatural and lax without a belt to secure the trousers on his hips.

This disheveled appearance in the father was disorienting to the child whose temperament, at even so young an age, required orderliness, neatness, coherence and civility.

"I said, son—*come here.*"

A rough hand at the nape of the neck. The child is plunged forward blindly.

Horace, on your knees.
Pray for the repose of your damned father's soul.

"Diseases are spread when the races promiscuously mingle"—so the child overheard.

First, a tremor in the father's hand. Then, tremors in both hands.

No, first was the anger: in the father's face, and then in the hand. Both hands.

Spittle-flecked lips. A line of greenish drool like pus on the chin.

Inflamed birthmark. Sometimes so violently scratched by the father, it oozed blood.

He'd been crouching at the foot of the stairs. As a child might crouch in play. But this was wrong, this was not play.

Smelling of whiskey, overcome by vertigo. Moaning, whimpering. *Son! Help me.*

In terror of Father yet he had no choice, he must come near Father as bidden. And Father's heavy grip on his arm pulling him off-balance, pulling him down.

God damn! God damn you.

A doctor was summoned. Not the doctor who'd been treating Horace Love for that doctor had been dismissed but another who was willing to come to the house on Charity Street like a servant, confer with the wife of the house, hurry up the stairs to the shouting man in the master bedroom; a younger doctor carrying his black valise, grim-faced, but resolute, with but a pitying glance at the child cowering in the hall.

In the bedroom, raised voices. The father's cries. A sound of struggle, a chair or a table knocked over.

The mother had not dared enter the bedroom with the doctor. How many times, the mother had been banished from the bedroom by the furious father.

Surprisingly then, or perhaps not so surprisingly, the doctor slammed out of the room, headed for the stairs. Close behind him the mother followed pleading, "Doctor—can't you help him?"

At the door trying to prevent the harried doctor from leaving—"But what about me? What about the boy? What will happen to us? Is Horace—*dangerous?*"

Stiffly the doctor said, "Mrs. Love, he is your husband. He is your charge. It is not for me to say if he is 'dangerous' or not. Good night!"

"But—Doctor—is he—his condition—*infectious?*"

Infectious! The word was so startling to the doctor, so obscene, he could not bear to acknowledge it. Stiffly he said, "Mrs. Love, please do not call me again. There are many other doctors in Providence whom you might summon for your husband's care."

In a state of anguish the mother followed the doctor outside, onto the front stoop of the house, but dared follow him no farther as he fled into the night without a backward glance.

* * *

In her small stubborn voice which was like the bleating of a sheep in reproach—*No thank you. I think not.*

Or sometimes gripping the phone receiver tight against her ear she would drawl—*No-ooo.*

That is not possible. We rarely dine out.

And the child—Horace, Jr.—he is nervous and not so fit for company.

After the father's death Horace's mother began to withdraw from even the limited society of her previous spinster-life. First, she ceased bringing Horace to the homes of Cornish relatives for somber, protracted holiday meals—Thanksgiving, Christmas, Easter—("holiday" being a word baffling to the child as it was supposed to mean festivity, joy); then, she ceased attending church-related activities like the St. John's Ladies Altar Society and Providence Episcopal Charities, and did not insist upon Horace, Jr. attending Sunday school classes. Yet, she continued to attend Sunday morning church services as devoutly as ever, bringing Horace with her as if their lives depended upon it.

Hiding her face in her hands, murmuring *Our Father who art in . . .*

Kneeling in the Cornish family pew, pleading as once she'd pleaded with the father . . . *thy kingdom come, thy will be done. Forgive . . .*

It was believed that the Episcopal church was (in the mother's words) the *highest church to Heaven,* of all the churches; superior to the Presbyterian church, the Lutheran church, the Baptist church, and, of course, the Catholic church. If there were other religions—(Jews? Muslims?)—they did not count at all. Yet St. John's Episcopal Church was a weak place, the boy sensed. The white-haired priest could not have defended the altar against an assault of *night-gaunts* if the malevolent creatures went on the attack and swarmed over it and for this reason Horace did not bow his head, did not shut his eyes to pray, for shutting his eyes could be a mistake, like reaching your hand into a pool of dark water in which (it was given to you to know) water-serpents might be waiting.

Little freak! Come.

By the age of ten Horace, Jr. had come to certain conclusions about religion—that is, Christianity. He saw that it was an adult preoccupation, not taken very seriously by most (male) adults, like his father; a habituated and uncritical way of not-thinking, cherished by women. He did not personally believe in a savior, for it seemed just silly that any god would care enough to save *him;* nor did he believe in the Christian devil who had become a cartoon. He felt a benevolent sort of pity for the pious Christian women who surrounded him—grandmother, aunts, great-aunts, cousins of his mother—inheritors of an attenuated, etiolated Protestantism, lacking passion and conviction. The father had more clearly held the religion in contempt—such admonitions to Christians as "loving one's neighbor as oneself"—"turning the other cheek" when struck. Once, the child had overheard the father declaiming to a visitor, each man with a shot glass in hand, that "survival of the fittest" was the "unwritten law of humankind."

" 'Do it to him before he does it to you'—eh?"

Laughing together, the men lifted their shot glasses to the gaping holes of their mouths, and drank.

Drawing back the bedclothes as he should not have done. And yet, it was done.

Fishy and glassy, semi-putrid congealed jelly with suggestions of translucency. Quite large, measuring perhaps two feet in radius, roughly cylindrical, vile-smelling, covered in greenish froth. Not immediately but after a few seconds the face—the features—defined themselves on the flattened surface, and became recognizable, irresistibly.

Fainting spells, mild convulsions. It was the Scots nanny who found him again collapsed on the carpeted floor, outside the master bedroom, eyes rolled back in his head and a fine froth at his mouth. In an era before fMRI scans the medical diagnosis was *possible/probable epilepsy.*

3. The Ebony Pen

And then, on the eve of his twelfth birthday, in a time of great anxiety and dread of the future, something happened that Horace Love, Jr. could not have foreseen.

In a drawer of his grandfather's desk which he had never dared to fully explore he discovered an Endura fountain pen in ebony black with gold titanium trim and stylus nib—a beautiful instrument that fitted his hand as if it had been custom-made for him.

Deeper in the drawer there was even an unopened bottle of black India ink. Just for him!

As a schoolboy Horace used a Waterman pen with a smaller nib, which his mother had given him; it was a serviceable pen, not very different from the pens other boys at the Academy used. And often they used lead pencils, as well. The *eraser* was a talismanic instrument, for it could be used to vigorously *erase* an error in pencil, as you could not hope to *erase* an error in ink.

All of Horace's schoolwork was executed with the Waterman pen and a variety of lead pencils. Along with being an exceptional student at the Academy, Horace Love, Jr. was praised by his instructors for the clarity and beauty of his penmanship. (Though Horace winced at such praise for if his classmates happened to overhear, their scorn would be merciless.)

But his grandfather's Endura pen was very special, obviously very expensive, and not to be glimpsed by others' eyes. It would remain Horace, Jr.'s secret, even from his mother.

Soon then, on the unhappiest of days Horace sought refuge in the exacting pleasures of copying the simpler of the illustrations in the antiquarian books, as well as copying passages of poetry and prose in the most gothic calligraphic penmanship—

First of all

The Killer fastens on him, then the Grabber,

Then Mountaineer gets hold of him by a shoulder . . . as the doomed hunter Actaeon, transformed into a stag by the furious goddess Diana, is attacked, mangled, torn to pieces by his own hounds who have no idea that the wounded creature is their master. How hideous! The stricken Actaeon makes a sound *not human, but a sound no stag could utter either.* There was something particularly horrifying about this metamorphosis so matter-of-factly described by Ovid and yet copying the lines with the gleaming black Endura pen provided a kind of comfort. As if, within the safety of a dream, he was calmly tracing the linea-ments of a *night-gaunt* through tissue paper.

Calligraphy is a measured art, as much for the eye as for the brain. It was a revelation to the boy that, as soon as he took up the pen, he began to feel hopeful, no matter the grotesquerie of the subject; and it seemed to be a fact that, so long as he gripped the pen, and guided it carefully across the stiff paper, there was no risk of a *night-gaunt* distracting him.

Soon, he was to discover that he had no need to laboriously *copy* Ovid, or Dante, or Homer for he could invent lines of his own. He began to write more rapidly, smiling as he composed, sketching demonic figures that, in actual life, would have terrified him, but gave him a curious pleasure springing from his pen. And soon, he had no need to commemorate the *night-gaunts* that haunted him, but could create his own.

Now there came a fever into the boy's blood, to create his own tales of monstrous metamorphoses. Page after page, notebook after notebook he filled with such tales, in which the logic of daylight was overcome by painstaking degrees by the barbaric madness of night; the narrator was frequently an individual of reason, civil, decent, often a scientist or a historian, committed to rationality even as waves of madness lapped at his ankles. For had not Horace witnessed his own father transformed over time from a handsome, fit, normal-seeming man to a furious ravaged creature with a lurid birthmark on his cheek, spittle gleaming on his chin . . . The boy's pen raced, to keep abreast of the voices in his head, and the clamor of his heart.

His schoolwork became of lesser interest. Other people, including even his mother, began to fade from consciousness; the Scots nanny had less power over him as he grew taller and more self-reliant, sullenly courteous to her, never rude, instinctively resistant to the *female.* He could no longer bear to be *touched*—as he could not bear to be interrogated. After school and on Saturdays he began to visit the beautiful old Greek Revival Athenaeum on Benefit Street with its gray granite façade and stately Doric columns, where patrons spoke in reverential whispers, like shades, and a sympathetic librarian allowed the tall grave-faced seeming-shy boy (whom the librarian may have known to be the grandchild of the late Obadiah Cornish, one of Providence's revered citizens and a most generous Athenaeum donor) to peruse books usually reserved for adults. And what seductive books these were!—first editions of Edgar Allan Poe's *The Narrative of A. Gordon Pym, Tales of the Grotesque and Arabesque,* and *Eureka*; Ambrose Bierce's *The Devil's Dictionary* and *An Occurrence at Owl Creek Bridge and Other Stories*; Bram Stoker's *Dracula* and *The Lair of the White Worm*; Henry James's *The Turn of the Screw.* Many a dreamy hour the boy spent in the high-vaulted reading room of the Athenaeum, scarcely aware of a scrim of golden late-afternoon sunlight that fell like a caress on the wall beside him.

In this place, no *night-gaunt* could approach him. In his hand the elegant Endura pen, moving rapidly across the lined pages of his notebook, a continual surprise, like a spring gushing out of muddied earth.

Ever longer and more ambitious, with tangled plots, arcane mythologies and vivid "poetic" prose, were Horace, Jr.'s earliest works of fiction. The Celtic ancestors of his mother's family whose portraits hung on the walls of the family house were transformed to Titans; his father Horace Love, Sr. was a lesser god, though handsome as a devil, dark-haired and dark-eyed and with a thin mustache on his upper lip, and a birthmark of the hue of dried blood and the size of a penny on his right cheek . . .

The boy's head clamored with such beings, that were both ghostly apparitions and more vivid to him as the persons he encountered. Often he would find himself struck by certain formations in the sky, in which deities might be observing him with sympathy, or with derision; it was not always clear if the Titans were in fact his ancestors, or the ancestors of his enemies. Nor was it clear that the dark-haired *night-gaunt* was a devil who meant him harm, or a devil who meant to empower him.

A glimmer of greenish spittle like a miniature jewel at the corner of Father's mouth.

Horace!—kiss your dear father.

Wanting to kick, scream. Claw at the hands that gripped him.

Did these adults not see that Father was only pretending to be dead, with quivering eyelids?

No choice. Could not resist. The Scots nanny gripped him hard beneath the arms. Forced to brush his lips against the ravaged cheek, the inflamed boil of a birthmark.

Screamed, kicked, writhed like a demented fish squirming out of the restraining hands, fallen senseless to the stone floor of the chapel.

"And are things well at home, Horace?"—Mr. Burns, instructor of English at the Providence Academy for Boys, spoke in a kindly and cautious way to the seventh-grader who stood before him with hooded, averted eyes.

Of course. Very well. Thank you, sir.

"It was very sad about—about your . . . But your mother is bearing up well, I hope?"

Of course. Bearing up very well. Thank you, sir.

Horace Love, Sr. had died years ago! It was nothing short of preposterous that the subject was being brought up now by this well-intentioned fool.

"You have seemed distracted lately in class, Horace. And your work—your grades—have not been . . ."

An awkward pause. Mr. Burns would have wished to touch the boy's arm, lightly; just a gesture, fatherly, concerned. But of course, better not. Always better to err on the side of caution than act on an impulse that might be regretted.

"Has anyone—threatened you, Horace? Harmed you?"

A curt murmur, a shake of the head. *No, sir.*

"You are sure, Horace? You can trust me, you know. If . . ."

Now the boy's eyes lifted to Mr. Burns's face, glaring, indignant. He was not a shy boy at all, it was revealed, though indeed he was a taciturn boy, and might go for weeks without speaking in class, unless his instructor drew him out; his face was long and narrow, as if his very skull had been squeezed, his cheekbones were sharply defined, his lips thin and pursed. He had been nervously picking at his face, at a small blemish or birthmark on his left cheek, that Burns had not noticed before, which was now oozing blood.

Seeing then the futility of such an interview, and perhaps the cruelty of it. For the child, tall for his age, with a slightly curved spine, spindly arms and legs, and those glaring sunken eyes, was both meek-seeming and rigid in opposition; in later years Burns would say of Horace Love, Jr., his most famous, indeed his only famous ex-student—*I did not quite realize, Horace was not to be fathomed. Not by me. Not by anyone who knew him. Not ever.*

On an obscure path in Prospect Terrace Park it lay motionless.

A small creature with dark feathers, stunted wings. A bird? A bat?

"Poor thing! What has happened to you?"—feeling a rush of pity and tenderness the boy stooped over the fallen creature.

The boy did not always like *living things*. Dogs with wagging tails that might succumb suddenly to a spasm of fierce barking, and lunge forward to nip and bite; sleekly beautiful cats that might suddenly hiss with bared, very sharp teeth. He disliked and feared aggressive birds like crows, ravens. Particularly he disliked and feared, in Prospect Park, the contentious waterfowl inhabiting the pond—Canadian geese, trumpeter swans. He did not especially like children including even his own young cousins whom (fortunately!) he saw rarely.

But injured creatures, ill or sickly like himself—for these he could feel a rush of emotion, near-overwhelming.

Stooping to pick up the wounded creature. Not a bird but possibly a bat, he thought it, wondering if it might be dangerous, for he'd heard of *rabid bats* and knew that it was dangerous to be bitten by one of these, and infected.

The little creature, that weighed virtually nothing, he held in the palm of his hand. Its wings fluttered—it appeared to be a large moth, with graceful wings, minutely detailed pearlescent markings. As if a miniature artist wielding a miniature brush had created a delicate lacework of beauty.

Gently he breathed on the moth, as if to suffuse it with life. Its wings began to quiver more rapidly, then to pulsate.

Lifting it to eye-level, that he might see it more clearly in the hazy light. *He has saved the moth!* But then suddenly he sees that the moth has a rudimentary face. A jeering face, a face of terrifying familiarity—even as the creature stings his fingers.

"No! Get away!"

He flings the moth down. Kicks at it furiously. The fluttering convulsing wings he brings his foot down hard upon. Oh, the sting hurts his fingers! Like a wasp's sting, so sudden, painful. He had not known that a moth could sting . . .

Running all the way back home, to steep Charity Street.
Wrought-iron fence, gate. Out of breath he slips into the house
by a side door used by tradesmen and servants, to discover that
the Scots nanny has not yet missed him, has given no thought
to him at all, as his aggrieved mother has not given a thought
to him in—hours, days?

In the sky above the house on Charity Street the Titans were
near-visible.

For long minutes enraptured Horace, Jr. gazed out from an
octagonal window on the third floor where no one could sneak
up on him and surprise him.

Even *night-gaunts* did not often appear on the third floor of
the house. Perhaps because the father had not ever climbed the
steep uncarpeted stairs to this floor which was comprised of
small rooms—servants' rooms (most of these empty)—and a
large storage room, an attic.

Here was a smell of dust, cobwebs, mice. A comforting smell
for it meant seclusion, secrecy.

At the octagonal window Horace could gaze into the depths
of the sky. A night sky, illuminated by the moon. For life, sig-
nificant life, was not of the day but of the night. Life was not
of the surface like the glossy skin of an apple, but deep inside
the fruit where seeds are harbored. Fascinating to him, as clouds
shifted, borne by the wind, and deeper dimensions opened,
like windows, or mirrors, to infinity. The Titan ancestors had
departed into the sky even as (somehow, the boy had not yet

determined how) they had descended into the earth. They were very ancient, before Time began. For there could not always have been Time—(the boy reasoned)—not as Time was measured in clocks and calendars. In the debased, ignorant twentieth century the ancient gods had become unknown even as they manifested their power in unpredictable seismic ways: earthquakes, great fires, war, pestilence, moral confusion among humankind. If Horace, Jr. stared very hard and breathed with enormous care he could make out their heroic/terrible figures in the clouds overhead that replicated to an uncanny degree the illustrations to certain ancient texts in his grandfather's library.

Ah!—his fingers twitched with the wish to write of his revelation taking up the black ebony Endura pen secretly kept in a pocket of his shirt against his heart.

"You know, dear child—it is not your fault."

Not his fault—what?

"Your father had an illness, that has not been yet diagnosed. His illness made him think wrong things about you, his son—but it was not your father who thought such things but the illness . . ."

Kindly, awkwardly Great-Aunt "Bunny" Cornish assured him when no other adult was near. Why such words were uttered to a five-year-old child already paralyzed with fear must remain inexplicable.

Unhappy is he to whom memories of childhood bring only fear and sadness.

In the high-ceilinged reading room of the Athenaeum library these words would erupt from his grandfather's pen onto the lined pages of his notebook like the water of an underground spring suddenly liberated, in sunlight.

In the master bedroom, he saw.

Barefoot in his flannel nightgown. A mischievous *night-gaunt* had led the boy into this forbidden place by the hand.

Averting his eyes. Eyes flooding with tears.

At first not knowing what the hideous thing could be atop the large canopied bed creaking like something in a windstorm: coiled serpents—in a ball?

Thick-bodied glittery-scaled serpents with diamond-shaped heads, tawny-glaring eyes with black, vertical pupils like slits, quick-darting red tongues—writhing, squirming, uttering small hissing cries: an obscene hideous ball, in spasms atop the canopied bed, in stupefied horror he backed away to run, run.

No escape. For where can you run.

Strangle you in my coils. Squeeze the mutinous life from you.

In lower Market Street where he oughtn't have gone.

A circuitous route to Charity Hill in the waning afternoon after school is a danger for always in the wrong quarters of Providence there is the danger of *them*.

Dark-skinned beings. Gypsy. Slant-eyed Asians—*Chinee* not to be trusted. As in a later decade *Japs* not to be trusted.

Native-born *Negroes*—descendants of *slaves.*

Well, some of these—*colored people*—are good upright Christian people, the women especially. Very good servants.

(In fact it is rumored that Obadiah Cornish's great-grandfather Ezra Cornish owned two slaves. Whom he'd called "indentured servants." Living right in the house on Charity Hill, in those quarters like rabbit hutches at the rear. In time, Ezra's abolitionist neighbors shamed him into releasing his slaves though [in fact] shrewd Ezra had not released them but sold the couple south.)

But others—*those others.*

. . . soon slash your throat as look at you. Animals!

He had known. He'd been warned. His mother's family—his relatives. Nor had his father been known to utter a kind or conciliatory word about *Negroes* to whom he referred by another word too coarse to be uttered.

And so now, in the very shadow of the historic old Market House (1773) Horace, Jr. has come to a halt. Cradling schoolbooks in his arms as street urchins (gypsies?) pluck at him emitting sharp cries he cannot decipher.

A young girl-urchin, scarcely ten, opens her soiled dress—bares her white, scrawny chest—tiny breasts, with small pinpoint-nipples—twelve-year-old Horace is astonished—he has never seen anything like this except in certain of the illustrations in his grandfather's library and then never of children so young. It is horrible to see, it is hideous, the aghast boy feels no sex-desire but only pity and sorrow, and fear.

No, no!—the urchins continue to pluck at him. Poke between the legs. The girl is squealing as if he has hurt *her*. (If a crowd gathers? If a police officer is summoned?) He begs them, *no*. Reaches fumbling into the pocket of his Norfolk jacket for the coin purse his mother has given him, a handful of fifty-cent coins, quarters, dimes in case of rain he needs to take a trolley to the foot of Charity Hill. With shaking fingers he snaps open the purse to give a few coins to the squealing girl and in that instant another of the urchins grabs the purse, beautifully stitched pigskin purse just the size to fit in the palm of the boy's hand, and all the urchins run away hooting with derisive laughter.

Long he will recall, the almost unbearable excitement of pressing coins into the girl's tiny hand just as—so rudely!—as he'd deserved—a crude boy-urchin yanked the entire purse from his fingers.

What do you mean, Horace—you lost your change purse?
   Lost—where? "Downtown"—?
   And why is your jacket torn? And why are you looking so—so white—as if you'd seen a ghost?

A *night-gaunt* has gripped his hand. Several *night-gaunts* like large bats flutter about his head. Leading him up the staircase in his stocking-feet, to the (shut) door of the master bedroom.

Father is but half-dressed. He is wearing a white smock so short, his bony knees show. There is something comical about a man, even a gravely ill man, in a short white gown, barefoot. On his wasted legs, tufts and whorls of dark hairs. On his cheek, the birthmark has become a lurid inflamed boil exuding heat.

With tremulous hands Father grips the son's head, to peer into his eyes. It seems that his eyesight has deteriorated—"Is this you, son? Has the woman been hiding you from me?"

And, "Open my trousers, son. On your knees."

. . . allowed then when it was (at last) finished to crawl away to safety coughing and choking.

To hide beneath the covers licking my wounds.

Devastated, ashamed! But knowing my story that had been taken from me was now mine.

Here is the explanation: Horace Love, Sr. had not been physically ill, or rather not only physically ill. His illness had been primarily *mental.*

A mental case. Precipitated by alcohol, alcoholism.

The term was flippant, disdainful. The boy had had the occasion of overhearing it—"mental case"—when adults hadn't realized that he was listening.

You were made to know that anyone who was *a mental case* was not genuinely ill, but only malingering.

Like soldiers who'd suffered from *shell shock* in the last war—the Great War.

Only a coward, weak and duplicitous.

Horace, Jr. hears, and resolves to *not ever* succumb to such weakness. Neither mental nor physical. *No.*

In desperation Mother barricades the master bedroom from inside. Every night. Perhaps aware that it is "over-caution." Father laughs gaily, kicking at the door. Sometimes he has a bottle of whiskey, or champagne, in hand; it is revelry he is offering to his frightened bride. Often gives up within a few minutes, with a shouted curse, and finishes the bottle himself. Sometimes he curls up on the carpeted floor just outside the door like a large slovenly drooling dog that shudders and twitches in its sleep, yet may well be dangerous. The barricaded bride will have to push the door open, pushing with her shoulder, to move Father's inert body, to get free of the master bedroom.

Or, the barricaded bride never pushes free but eventually, or perhaps soon, allows Father to take possession of the room, and of the bride.

"You see, Horace. You must never marry."

And: "It is very wicked, to even think of marrying. My mistake must not be repeated. Our diseased lineage must die out with your generation."

Through the attic window the child could see glittering rivers— the Providence, the Moshassuck. In a dream it was promised to him that he would one day sail with his Titan ancestors along a river, into the vast Atlantic Ocean and to the very horizon where the earth meets the sky.

How does he know, how does wisdom come to him?—out of the nib of the grandfather's ebony Endura pen that pulses with its secret energy.

Finally then, the mother has died.

A mild shock, to realize that her name was *Gladys—Gladys Cornish Love.*

The woman he'd known as *Mother.* And all along, it was *Gladys* she'd been born, whom he'd never known.

On the marble grave marker in St. John's Episcopal Cemetery *Gladys Cornish Love Beloved Wife and Mother.* And beside her *Horace Phineas Love Beloved Husband and Father.*

There were not many mourners at the funeral service in St. John's Episcopal Church. Most of the mother's relatives had died or were too elderly and ill to attend; the very atmosphere of Charity Hill had changed, for the old Providence families who'd once lived in the mansions had disappeared also, their heirs had sold the properties or, in some egregious instances, boarded them up and abandoned them, or sold them at auction, for taxes. *The riffraff is at our very door*—Horace's mother used to say; and so it was true, or nearly. But Horace had paid little heed for it was the siren call of his own writing that filled his head like a howling of Antarctic winds even at the hour of his dear mother's demise.

Here was a surprise following the funeral service at the church: an elderly woman hardly more than five feet in height, but stately in bearing, with a fine-creased face, and faded blue eyes, came to him to touch his wrist and to proffer condolences in a voice that made Horace feel faint, for it was so familiar.

"Horace? D'you remember me?—Adelaide MacLeod."

Adelaide MacLeod. He had never heard the name before, he was certain.

"I was your 'nanny,' when you were a boy. And for some years afterward, your mother's companion. But, you know, your mother was not so easy to get along with, in later years, and so— we became estranged, and I was no longer welcome at Cornish House. Only by chance did I hear of her death, which is very upsetting to me as I'd hoped that, one day, Mrs. Love might have summoned me back . . ."

With slow-dawning recognition Horace listened. Could this be—this elderly white-haired woman, so much shorter and frailer than he recalled—the Scots nanny?

"I—I—yes, I—remember you . . . Of course, you are 'Adelaide . . .'"

Even as an adult it was very difficult for Horace to enunciate the name which he'd never spoken as a child. As for "MacLeod"— he was sure he'd never heard it.

With an air of reminiscence and perceptible reproach the Scots nanny continued to speak; for it was wounding to her, Horace gathered, that his mother had sent her away in an outburst of temper or spite, as she'd often done in recent years with other servants, acquaintances and relatives; lashing out even at her only son Horace, screaming at him to *Get away! Get away to Hell and leave me alone.*

He would grieve for Mother as he recalled her, many years before. Or rather, as he'd wished to recall her, when he had been a young child and she had seemed to love him, if but in the interstices of her anguished love for his father.

Badly wanting now to escape Adelaide MacLeod, who was revealing herself with every minute as desperately alone, lonely and (no doubt) impoverished; for Horace could see that the clothes the white-haired little woman was wearing were shabby, if genteel; and her kidskin boots were soaked through.

"It would mean much to me, Horace, if—if we might . . ."

These words Horace pretended not to hear, turning from his former nanny with a smile of forced heartiness, and waving goodbye to her—"Very good to meet you! Mother would be grateful to know that you remembered her."

No. Not ever.

The prospect of seeing "Adelaide MacLeod" another time filled Horace with dismay. He did feel sympathy—pity—for the lonely old woman but he could not bear it that the Scots nanny knew so much about his private life, and the private lives of his parents.

That look in the faded blue eyes!—loneliness, sorrow.

He would not see Adelaide MacLeod again (indeed, Horace saw virtually no one) but yes, he would contact her. Even in his estrangement from his old life Horace was a gentleman, and could be generous; though he had very little income from his writing and from what remained of his parents' estate, scarcely enough to feed himself, he would set aside a small amount of money to send to Adelaide MacLeod each month. He hoped for the rest of her life.

What a good, kind man you have come to be, dear Horace!— Adelaide MacLeod writes to him, each time he sends her a check. *A Christian after all.*

Weird tales he would compose to contain the unspeakable wonders of *weird love.*

In the high-ceilinged reading room of the Athenaeum library amid patrons like himself *of good Providence stock*, he would compose his *weird tales*. In a courtyard of the Ladd Observatory where no one would observe him, or, if observing, would not give him, gentlemanly-looking, an "old soul" in oversized clothes bearing the dull glaze of time, a second glance. On a stone bench in the rear grounds of the Butler Hope Psychiatric Hospital where Horace Love, Sr. had passed away many years ago when he, Horace, Jr. had been but five years old.

What exhilaration, what joy in the grandfather's pen! Black ink spilling in the most intricate (silent) speech, enthralling to the writer.

Such a lot the gods gave to me—to me, the dazed, the disappointed; the barren, the broken.

And yet I am strangely content, and cling desperately to these sere memories . . .

Bearing the talismanic pen Horace is (more or less, usually) safe from *night-gaunts*. So caught up with the mesmerizing spell of his *weird tales*, he is capable of forgetting them for hours.

Empowered too, as he impersonates *night-gaunts* in human shapes. As if wearing a mask, and even his voice acquires a more confident timbre.

At the Butler Hope hospital, making inquiries. In the guise of "Jerald Ryerson, Esq.," a Providence attorney representing the Gladys Love estate, with questions for the chief administrator of the hospital phrased in the most gentlemanly cadences, polite, unassuming and yet emphatic, asking if the medical record of the deceased woman's husband Horace Love might be available after so many years. (Unfortunately no, the attorney is told: the medical records of the deceased are destroyed after a decade.) Well, then—is there anyone on the staff, an older nurse perhaps, who might recall Mr. Love?

Indeed yes. As it happens there is one individual, not a doctor but a white-haired nurse, in fact, a nurse-supervisor, who does remember Horace Phineas Love; and who tells Horace, Jr. that the case was "very sad, for little could be done for the suffering man, as the illness had advanced too far before being diagnosed, and had altered his brain, as it does in such cases . . . It may seem surprising that Mr. Love was very quiet much of the time, after his outbursts. As he grew older, and more ravaged, an outburst would exhaust him, and render him almost catatonic, like a statue. He had no appetite and had to be fed intravenously which presents problems, an irrational patient will pull out tubes if he isn't restrained, and can be dangerous to himself and others . . ." Seeing the attorney's respectful but puzzled expression the white-haired woman says, in a lowered voice, "It was syphilis, you know. Undiagnosed for years."

Syphilis! The attorney stares speechless.

"Untreated syphilis. Mr. Love must have procrastinated going to a doctor and even then, he may have delayed treatment. Of course there was a 'cure' for the disease then but there was such social opprobrium attached to the disease, many of the afflicted simply refused to believe the diagnosis, and were too ashamed to tell anyone else, like family members. People did not want to know. Families did not want to know. A wife—ah, a wife!—would not want to know though of course the wife is the one who must know." The nurse pauses, choosing her words with care; saying, with reluctance, "Mr. Love's poor wife was likely 'infected' too. But I don't believe that she was a patient here."

"And—children? If she'd had children?"

"Well, possibly. I don't like to say 'probably.' If the poor woman had had children after the infection, if the husband had not been diagnosed yet and there were marital relations between them, almost certainly the child was at risk of being infected."

"I see." A grave pause. Mr. Ryerson adjusts his eyeglasses, frowns just perceptibly. His lips draw back from his teeth in a rictus of a smile. "And how, in the child, would the infection manifest itself?"

He was the pollution—you were the helpless victim. From his loins he injected his poison into you, in your mother's womb.

They would keep it a secret, would they?—the father's terrible illness, that rotted his brain. And the mother's brain, in time.

4. *Weird Love*

Swiftly words erupt from his pen. Black-inky words, beautifully formed, transcribing an old tale of anguish. *All have died now on Charity Hill. There is peace.*

In the interior of the (private, prestigious) Athenaeum library where for long hours he sits utterly content, writing.

Ah, writing! Here is an activity so much more rewarding than mere *living*.

"I am very happy here, Mrs. D___. Thank you."

(Mrs. D___ is one of the friendly librarians. Always a smile for the gentlemanly Mr. Love, grandson of Obadiah.)

"We are very happy to hear that, Mr. Love. But why?"

"Because"—glancing about almost shyly—"because we are all dead here, and there is peace."

In Latin class at the Providence Academy, each year the instructor would note the Ides of March: 44 BC, death of Julius Caesar.

Though it is but superstition—(and Horace Love is a thoroughly rational, not-superstitious man)—always as March fifteenth approaches he feels a frisson of something like—premonition?

This year, a demon seems to have leapt into his pen—a *night-gaunt?* He feels the extra surge of energy, like a shot of adrenaline to the heart.

What pleasure in the pen flowing swiftly and unerringly across the lined pages of his notebook! Months have passed since the mother's death—years have passed since the father's death—and yet (it might almost be claimed) very little time has passed inwardly. For the (now-adult) survivor the experience of writing is like making his way along a path by the light of a quarter-moon: he can see enough of the path before him to make his way safely though in fact he is surrounded by shadows on all sides.

The gift of "weird sight" is that you see just as much as it is required for you to see. Beyond that, you have no need.

While others, neither accursed nor blessed, see far less of the path before them, and know virtually nothing of the darkness that surrounds.

Many Waterman pens he has worn out in the course of his lifetime; yet still, for *weird tales,* he uses Obadiah Cornish's Endura pen, though it is not so striking as it had been; the nib many times replaced, the gold titanium trim worn from his fingers.

Sometimes the pain is not bearable.

(But why has he written this line? It does not belong in the novella he is writing, set in the Antarctic in the present time and in the Cretaceous age of many millions of years ago.)

Of course he has infected you. You could not have been born except by way of infection. You yourself are infection.

Despite clanking radiators like panting beasts the reading room of the Athenaeum is drafty in winter months. Patrons tend to dress warmly in thick sweaters. Like a reptilian creature

Horace, Jr. has difficulty retaining heat; in a cold room his temperature tends to drop, and his fingers become stiff and unwieldy. So, out of practicality Horace has taken to wearing leather gloves with the forefinger and thumb of the right glove cut away, to facilitate writing. (The gloves are supple, thin black leather, once belonging to Horace, Sr.)

Indeed, Horace, Jr. often wears clothing formerly belonging to Horace, Sr. laid out for him by his mother years ago. She'd fretted that such "perfectly good"—"high-quality"—clothing could not simply be donated to Goodwill, when Horace, Jr. could wear it; despite the clothes being not quite right for him—too short in the sleeves and trouser legs, too loose otherwise. (For Horace Love, Sr. was a much heavier man than Horace Love, Jr., as well as two or three inches shorter.) Black woolen overcoat, with worn cuffs; dark woolen suit coat and (mismatching) dark woolen trousers; waistcoat, loose at the waist; belt, with inexpertly notched new holes, to fit Horace, Jr.'s narrow waist. The white cotton long-sleeved shirts are not starched, for Horace, Jr. washes them himself in a sink; their cuffs have grown discolored with ink which no amount of scrubbing can erase.

Sometimes there are experiences which scar too deeply to permit of healing, and leave only an added sensitiveness that memory re-inspires all the original horror.

On exceptionally cold days Horace, Jr. wears a black felt fedora of his father's in the library, though (he believes) it is not good manners for a man to wear a hat indoors, in the presence of women; murmuring *Excuse me!—hope you won't mind* . . . with an apologetic smile that exposes uneven stained teeth.

Kindly Mrs. D___ assures Horace Love, Jr. that it is perfectly all right—of course. For years the librarian has observed the unusually tall, gaunt gentleman with a boil-like birthmark on his cheek and sunken, intelligent eyes, in old-fashioned ill-fitting clothes, who spends many hours a week in the library, in the reading room, occasionally in the reference room, taking notes, writing furiously in a notebook. He is a nervous man, but excessively well-mannered. His smile is a fierce but restrained grimace. His breath is faintly sour like something that has rotted and partly decomposed. From random remarks of his, both modest and boastful, she has gathered that these "manuscripts" are "typed up" at home, by Horace, Jr; he has said that he could not entrust a typist to type them, and that he is "constantly revising" as he types. His great literary hero, he has said, is Marcel Proust—for Proust's *explorations into the labyrinth of Time, which is our only true subject.*

It is Mrs. D___'s vague understanding that stories by Horace Love, Jr. appear occasionally in magazines, though no magazine displayed in the library has ever contained any story by Horace Love, Jr., so far as she has discovered; and those magazines that do publish his work, if indeed they exist, are not (evidently) of a quality to be displayed in the periodicals room of the Athenaeum.

Out of curiosity Mrs. D___ has asked Horace for a copy of a magazine publishing his work, and Horace promised that yes, he would bring a copy to her—soon! But out of shyness, or embarrassment, Horace has not (yet) brought his librarian-friend a copy of *Weird Tales* in which his strongest work has appeared.

Many days, after hours of vigorous writing, when his (gloved) hand begins to ache, Horace, Jr. feels a thrill of exaltation. One day, he believes, the name *Horace Phineas Love, Jr.* will be as much revered in Providence as the name *Cornish*.

Though it is not likely, Horace concedes, that any street or park would be named after him, as a street and a park are in fact named after his mother's relatives: Cornish Street, Cornish Park. Such a concession is a check to his exaltation for invariably if Horace's spirits soar like a balloon, there must be a brisk tug on the string to bring the balloon down closer to earth.

On the ground floor of the library there is a men's lavatory which Horace has no choice but to use. Shielding his eyes from the freakishly tall, thin, white-faced apparition in the mirror, a *night-gaunt* brazenly staring at him . . .

Wanting to protest—*But I am not one of you. I have not succumbed to your despair, I am still alive.*

Wanting to declare defiantly—*What I have written will endure. Beyond any of you.*

On this day shortly after the Ides of March 1937 Horace finds himself at the checkout desk of the Athenaeum, where a queue has formed just before closing time. In the truncated light of late winter it is already quite dark outside at six P.M., as he can see through the tall windows. Horace is taking out several books he has not yet read, though by this time it is a rarity for him to have found any book in the Athenaeum collection which he has not already read, or indeed owns; he has purchased so many books, most of them secondhand, that he has not had time to alphabetize them, and so these "new" books have been added to his grandfather's considerable collection, in so haphazard a way that Horace often can't locate a book he is reasonably certain he owns, and so must check it out of the library. "Thank God for the Athenaeum!—no riffraff here," Horace remarks to patrons in the queue, who smile fleetingly at him, as if his humor is embarrassing; some of these, the older individuals in particular, are familiar faces to Horace as (he supposes) his is a familiar face to them. For they have shared this interregnum of history with one another even if they are not known to one another by name: all share a common bond, a kindred sense of the paramount importance of books, the life of the mind and the imagination, the life of *print*. Horace wants to think that he has been writing his *weird tales* of *weird love* for these readers, and for others like them, though they are not much aware of his work—yet . . .

How otherwise can I speak of my love. My writing, my books, my weird tales are my love. It is weird love I offer you.

And why?—because I love you. Because there is no other way.

It is true. Never could Horace have uttered such truths aloud. Only through the mouth of the mask fitted tightly over his face.

But here is a mystery: Horace's fellow patrons are not behaving with their customary politeness. Rather, with uncharacteristic rudeness. Not only do they fail to acknowledge Horace's innocuous remark, they are pushing past him in the queue, oblivious of his very presence. Inwardly he protests *Excuse me? I have been waiting here also . . .*

Of course Horace is too courteous, too much the gentleman, to object out loud. With an ironic self-effacing shrug he allows the others to move ahead of him, to check out their books from Mrs. D___; and finally, when the last of the patrons has left, and Horace approaches the checkout counter, to his surprise Mrs. D___ ignores him also, putting away her stamp pad, briskly shutting drawers. Ever thoughtful of Horace Love, on this blustery March evening when a faint wind howls about the rotunda in the foyer, Mrs. D___ seems unaware of him entirely. She shudders, a chill passes over her. Another librarian says, "What is it, Elisabeth?"

"I—I—I don't know . . ."

"You seem so—cold, suddenly."

"Just suddenly, yes. I—I am . . ."

Horace realizes, then.

Stepping back he realizes. *He!*—he is the sudden chill.

It is a gentlemanly gesture, to leave the Athenaeum at once. It is an uncouth act, to disconcert the lady librarians any further.

Without a word Horace hurries outside. He has left behind the precious library books he'd wanted to check out, he has brought only his precious notebook with him clasped tight against his chest. On his long legs staggers out of the building just as the door is being locked for the night by a custodian.

On the stone steps, gusts of wind. Overhead, a full moon. Horace runs into the street, he is both frightened and exhilarated, like one who has stepped across a threshold in full knowledge that a door will slam shut behind him, and lock against him irrevocably.

Was it here, on Benefit Street, that the little gypsy-girl had plucked at his wrist? Or no, that had been Market Street, and long ago.

The wind, the wind!—blowing Horace stiff-legged in his long flapping overcoat along Benefit Street, over the trolley tracks, to the foot of Charity Hill. More slowly then he climbs the cobblestone street past the large darkened houses of his neighbors set behind wrought-iron fences to keep out strangers, to thwart even the curious eyes of strangers, another steep block to the small mansion of sandstone, brick and iron in which he has lived out his life of forty-six years. Thinking—*Why, this has been my happiness. The only world that could have sustained me.*

Thinking, with a fluttering in his bony chest—*My "weird tales" will make their way into your hearts as in my person I could never have done . . .*

At 33 Charity Street the wrought-iron gate appears to be locked though (Horace is certain) he has not troubled to lock it in twenty-five years. Rust of the hue and texture of brine exudes from its iron pores. He is perplexed, surprised. What has happened? Why?

There has been some mistake, has there? He has been locked out of his own house—by whom?

He shakes the bars. He will certainly gain entry, he cannot be kept out of his own home.

But what is that?—a *face*?

Seeing in a high, octagonal window beneath the eaves of the old sandstone house something pale and blurred hovering just beyond the glass.

Acknowledgments

"The Woman in the Window" originally appeared in *One Story* (2016) and has also appeared in *The Best American Mystery Stories 2017*, ed. John Sandford (Mariner Books, 2017) and *In Sunlight or In Shadow: Stories Inspired by the Paintings of Edward Hopper*, ed. Lawrence Block (Pegasus, 2016).

"The Long-Legged Girl" originally appeared in *The Kenyon Review* (2017).

"Sign of the Beast" was originally published by Amazon Original Stories (2017).

"The Experimental Subject" was originally published by Conjunctions.com (2017).

"Walking Wounded" originally appeared in *Conjunctions* (2015).

"Night-Gaunts" originally appeared in *The Yale Review* (2017) and contains isolated lines from H.P. Lovecraft's work, notably "The Outsider," "The Shunned House," and "At the Mountains of Madness."